# MARS 2194

## Tales From the

## Next Frontier

JACK STORNOWAY

While every precaution has been taken in the preparation of this book, the publisher assumes no responsibility for errors or omissions, or for damages resulting from the use of the information contained herein.

MARS 2194: TALES FROM THE NEXT FRONTIER

# Table of Contents

# King of Mars

The twenty-odd red concrete houses that formed the colony of Milanković Crater huddled, dwarfed and miserable, below the towering sand-dunes at the center of the crater. The lofty circle of ruddy mountains far in the distance with their sand choked ravines and massive outcroppings of rust-red rocks, formed an enclosing wall as impassable as any Eve Johns had ever seen. There was only one road out of the crater, a ten kilometer long dust trail that ran up one of those ravines. They'd spotted it on approach, they always looked for exits when heading into a colony they didn't know. Even so, those crater walls were over sixty kilometers from the dunes at the center of the crater, and hundreds of kilometers from the next colony.

Eve Johns had run it through her mind many times in the past couple weeks, and each time she had come to the same conclusion, it was hopeless. There was no way to escape on foot, even if she made her way to the rim, and up to the surface, she was still hundreds of kilometers from civilization. There was only one way to escape, by air.

There were three aircraft in the crater, and all of these belonged to Tadeusz Warszawski. One was the airship that he used for occasional trips to Ciudad de Arcadia, to carry out ore and bring in supplies. There were also two prospector auto-gyros, but they were far too small to reach much beyond the crater rim. Yet she had to escape, and immediately.

Returning to the bedside, she looked down at her dying husband. Lovable, impractical, and a dreamer with an always restless heart, Ozzy Mac-an-Bhaird had never been able to remain still. Now, this isolated crater in a remote region of Mars had trapped him, and once there he could not leave.

Two things were trapping them there. The first was his health, which failed rapidly in the cold dreary world of Milanković Crater, where the long winter had set in, and the heat of the distant Sun was hardly felt. If it been his health alone, Eve could have managed. The other problem was Tadeusz Warszawski.

From the moment they disembarked their airship at the old Milanković Colony landing pad, and Eve turned to look into the tiny hazel eyes of the short yet very muscular man, she had been frightened. Right then she asked her husband to leave, knowing that this was not a place that they should stay.

He didn't see it, asking, "Why Eve? We just got here, and this is hundreds of kilometers from anywhere else! We can meet the locals, can't we?"

"No Ozzy please! Let's go find somewhere else."

Her husband had turned to face Tadeusz, and his pale face smiled under the respirator mask. "I'm afraid my wife doesn't like it here," he stated.

"Well," Tadeusz replied. "It is not so much a good place for women, that is true. But there is gadolinium here, and so we are living here."

"Gadolinium?" Eve's heart sank at the eagerness in her husband's voice. She wondered what he'd do if he found it. Nobody ever cared less for the idea of getting rich, but to her husband the concept of finding any precious metal was so much more than credit. It was history, destiny, fate, the reward that would somehow repair the life that lady luck had abandoned.

"There's gadolinium here?" Ozzy asked.

"Yeah, a whole lot!" Tadeusz turned and waved a hand at the crater around them. "This crater was made by a gadolinium rich asteroid! It is the best source of gadolinium on Mars, maybe in the entire system! Was that why you came here? You can prospect if you want to, but KGHM Polska Mars has exclusive rights to mine the ore."

Was there anxiety in the short man's voice? Eve looked at him again, and felt such revulsion that she could barely stand to be near him. Stalking along beside her husband, Tadeusz had been dwarfed by Ozzy's huge body. Tadeusz face was thin and hawk-like under his thin brown beard. Wrinkles ran out in a network of tiny lines from the corners of both eyes, eyes that were small and cruel. His gloves were filthy, and his black thermal-still-suit and duster were covered with red dusty grime. Then she saw it, holstered to his right hip, a laser pistol.

It wasn't until later that Eve wondered why none of the other people in the small colony had come out to greet the visitors. They couldn't get that many visitors out here. It would've made sense for them to want to trade, but no one came out. Eve did notice one pale emaciated woman looking out the window of one of the red concrete houses, who immediately closed the shutter when she saw Eve looking at her. Eve assumed the woman was shy. She should have known better.

At midnight they were still at the bar with Tadeusz. The bar was the only restaurant in the colony, although it looked like it had started out as a company cafeteria, and deteriorated into a bar over the decades. The bar was in the only large building at the colony, the old corporate station. Once it had been used for everything from a control tower to direct shuttles down from orbit, to a store house. Now it was called Warszawski's Station, home to Warszawski's Bar, and Suleiman's Trading Shop. Suleiman was the only other person they met that first night, an Arabian trader that lived with the colonists. He rarely spoke, but when Tadeusz and Suleiman shared a look Eve realized there was more being said silently than out loud. After the sun set, lights appeared in some of the red concrete buildings, but no one seemed to be interested in visiting the bar.

Ozzy got unusually drunk on Colmbian aguardiente, which seemed to be the only alcohol in the bar, and then Tadeusz offered the station's one and only hotel room above the bar to them for the night. Eve wanted to return to their bedroom in the airship, but Ozzy was having a difficult time figuring out which way was up, so she thanked Tadeusz for his generosity, and helped Ozzy up the stairs. In retrospect that should have been her second clue, Ozzy was known to drink, but never to get completely wasted. Perhaps if she hadn't been drinking too it would have occurred to her that Tadeusz might have spiked the with something stronger than alcohol.

In the morning, their airship was gone.

Eve had just woken up, when she looked out the window at the landing pad where the airship had been docked the night before and saw it wasn't there. Terror ripped through her like lightning. She jumped on Ozzy and started shaking him awake. Ozzy Mac-an-Bhaird's face went paler that usual when he saw the landing pad with just Tadeusz's airship docked on it, and for the first time in a long time, he was afraid.

They pulled on their still-suits and respirator masks without bothering to grab their dusters and ran out to the landing pad looking frantically around in case the airship had drifted off. If it wasn't docked correctly it could have drifted off, but in over ten years of owning the airship Ozzy and Eve had never failed to dock it correctly. Tadeusz came out of the station, rubbing his red eyes. "What is wrong? Why are you running around out here?"

"Our airship's gone!" Ozzy yelled. "My God man! What'll we do? What could've happened?"

"Wind, maybe. If it was not docked right, maybe it drifted," Tadeusz suggested. "Or maybe a thief stole it. I will go see if anyone is missing from the colony. It is no good standing out here. Come in and we will eat. Then we go look for your airship with one of my auto-gyros."

It sounded right, but when Eve's eyes met Tadeusz's she saw something else, something that looked like victory.

Despite his obsession with precious metals, her husband was genuinely worried. Ozzy knew the rim-walls were virtually impassable, and the lowlands beyond were treacherous. Walking to the next colony was impossible. By the end of the day, they realized that the airship was gone, and they were not going to find it. None of the colonist were missing, and so Tadeusz surmised it must have drifted off. The wind had been blowing to the southeast, and they surveyed the crater to the southeast as far as the rim-wall. The auto-gyros weren't able to scout further, and Tadeusz insisted that if it drifted out of the crater it could be hundreds of kilometers away. There was no chance of finding it even if they searched in his airship, which he did not have time to do.

"Could you fly us down to Ciudad de Arcadia?" Ozzy suggested that evening. "You have an airship, and we can't stay here. I have credit at my bank in Sirenum, I could get access to it in Ciudad de Arcadia. Get us there and I'll pay you well."

"Alright," Tadeusz replied thoughtfully. "But you will have to wait until I go for supplies. A couple weeks, maybe."

The weeks passed and Tadeusz said nothing about leaving. Ozzy had lost track of the days, prospecting in the region south of the dunes. Tadeusz had said the region north of the dunes was thoroughly mined out during the Corporate Era, but if Ozzy found any deposits to the south of the dunes, Tadeusz would see that KGHM Polska Mars gave him a 5% royalty.

Ozzy and Eve had moved into one of the old abandoned red concrete houses, as it turned out only about half the houses in the small village were still inhabited. The solar panels installed in the roof still worked, so they just needed to jump start the house's oxygen recycler with some algae from their respirator masks. It took almost a week for the house's oxygen recycler to grow enough algae to get the oxygen levels in the house high enough that they could remove their respirator masks. It took longer to warm the old house up. It was winter in the northern hemisphere, and the only source of energy the house had was its solar panels. The walls of the old red concrete house had electrical heating built in, but the solar panels weren't receiving enough light to heat the house to much above freezing.

About a week after they arrived in Milanković Crater, Ozzy started to complain about a strange electric feeling in his skin. A couple days later he was incapacitated in his bed, unable to move due to shooting pain in his muscles. There was no doctor in Milanković Crater, but the priest came to their house to check on Ozzy. He lived in the old Corporate Era Catholic Church, however he didn't appear to have any formal training. He said Ozzy's condition looked like Gadolinium poisoning. It was a condition that sometimes affected miners, and should subside in a few days.

"I'm sorry, Eve," Ozzy said after the priest left. "When I get well, we'll get out of here and I'll make it up to you." He coughed, and his teeth started chattering.

"Get some rest honey," she replied. He smiled and relaxed, breathing more easily. She sat there in the cold, a thirty-two-year-old woman who had failed in life, and fled with her husband, a lifelong prospector, to end up here, in a virtually abandoned crater in one of Mars most remote areas.

Her parents had been British colonists that had settled in Sirenum colony, half way around the planet. Her husband's parents had been the same, and she'd met him in Sirenum when they were in Icaria College. Ozzy and her both had an interest in the early prospectors, although in Ozzy's case it was more of an obsession. Those early explorers who worked for the corporations before the Mars Treaty had divided the planet into colonial zones. They who explored an unknown world with no hopes of help if they ran into problems. It was a romantic notion, an unreal concept of Mars only a century earlier.

Unfortunately, as obsessed as he was with the early prospectors, Ozzy never seemed to find a great stake of his own. For more than a decade, they'd searched the isolated regions of the planet, but everywhere they went, someone had beaten them there. They'd lived in the old Russian airship they'd bought real cheap in Daedalia, as the revolutionaries drove the Russian government from Mars. They'd lived on that airship for more than a decade, and now it was gone.

Ozzy Mac-an-Bhaird had made his fair share or poor decisions, and he'd never had much luck either, but he always met the morning with a smile, and fixed his eyes on the horizon. Ozzy had planned the trip north to explore the lowlands, as they'd spent almost a decade floating across the southern highlands and had little to show for it. They'd prospected at various places as they moved north of the equator, but found nothing of consequence. If they could find a major deposit of a rare metal they could sell the location to one of the mining corporations in Ciudad de Marte, and they'd be setup for the rest of their lives. It was the dream of every prospector.

But now they were stranded here in this dismal crater, and Ozzy was very sick. Eve put her husband to bed and went to the station for medicine.

"Medicine?" Suleiman asked. "We don't have much medicine. I can get you something for the pain, and some vitamins. If he starts vomiting we have something for that, or for diarrhea. Not much else."

Tadeusz came into the shop and Suleiman wandered off to a store-room to get some painkillers. Despite her dislike of the man, she forced herself to stand still, but couldn't look Tadeusz in the eye.

"You know," Tadeusz broke the silence. "You and me should be friends. The winters here are very cold and very long, more than an Earth year long."

In the store-room Suleiman started chuckling.

"That won't be happening Mr. Warszawski. When my husband gets better, we'll leave."

"And if he does not get better?"

A jolt of fear shot through Eve. "He will," she said firmly. "He'll get well, and then we'll leave."

"Maybe," Tadeusz said grinning at her, his teeth yellow and broken. "If I take you to Ciudad de Arcadia. But, maybe I will just keep you here. More workers is a good thing."

"That's ridiculous!" Eve looked directly at him for the first time since he'd entered. "You couldn't get away with that! What about the authorities?"

"The Sudamericans?" Tadeusz laughed with genuine amusement. "They do not come here. This is a Corporate Mining Zone from before the Mars Treaty. We are autonomous. Do you know why the people here don't talk to you? Because I told them not to! Do you know why they stay here at this mine? Because they can not get away either! They are mining gadolinium for me and Suleiman and they are not even paid! I feed them, and Suleiman ships the gadolinium back to Arabia without the Sudamericans in Ciudad de Arcadia, or anybody in Europe even knowing! KGHM Polska Mars went bankrupt decades ago! I pay no taxes! In this place I am a king! And these are my subjects. And now you are my subject also. This place is so far from the other colonies that nobody ever comes here, and nobody ever leaves."

Two days later Ozzy was dead.

He died suddenly in the night, but was rational until the end. The evening before he died, he told Eve something he had been keeping to himself. It seemed he knew he was going to die. "Eve, I know what happened to the airship. Tadeusz towed it away. He hid it on the north side of the dunes. One of the miners told me that last day prospecting."

"It's alright Ozzy, we'll find it," she said gently. The thought of the distant rim-walls that trapped them filled her with horror. In all of Mars, there could be no more desolate place than this crater out in the northern lowlands.

"We'll manage," she whispered, but she knew he was dying.

They buried Ozzy Mac-an-Bhaird in the old Catholic cemetery dating from the Corporate Era at the edge of the colony. The priest gave a eulogy in Polish. Most of the miners were at the funeral, there wasn't much the way of entertainment in the crater. It became clear that no one in the crater wanted much to do with her. They were all thin, obviously malnourished and terrified of Tadeusz and Suleiman.

She found out that there were only ten men and six women in the colony. Four of the men were Sudamericans, and six were Polish, descendants of the old corporate mining colony. The six women were all Polish except one, a Persian woman from the old Iranian mining colony in Hyperborea, far to the north. The Sudamerican men and Iranian woman had been hired by Tadeusz in Ciudad de Arcadia. Homeless people with no family, and no one to miss them.

After the funeral, Eve talked with the miners while Tadeusz and Suleiman ignored her. Tadeusz and Suleiman had the only weapons in the colony. Besides the laser pistol that Tadeusz always carried, he and Suleiman had sonic blasters, and Suleiman also had a laser rifle. She found out that Tadeusz had killed a man just a week before she had arrived with Ozzy.

Eve realized Tadeusz's greatest fear as she spoke to the few miners that would talk to her. She remembered Tadeusz's anxiety that first night when Ozzy and her had arrived. Here in his little kingdom, he ruled supreme while the miners slaved for him and depended on him for food and water. He controlled the only means of escape, as well as the only source of food, drugs, and liquor. He had complete control. Most of the miners didn't even have a still-suit, they wore homemade clothes sewn together from the carbon-fibre sacks the food came in. Several even shared old respirator masks, meaning only one could go outside at a time.

"What about the auto-gyros?" she asked a miner named Dariusz. "Couldn't you steal one and get away?"

"No chance!" he answered. "Warszawski's airship is faster than any of the auto-gyros, and he would catch us before we made it to the rim-walls. Besides, where could we go on the supplies we have? We are a long way from any other colonies."

During the morning before her husband's burial, she tried to remember exactly what the map-display in the airship had shown when they'd landed. The crater was in the northeast sector of Arcadia Colony, and far to the south was Marte Colony. There wasn't much else on the chart. The northern lowlands were never-ending sea of sand-dunes occasionally pock-marked by the odd crater. It was nothing like the rugged highlands where Ozzy and her were from.

A dust storm blew into the crater as the funeral service was finishing. She started walking away as soon as the frail old priest finished the eulogy. When the grave had been filled Tadeusz found her in the bar talking with a few miners. They disappeared as he approached.

"Get your things together," Tadeusz ordered. "You are moving in with me."

The day had been emotional enough, and Tadeusz was the last thing she needed. It didn't take much to bring her to tears, but she intentionally milked it for all it was worth. "Oh, not now! Please!" She sobbed hysterically. "My husband just died! My husband! My Ozzy!"

She made the most unappealing spectacle of herself she could, and finally, disgusted, Tadeusz shrugged it off. "Fine, tomorrow then," he declared and trudged away.

Eve was packing up her husband's still-suit a few hours later when she found the knife. He must have planned to use it himself because he hadn't mentioned it to her. She didn't recognize the knife. It wasn't from the airship, which meant he had acquired it since they'd landed. It was bright and gleaming, and obviously hadn't been lying out in sand-storms. The thought filled her with excitement. If one of the miners had given him a knife, she might have an ally in the colony, someone else who wanted to escape. How could she figure out who it was?

The knife gave her courage. The thought of killing Tadeusz came to mind, but she dismissed the idea immediately. He was too strong, and he wore an insulated carbon-fibre suit that would be difficult to stab through.

Then she remembered the drugs. Her husband had landed prepared to trade, carrying a small satchel of cocaine, and a few cartons of marijuana and tobacco cigarettes. The drugs were legal in the Sudamerican colonies, and common enough in the major centers, but out here invaluable. She had seen how avidly the miners clutched the tiny packets of marijuana and tobacco cigarettes that Tadeusz passed out. Maybe that was how her husband got the knife.

For a long time she wondered about the rim-walls of the crater and the vast flat lowlands beyond. If she could manage to steal an auto-gyro, she could probably get to the other side of the dunes, and there hopefully she could find her airship. She wouldn't need food or water to get that far. The thought of the time it would take to find her airship versus the time it would take for Tadeusz to catch up in his airship worried her. She doubted she could do it, but she had to try.

Eve turned off her light to go to bed, but before she got to her bed, the airlock chime sounded. Eve approached the airlock cautiously not wanting to make a sound in case it was Tadeusz. She looked through the airlock view-screen and saw one of the ragged colonists standing outside.

"Mrs. Eve Johns? This is Gol-nasrin. You have marijuana?" the colonist asked as Eve opened the airlock.

Gol-nasrin was the Persian woman from the old Iranian mining colony in Hyperborea, far to the north. Eve remembered Gol-nasrin from the funeral. She remembered Gol-nasrin's eyes as she'd turned away, and how they had seemed compassionate.

"Yes, I have marijuana! Come in out of the cold!"

"I can not stay!" Gol-nasrin said stepping into the airlock. "He will come soon. He cannot see me here! He will kill me!"

"Gol-nasrin, can you get me out of here? Can you? Please!"

The Persian woman was silent.

"Can you get me to our airship? My husband was told it was anchored on the north side of the dunes!"

"The dunes? Yes. Your airship is there. I saw it while prospecting." There was sudden eagerness in Gol-nasrin's voice.

Eve was almost frantic. "Yes Gol-nasrin! Take me to my airship and I'll give you all the marijuana on board! Can we take an auto-gyro?"

"No, the auto-gyros are too loud," the finality of Gol-nasrin's voice was a blow to Eve. "Maybe we can walk, are you fast? Can you walk fast? Can you climb?"

"Yes, definitely!" Eve replied, "How long would it take on foot?"

The airlock chimed again, and Gol-nasrin slipped into the closet next to the airlock where Eve's still-suit was hanging. The lights were still off, and Eve quietly slipped into bed. A light shone in the window, and a minute later the airlock outer door opened, then the inner door, and Tadeusz was in her house.

Eve heard Tadeusz's feet walk across the room, then she felt him staring down at her, breathing roughly. His rank body-odor was unmistakable. He stood listening, and she kept her breathing deep and regular, hoping he would not try to wake her, for more than one reason. She had the knife in her hand, but doubted it would help. Suddenly a light flashed on her face. After a minute of examination, he turned it off and walked away. Eve lay rigid listening to the airlock doors open and close, before she got up.

Before she got to the airlock Gol-nasrin stepped out of the closet and whispered, "I take you to the airship, and you give me the marijuana, yes?"

Eve quickly put on her still-suit. She pulled on her duster and thrust the knife into her still-suit pocket. It was only a few minutes before they exited the airlock, and Gol-nasrin pulled her towards the dark dunes. The two moved rapidly into the darkness. Almost before she realized it, they were working their way across the red rocks, rising from the drifting sands. Gol-nasrin was jumping quickly from rocky outcropping to outcropping. Eve had a problem keeping up, and then missed a rock and landed in the sand. She sank up to her waist in the loose dusty sand, and Gol-nasrin turned back to help pull her out.

"You must be careful," Gol-nasrin stated as she pulled Eve onto the rock she was kneeling on. "You can sink right into this sand past your head."

Eve knew why Gol-nasrin was traveling by rocks, but she wasn't used to this type of travel. There were no sand seas up in the highlands where she'd spent most of her life. Although she knew about the sand-traps, she'd never fallen into one before. She didn't bother responding to Gol-nasrin suggestion that she be careful. There didn't seem to be anything to say to that. She followed Gol-nasrin across the rocky outcroppings, going slower and more cautiously. Gol-nasrin seemed somewhat annoyed by their slow progress, but Eve didn't want to fall into the sand again.

They reached the end of the rocky outcroppings they'd been on, and nothing but sand stood between them and the dunes. Gol-nasrin turned back to Eve and said, "Follow me exact, or you fall in." Then she started out across the sand, sinking knee-deep into the ruddy dust.

Eve had no idea how long they struggled and fought through the knee-deep sand. Time and again she slipped in the sand, as if they were walking along the top of a rocky outcropping just beneath the sand, a rocky outcropping that sank in each direction. She managed to catch herself each time she slipped, but each time Gol-nasrin paused and turned back. They were clearly making terrible time. Eve kept going, fighting with the strength of desperation in every step. Suddenly, rocks emerged from the sand in front of them, and Gol-nasrin was climbing up onto them.

Once on the rocks Eve turned to look back, and realized they were partway around the dunes. The colony was no longer in view, and she was amazed they'd already traveled that far. Before them, another string of rocks broke through the sand leading out of view. Overhead, Phobos was high and provided some light on the rocks ahead of them, but the Persian woman wasn't looking at the moon or the sand dunes. She was moving swiftly out cross the rocks bounding relentlessly. From time to time she glanced back. Was she expecting Tadeusz so soon? They made better progress now. Gol-nasrin did not waste time. She led swiftly and

Eve almost lost view of her many times. The Persian woman was obviously terrified.

Leaving the rocks behind, Gol-nasrin led Eve along a steep, sandy path leading up the dunes. Once they started to climb the sand became firmer, and soon they were only sinking ankle deep. Eve knew they were running out of time when she saw the eastern horizon was beginning to glow orange. Despite the night of travel, she had the feeling they hadn't gotten far enough.

From time to time Gol-nasrin stopped. She looked ahead but appeared to be listening for something. Eve was fighting exhaustion now. Not only had they encountered the roughest travel she had ever known, but they had also kept a pace she was not used to. Yet the Persian woman showed no evidence of fatigue and no intention of slowing down. It was clear she knew if they were caught, Eve might be taken back to the colony, but she would be shot on the spot. Gol-nasrin turned now, changing her course to proceed more directly north, but her eyes continued to watch toward her left.

Was the fact that they had to go down the sand dunes what Gol-nasrin feared? Tadeusz could guess their route or maybe follow their tracks. He could use the airship to come around the dunes and head them off. It would be easy enough to do, and in as little as an hour he could render their night of struggle pointless.

The ridge they had been following dipped

sharply down into a fantastic sandy gorge. Here the rocks were scarce, and Gol-nasrin started sliding down the gorge. Eve realized that the slide was intentional, and followed suit. It only took a few minutes to reach the floor of the crater, where they slid into the sand up to their knees. Ahead of them was another stretch of rocks leading off towards the west. They clambered onto the rocks as the sun burst over the eastern horizon.

The rocks curved sharply to the left in front of them, but remained low allowing them to move quickly. In the daylight she understood Gol-nasrin's urgency, there was no cover here. If Warszawski's airship passed over, there would be nowhere to hide.

Gol-nasrin started moving fast again, with only a glance back at Eve, nearly running wherever the rocks were even enough to permit it. At times they had to climb over great tumbled masses of red boulders, or walk cautiously across sand-smoothed rocks, some of them covered with encroaching sand drifts.

They came around the edge of a sand dune, and there Eve's airship sat with the carbon-nanotube envelope folded down onto the roof of the gondola. Eve's heart sank, Tadeusz had deflated the airship, it would take hours to get it into the sky.

"Your airship," Gol-nasrin stated as they started towards it. "You give me marijuana on the airship?"

The old Russian airship was sitting in a deep canyon that the wind had carved into the north face of the sand dunes. A good place to hide an airship Eve realized, but a difficult spot for her to pilot out of, even with Gol-nasrin's help. The airship would have to be floated straight up out of the canyon before it could be turned into the wind. A strong gust could blow the airship into the canyon wall before they cleared it. It wasn't going to be easy.

Eve ran across the rocks and shallow sand to the airship. When she got to the airship she ran up the ramp into the cargo-bay that Tadeusz must have left open. The airship was powered down, and the airlocks left open, exposing the interior to the frozen Martian air. Eve quickly made her way to the cockpit to check the fuel-cell status: 100% charged. Good.

"You can take us away now?" Gol-nasrin asked.

Eve could see that Gol-nasrin was more terrified now that they had reached their destination. Terrified because, unlike the stretches of sand and rock, this was a place where Tadeusz would definitely look for them. She thought of the difficult job of floating up out of the canyon, of how the airship could get pushed sideways into the canyon walls by even a strong breeze. She realized how impossible it would be to get it fixed out here. The sun was already above the horizon, they didn't have time to waste.

"I can try," Eve decided. The thought of the canyon walls frightened her. She had spent many years flying this airship all over the southern hemisphere, but never without her husband. She took a deep breath and reached out for the switch to start pumping hydrogen into the air-chambers above. Nothing happened. She tried again.

The moment she touched the console, she heard it. Off in the distance, but not distant enough, was the low rumble of airship engines. It had to be Tadeusz's airship. She turned, and saw it through the cockpit window drifting into view above the canyon wall.

"Quick, we must hide!" she said to Gol-nasrin, but the Persian woman was already headed for the ramp. She hit the sand and ran for the rocks. Eve, desperate to know why the airship pumps didn't start up, opened the console and glanced into the circuitry inside. The neural processor had been pulled out, and without it, the airship was dead. Tadeusz had made sure that no one was taking the airship out of the crater, at least not without his approval. She closed the console and ran.

Outside the window, she saw Gol-nasrin moving frantically across the rocks. She was leaping across a sandy stretch when the laser beam cut her in two. Tadeusz's airship was drifting down towards them, and standing on the lowered ramp was Suleiman, holding his laser rifle!

"Gol-nasrin!" Eve screamed instinctively, but

it was too late, she had already seen Gol-nasrin fly into two parts. She thought quickly about the situation. Tadeusz's airship was landing behind hers, and Suleiman would cut her down if she ran for it. She had to hide. They couldn't know for sure she was there. She ran to the bedroom. Tadeusz and Suleiman hadn't found the stash yet, the door was still closed. She reached for the hidden button, and popped the door open. Fortunately it was entirely mechanical, as Ozzy had been paranoid about DNA sensors. She stepped into the closet sized stash Ozzy and her had built to protect their assets from over-zealous colonial inspectors. Everything was still there so Tadeusz and Suleiman clearly hadn't found it.

She heard the sound of foot steps running up the ramp as she slid the stash door closed, inside she turned on a small lamp that they kept for emergencies. Around her were the drugs her and Ozzy had been using as currency, some ore samples they'd collected, and their rail-gun. She quietly picked up the rail-gun and turned it on. The electromagnetic field caused her skin to itch inside the still-suit. It was fortunate that Ozzy insisted they always kept it loaded, because loading the mag made a loud clicking sound, and Suleiman's voice was suddenly in the bedroom right outside the stash.

"She's not in here either!" Suleiman shouted.

"She has to be," Tadeusz's voice called back from what Eve assumed was the cockpit. A few

seconds later his voice sounded from the bedroom, "Why would Gol-nasrin come here by herself. She could not know how to fly an airship."

"Maybe she was just looking for things to
steal," Suleiman suggested. "Probably drugs, I
think they gave her some a few days ago, she
has not been coming around at night."

"If she did not come out here with Gol-nasrin,
then where is she?" Tadeusz demanded.

"Maybe she sank in the sand," Suleiman suggested.

"She could be hiding here somewhere,"
Tadeusz stated.

"Where? This airship is tiny, there isn't even a
full cargo hold," Suleiman argued.

"Yes," Tadeusz seemed to agree hesitantly,
"We will come back here with a plasma torch,
and cut up this ship. If she is hiding here we will
find her."

"You do not want to sell the airship?"
Suleiman asked.

"No, too many questions," Warszawski answered. "And we can not have two airships here
in the crater, the workers will escape."

"Yes, we should get back and make sure they
are working," Suleiman stated. "And make sure
she is not back their trying to organize an escape."

"Yes, if she is here, there is no way that highlander bitch can find her way back around the dunes. I think will kill..." Tadeusz's voice trailed off, and a few minutes later Eve heard the dull roar of Tadeusz's airship engines come to life, and then drift away. Eve stepped out of the stash into the bedroom, and then crept to the window. Tadeusz's airship was floating over the canyon wall and was soon out of sight.

"Highlander bitch?" Eve repeated to her self. "We'll see about that."

Eve started to laugh. She was standing in her home of the past decade, an airship that might as well be dead. The only way she could get it functional again was to make it back to the colony, across sand-pits that could swallow her whole, and then get the neural processor back from Tadeusz before the computer starved to death, and before the algae in the in the air-ship's oxygen recyclers and fuel-cells starved.

From somewhere inside her there came a deep swell of emotion, and she screamed. Some of it was from the loss of her husband. Some of it was fear of these terrible people. Some of it was just anger. Most of it was a nameless emo-tion, something primal, the feeling that an ani-mal might have, when after being chased into a corner, it turns to attack its predator. That emo-tion, when not only does it need to fight, but a switch in its mind has been thrown, and now it wants to fight.

After she screamed, she sat down, and thought about the situation. If she stayed at the airship, she'd either freeze or starve. She decided to begin back to the colony at once, and travel as far as she could before the sunset. She slung the rail-gun over her shoulder and headed for the door.

Morning found Tadeusz waking up in pain. He had clumsily fallen off one of the rock outcroppings that Gol-nasrin and Eve had negotiated in their escape the previous day. Tadeusz had twisted his knee, and now the swelling had become serious and excruciating. He took a swallow from a bottle of aguardiente he'd half finished the night before and limped to the station airlock. He stepped out into the brilliant dawn that caused him to close his eyes, waiting for them to adjust to the light.

Today he and Suleiman would have to finish what that damn woman had started. Regardless of the pain that shot through him every time he took a step, regardless of the hangover pounding in his temples, he'd find Eve Johns, and if he couldn't make her come back with him, he'd kill her. He'd eventually kill her anyway, but it would be more fun if he brought her back alive.

He surveyed the massive dunes to the north. Time to get moving. He shook his head, trying to clear it, but that movement made his vision blur.

Suddenly Tadeusz's legs fell out from under him, and he went face first into the sand. He lurched around, trying to get up even as the sonic booms of the rail-gun rounds echoed back from the sand dunes. Looking down, he saw blood streaming from holes where his knees had been. His still-suit was ripped open, and his legs below the knee were missing. He pulled his laser pistol from his hip.

Eve stepped out from behind one of the red concrete houses, the sights of her rail-gun trained on Tadeusz. Suleiman charged out of the station airlock, sonic blaster in hand, and Eve shot a burst of holes through his torso. Then she started towards them both.

Tadeusz started to raise his laser pistol, but Eve spoke before he could aim it, "Don't do it! I won't kill you if you toss it."

Tadeusz was clearly trying to raise the pistol, but lost consciousness, and the pistol fell into the sand.

Eve picked up the pistol, and then walked over to Suleiman's body and picked up the sonic blaster. She eventually found the neural processor in Tadeusz's airship. It wasn't until she turned on the engines for Tadeusz's airship that some of the miners came out to see what had happened. She went to the cargo bay and lowered the ramp.

"I'll leave this airship in the canyon on the far side of the dunes," she shouted to them as they approached Tadeusz. They looked up at her as she turned and disappeared back into the airship. The last time she looked back, they had walked over to where Tadeusz and Suleiman lay in the sand. They had picked up rocks, and as Eve turned her attention back to the airship controls they fell savagely onto the King of Mars and his business partner.

# Loyal Soldier

Above the motel, the sandstorm raged through the night. The small motel was in the valley of Claritas Fossae, near the Solis-Sirenum border on Mars. The valley provided some shelter from the sandstorm, which made the sky above impossible to navigate. The settlement of Claritas was several decades old, founded as a potato farming community to take advantage of the silty sand of the ancient riverbed, and water-ice in a local aquifer. sMost of the settlement was greenhouses, the only other buildings being the potato processing plant, the vodka distillery, and the motel which included a small pub.

Shoulders hunched against the sandstorm, the rider stared at his bike's multi-spec display as he flew through the darkness of the valley, hugging the ground to keep below the worst of the storm. It was January in 2194, and the worst storm of the summer was raging across the Solis Planum, swirling down into Claritas Fossae and blasting everything in its path.

Suddenly the shape of a human appeared in the multi-spec display. It was almost a hundred metres from the settlement, so he decided to stop and see if this person needed help. It was a woman standing in the valley in a thermal still-suit covered in a duster, like the rider was wearing. She had a flashlight in her hand which she started flashing as the rider drew close. The rider slowed, his bike's turbo-fans kicking dust in every direction. He landed his bike a couple metres from the woman and dropped a hand beneath his duster.

"Hello, are you Nuka Strange?" the woman inquired moving quickly to the bike. Her accent was American, like the rider's. Her build was thin, her stature tall, and through her respirator-mask the rider could see she was pale skinned, the signs of someone that had spent her entire life on Mars. The rider decided she was probably born in Solis, as Solis had been an American colony before being sold to the Canadians during the war.

"Nuka Strange?" He replied bewildered by the question. "No, I'm not Strange, why would you be out here looking for Nuka Strange?"

"I work at the pub in Claritas. There are some mercenaries in the pub and they're talking about Nuka Strange. They think that Nuka Strange is flying to Sirenum tonight and storm will force him down into Claritas."

"And you came out here to meet him?" the rider asked, stressing the word 'him' as Nuka Strange was a woman.

"Yes. The mercenaries are planning to kill him. I'm hoping to warn him," the Martian woman answered.

"How much do you know about Nuka Strange?" the rider questioned.

"How much do I need to know about him?"

the woman retorted. "I don't want anyone to be murdered in Claritas, not even an American."

"Fair enough," the rider responded. "I'm headed into Claritas for the night, I could-"

The rider's voice broke off sharply as two people came running through the sandstorm. Both were running at that strange gait that indicated they had recently arrived from Earth and hadn't yet adjusted to Martian gravity. Neither were wearing still-suits, instead wearing those thick puffy coats the Earth people liked. They had to be the mercenaries. As they got close the rider saw they were both dark skinned, and not the faded grayish-brown of dark-skinned Martians, but vibrant dark browns endemic to Earth. The leader was a tall woman, very dark skin, almost black. The other one was a dark-brown man, almost as tall as the woman.

"So here you are!" The Earth woman shouted to the Martian woman over the sound of the swirling sand storm. "Why are you out here?"

The Earth woman grabbed at the Martian woman's shoulder and the Martian recoiled in fear. Instantly the rider jumped from his bike and stood between them. In his right hand was his laser pistol, and in his left a plasma dagger glowed brilliantly. "Back off! She came to bring me a message, and it's private!"

"Who are you?" the Earth woman asked in a Guinean accent. She stepped toward the rider obviously not intimidated by either the pistol or dagger. She hadn't reached for a weapon, and was instead trying to get a good look at his face through his respirator-mask. Suddenly there was that look of shock people got when they recognized him, followed by something that people never did, a smile. "Don't worry about this one Bala. I know him. He will not be a problem. Will you General?"

She didn't wait for an answer, she turned and they headed back towards the settlement. Once they were out of sight, the General turned to the Martian woman and asked, "Can I give you a ride back to the pub?"

He climbed back onto his bike, and she climbed on behind him, wrapping her arms around his waist. He turned back to her before turning on the turbo-fans, "It's probably best if you don't mention what happened here to anyone."

"I understand," was all she managed to get out before the fans started up and drowned out anything else she would have said. He dropped her at the front airlock of the pub and then flew over to the parking lot of the adjoining motel. After parking his bike, he walked into motel lobby, and inhaled shallowly as he removed his respirator-mask. The motel air smelled musty, and the rider assumed they must not get many guests if they didn't bother checking the algae filters regularly.

He walked over to the wall display under the 'Concierge' sign and registered a room under an alias, then inquired, "Do you have a reservation for a Nuka Strange?"

"We do not currently have a reservation for a Nuka Strange," the concierge computer replied in an American accent.

The general shook the dust off as he removed his duster, the large overcoat commonly worn by Martians to protect their still-suits from sand damage. His dagger, pistol, and com were all within pockets in the duster. Once he felt civilized he walked over to the door under the sign 'Lucasta's Taproom.' The two mercenaries from Earth were just entering the pub through the airlock on the other side of the room. They both looked up at the general as they took off their respirator masks, then walked over to one of the tables. The general walked over to the bar, hung his duster and respirator mask on a hook, then sat down at the bar. The woman he'd met outside had walked over to the mercenaries with a couple vodkas, and so he turned on the bar's menu-display and started scrolling through the options. Most of the food was potato based, as was the vodka no doubt. There were few vegetables on the menu, and the only meat was soy-based. The potato based foods were cheap, but anything else was quite expensive, even by Martian standards.

"Can I get you something?" the waitress asked returning to the bar.

"What would you recommend?" the general

asked.

"Our potato pancakes are excellent," the waitress answered. "As are the baked potatoes, possibly the best on Mars. They're fresh, grown right here in Claritas."

"Sounds good, how about the mushrooms in the mushroom gravy?" the General asked.

"The mushroom gravy is imported from Lassell," the waitress answered. "Everything on the menu that isn't potato is imported from Lassell or Solis City."

"Well, I'll have to take your advice, and try one of your baked potatoes with the mushroom gravy, and the soy-burger on potato bread. Do you have any cheese or ketchup?"

"We do have ketchup available, and some cheese imported from Lassell," the waitress answered cautiously, "but, it is quite expensive."

"I expected it would be," the General stated. "I'll have both on the burger, and what do you have to drink other than vodka?"

"We have raspberry juice and saskatoon-berry juice," the waitress answered. "And, if you have the credit, some strawberry wine."

"Strawberry wine?" the General repeated in surprise. "From Sirenum?"

"I don't know where it's from," the waitress answered evasively.

"It's alright, I have Arean citizenship," the

General stated. "I won't be reporting you. Besides it's been a decade since I've had any strawberry wine. I'll have a bottle."

"Alright, I'll enter the order," the waitress stated. "Once you pay, the order will go through to the kitchen."

The general accepted the price on the menu-display in front of him, and added a generous tip. The waitress smiled and then left the bar to get the strawberry wine, which was stored somewhere else. Once she'd left, the pub seemed quieter and behind him the general overheard the voices of the mercenaries.

"...no way they can make it through to Sirenum in this storm!" the woman was saying in a Guinean accent. "And there are no other settlements in the region, they will have to stop here. I guarantee it Bala, by the end of the night you will owe me $500."

"For what we are to be paid, it is a small sum," the man replied in an Indian accent. "Assuming you are correct about them coming here. If not Nkiru, you will loose $500 and I at least have my drinks paid for."

"Gita reported they left Lassell six hours ago," Nkiru continued in her strong Guinean accent. "The storm has only got worse since they took off. They will have to land here."

"Good," Bala continued in his Indian accent. "The sooner we depart this frozen rock the better."

They didn't seem to have any interest in the old general at the bar. He was still young enough to be formidable in a fight, but old enough that his age was showing. His long dark-brown hair was graying. He had lost some weight since his prime, but he was still muscular, and more importantly he had years of combat experience locked into those muscles. That Guinean woman had recognized him, so she had to know he'd die hard, and not alone. He was a lot shorter than either of the mercenaries, a common trait of Martians of his age, caused by chronic childhood malnourishment.

"So what's an Arean general doing in a Canadian colony?" the waitress asked returning with the strawberry wine.

"Thinking of reporting me?" the Arean general asked with a grin.

"I doubt that would be advantageous," the waitress said pouring a glass of the contraband wine. "Besides you have an American accent, so you're probably from Xanthe. And that would be of no interest to the government in Solis City. And you didn't answer my question. What is an Arean general doing in a Canadian colony?"

"It's complicated," the Arean general answered lifting the strawberry wine to his lips. It was Sirenian, he hadn't had Sirenian strawberry wine since the war. It tasted like it was from Icaria, the old British colony. This little settlement must be selling potato products to the Areans. They were close enough to the Sirenum border that they could cross it without the government in Solis City knowing. A useful fact to remember. The wine was good. The meal came. The burger was passable, and the potato was excellent. He hadn't eaten a non-frozen potato in years. Canadian laws limited which corporations could grow which plants in their Martian colonies. The result was a high price for food throughout the colonies, and high profits for the corporate headquarters back on Earth. It also resulted in each colony having a different diet, depending on which foods were locally available. The other Earth colonies all had similar laws, it had been one of the main reasons for the war.

In the background the mercenaries were talking, but not saying anything important. Nuka Strange, the Arean general knew the name well. Last he'd heard, she'd moved to Solis from Canada, supposedly to plan the Canadian government's invasion of the Arean Confederacy. The Confederacy had been beleaguered by criminal syndicates since establishing independence, and the Canadians were apparently trying to organize an insurgency as prelude to invasion. Nuka Strange was the perfect person to organize the insurgency, she was the former Director General of the National Security Agency. Strange had fled to Canada as a refugee along with most other members of the American government and corporate elite as the Eco-Revolutionaries seized control of America. The corporate regime in Canada was more stable, and the Canadian government was aggressively funding a counter-revolution in the former United States.

If Strange was sneaking across the border into Sirenum, she was defecting to the Ares Confederacy. If she was defecting, she had gone Eco. If so, Ares was about to gain a major asset. Strange was reputed to be both a brilliant strategist and a shrewd diplomat. She must have lost most of her corporate assets if she was going Eco. Obviously someone knew she was defecting if they'd sent mercenaries after her. The mercenaries were from Earth, so it was probably someone in Canada, likely one of the American families. It couldn't be anyone in the Canadian government, because they would have just sent the Solisian Police to arrest her. Whoever it was, these mercenaries appeared to be working with someone travelling with Strange; someone called Gita. They were correct about the storm, no small aircraft could fly through this storm. If they were up there they would be looking for a place to land.

"Who is that general?" Bala asked, suddenly drawing the Arean general's attention back to the mercenaries' conversation.

"You do not recognize him?" Nkiru asked. "It took a month to get here from Earth, what did you do during all that time?"

"A couple of the stewardesses," Bala answered. "You spent the time looking at pictures of generals?"

"I spent the time studying the region," Nkiru stated. "That is General Milburn Rome."

There it was. The name that had haunted him since the war. He had aged a bit since the war, and not everyone recognized him anymore, especially the younger generation. But that name, everyone knew that damned name. He tried to ignore them and focus on the meal he was eating, but he could feel his face turning red. Even after more than a decade since the war's end, he still got angry whenever he heard people talk about him. None of them knew what he'd done, yet all judged him.

"That is General Rome?" Bala stated in disbelief. "Did they not shoot him after the war?"

"No, he was given immunity," Nkiru answered. "All the soldiers under his command were given immunity."

"I would have just shot them all," Bala stated.

"Then they would not have surrendered," Nkiru replied.

"Do you think there is a price on his head in the Confederacy?" Bala inquired.

"Probably," Nkiru answered. "But we do not have time to do anything about it. As soon as Nuka Strange is dead, we are to return to Earth. Our client is very clear on that point."

"How would they know?" Bala asked.

"How do you expect to claim a bounty on Milburn Rome without our client finding out?" Nkiru countered.

"I see your point," Bala conceded. "Well, at least we do not need to worry about him interfering. Not someone like him."

There it was, the judgment. The same judgment every time, by everyone. A coward who sold out the Eco-Revolution in Solis to the corporate backed Canadian troops. He noticed his hand was trembling slightly from the anger welling up inside him, and lifted the fork he was holding to his mouth.

"More wine?" the waitress interrupted the Arean General's dark thoughts. How much of the mercenaries' conversation had she overheard? Probably all of it.

"No thanks," General Rome replied. The least he could do was remain civil. "What do you have that's non-alcoholic?"

"Raspberry juice and saskatoon-berry juice," the waitress replied. "Or water of course, quite cheap, there's a large aquifer below us."

"Cheap water?" General Rome chuckled. Free Water was one of the promises of the Eco-Revolution. "I'll try the saskatoon-berry juice. Where do you import that from?"

"We get it from Lassell," the waitress answered. "It just became available, it's quite good."

"Any idea where it comes from?" General

Rome asked. "Is it imported from Earth?"

"Oh no!" the waitress answered. "The University of Saskatchewan is sponsoring a new farming community in Noachis, where they are growing saskatoon-berries."

"Ah, that's how they managed to get around the bio import laws," General Rome realized.

"Yes, we've heard they're also experimenting with canola and lentils," the waitress stated. "Unfortunately they're only marketing the saskatoon-berry juice, and saskatoon-berry jelly so far."

"It's still progress," General Rome observed. "The first new plants on Mars since the war, or at least the first one's I've heard of. It might-"

"Did you see that?" Bala suddenly demanded jumping to his feet.

"What?" Nkiru asked also rising to her feet.

"A light! Something is landing outside," Bala stated headed to the airlock. "I saw it moving through the sandstorm, just for a second. It looked like it was heading down to the motel landing pad."

General Rome waited until the mercenaries were in the airlock before jumping to his feet and grabbing his duster and respirator mask. "I'll be back," he said to the waitress as he ran to the door into the motel. He swung the duster over his shoulders as he stepped into the lobby airlock, then pushed the respirator mask to his face as he hit the button for the outer air-lock door. As he stepped out into the swirling sand, he pulled the strap of the respirator mask over the back of his head, and the mask pressurized. Across the lot a vehicle had just landed. All Rome could see through the sand were the lights, but based on their spacing it had to be a truck or a bus.

He saw the shapes of the mercenaries moving around near the pub's airlock, and ran out into the sandstorm at a right angle to the vehicle so the mercenaries wouldn't see him. When he couldn't see them any more, he curved back towards the vehicle. It was a bus, a long range transport, the type usually used to connect smaller settlements to major hubs. Someone was climbing out, several people. General Rome ducked under one of the short wings that supported the turbofans, and crept up behind the new arrivals, he couldn't see the mercenaries anywhere. Rome pulled out his pistol and dagger, but left the dagger's plasma-blade turned off as the light would immediately alert everyone to his presence.

The new arrivals were talking with American accents, but not local ones. The accent in Solis was based on the New York Dialect while the Xanthe accent was based on the Western American Dialect. One of these new arrivals could be from Xanthe, but the others were clearly from Earth. A man with a Southern accent, and a woman with a New England accent.

"This fucking planet!" the woman with the New England accent swore. "I can't believe anyone wants to live in this shit!"

Definitely Earth-born. They ran towards the pub airlock. Rome still couldn't see the mercenaries anywhere. He waited a couple minutes for movement but couldn't see anything through the sand so ran back to the motel airlock. He pulled off his mask and duster, and shook off the loose sand before casually walking back into the pub. The three Americans were sitting at one of the tables, and the waitress was explaining why the menu was so potato-based. There was no sign of the mercenaries. Rome sat at the bar in the same seat he was in earlier, and ordered another saskatoonberry juice through the bar's menu-display.

The waitress returned to the bar somewhat flustered by the Earth-borns' bewildering questions about foods they didn't have in Claritas, and poured Rome's juice before mixing the Americans' drinks. Rome took the juice and sipped it, before pulling out his com. He looked up Nuka Strange in the database, she was an Alaskan Inuit, the pale skinned woman with the western accent. She wasn't saying much at the table, neither was the brown woman with the New England accent. The tan skinned southern man seemed to be doing all the talking, mostly complaints about the storm and the food. None of the conversation seemed related to their destination, but if they were here, there was only one place they could be going.

The mercenaries reentered the bar and looked around casually. They were trying to look like locals just come in from the storm. It would have been more convincing if they weren't dressed like tourists. The Americans were dressed the same, they probably wouldn't notice. The mercenaries sat at the same table they were at earlier, and called the waitress by her name, which was apparently Joanie, asking for Red Swirls. They must have asked her name earlier because she wasn't wearing a name badge. The Red Swirl was the Vodka Raspberry mix Joanie had told Rome about earlier. It was apparently the local favorite, Rome had over-heard Joanie telling the Americans the same thing as he walked in. Nuka had ordered one, the other two had ordered straight vodkas after a lengthy explanation from Joanie as to why they didn't have any beer.

The door to the motel opened and Rome's shadow walked in. That complicated things. The tall thin black man took a seat at the opposite end of the bar. He had been following Rome for years, although they never bothered talking. He was Martian born of African ancestry, almost as dark as the Guinean mercenary, but that faded shade of grayish-brown that differentiated the locals from the tourists. He'd heard the man's accent many times, he was Solisian, like Rome. He looked at the menu and ordered a couple baked potatoes and the Red Swirl that Joanie suggested. Another sign that he was Martian, as was the still-suit and duster he was wearing.

Rome needed to expedite things, everything would go sideways if his shadow learned who the Americans were. He got up, slipped on his duster, and walk towards the airlock, then paused looking at the table of Americans. "You're lost, aren't you?"

"Fuck off," the Southerner answered.

"You know you're in Solis now?" Rome asked. "You'll get arrested if the Canadians find out you've crossed the border."

"We haven't-" the Southerner started.

"Thank you," Nuka Strange cut him off. "We got lost in the storm. The GPS was blacked out."

"I recommend you cross back before the storm passes," Rome said walking over to their table. "Or you might get stuck here like the rest of us."

"You're Arean?" Strange asked.

"Yes," Rome answered, "but I haven't been in the Confederacy for years."

"Why don't you just cross during a storm?" the Southerner asked.

"I don't have a vehicle capable of making the crossing during a storm," Rome answered.

"We don't have room for hitchhikers," the New England woman stated.

"Fare enough," Rome said turning to leave.

"We could make room," Strange proposed.

"Where are you from?"

"I have a house in Pickering," Rome stated, not actually answering the question.

"The capital," the Southerner said in a tone Rome didn't quite understand. "Well ain't that special!"

"The current capital," Rome observed.

"You think the legislation will pass?" Strange asked.

"I have no doubt," Rome said, sitting down at their table. "It's what we've been planning since the war."

"Governments have no business building cities," the New Englander stated. "If cities don't grow organically around natural resources then they won't be economically sustainable, and will suffer from endemic unemployment."

"You might want to keep that Smithian propaganda to yourself inside the Confederacy," Rome stated.


"It doesn't apply anyway," Strange observed. "The Confederacy won't have an unemployment issue for centuries."

"They'll never raise the credit to terraform this planet," the Southerner dismissed Strange's statement.

"I don't think you understand resource based economics," Rome observed.

"They don't need capital," Strange agreed. "Just people willing to work on an impossible dream."

"It'll fail just like Marxism," the New Englander dismissed Strange again.

"Maybe on Earth," Strange agreed. "But not here. The Martians have no choice but to make it work. They need a viable biosphere, and they believe in the dream."

"The Confederacy will never get the colonial governments of Earth to go along with it," the Southerner stated. "And you can't just terraform part of a planet."

"You're right, Avi," Strange agreed. "You can't terraform just part of a planet, and once this planet's biosphere starts to spread into the colonies, what do you thing will happen to the colonial economies?"

"Total economic collapse," the New Englander observed. "But they'll never get the biota to pull it of."

"They will," Strange disagreed. "There will always be someone willing to run a blockade for money."

"And as the colonial economies collapse, the eco-revolution will spread," Rome added.

"They don't have enough people," the Southerner named Avi argued. "They don't even have people to populate this new city they want to build."

"They have an open door policy regarding immigrants, and no eugenics laws, meaning people who can't get permits to have children on Earth will flock here," Strange stated. "Assuming any country chooses to recognize them and open trade."

"And no country will," Avi stated triumphantly.

"America will," the New Englander said. "We have a population surplus, you know it's just a matter of time before the Confederacy agrees to formal relations with the new American government."

"And those immigrants will find ways to smuggle in seeds," Rome added. "The revolution is complete. Now manifest destiny."

"You sound like that windbag Dalton," Avi stated.

"You might want to keep your opinion of Dalton to yourself as well, when you're in the Confederacy," Rome observed.

"You're a fan of Dalton?" Strange asked Rome directly.

"Why else would I have fought for him?" Rome answered equally directly.

"Then why did you surrender?" Strange asked.

Unusual. People didn't ask that question. They assumed the answer. "Why do you think?"

"Survival," Strange answered. "But not yours."

"What are you two talking about?" Avi demanded, bewildered by the conversation's sudden change in direction.

"This is General Milburn Timothé Rome," the New Englander stated, clearly following the conversation.

"It was unwinnable. The army was done," Rome answered Strange's question. "The economy was in ruins, industry stalled, no meds, no food. There was mass starvation and rampant cannibalism. We couldn't fight anymore."

"General Dalton did," Avi stated rejoining the conversation.

"Did he?" General Rome asked briefly turning his attention to Avi.

"There were no major battles after General Rome surrendered," Strange observed.

"Six months of fire fights, and then an armistice," Rome agreed.

"So Dalton was done too?" the New Englander inquired.

"Everyone was done," Rome stated. "The Americans, Chinese, British, and Russians had been driven off world, and the Canadians, Brazilians, and Sudaméricans hadn't sent reinforcements for over a year. There was nothing left to the war but random bombings, and starving orphans."

"So you're not a coward, you're a humanitarian!" Avi declared contemptuously.

"Politics," Strange surmised.

"Politicians," Rome corrected.

"What?" Avi asked.

"The Canadians needed a win to begin negotiations," Strange surmised.

"Something for the public," Rome added.

"Spin? You surrendered for spin?" Avi demanded in disbelief.

"Food, I surrendered for food," Rome stated. "The spin just allowed the Canadian government to formulate an exit strategy."

"Sounds like retcon BS," Avi stated.

"Sounds like truth to me," Strange disagreed. "Why you? Why not Dalton?"

"I'm more pragmatic than Dalton," Rome answered. "He'd never surrender. For him it would be giving up on the dream."

"Not for you?" Strange asked.

"I wasn't the dreamer," Rome stated.

"Can he be trusted?" Strange asked.

"Yes, but he needs a lot of help," Rome answered.

"I know. The Confederacy has no trade or

diplomatic relations," Strange stated. "America tried to open diplomacy last year, and the Arean senate rejected it."

"Areans still see America as the enemy," Rome explained. "I suggest an alliance. If America agrees to invade Sudamérica, then the Areans can invade the Sudamérican colonies up north."

"Thank you," Strange accepted the advice and then moved on to the more pertinent issue. "So, who's working with the mercenaries?"

"Gita," Rome answered, quietly pulling his pistol from its holster beneath the table.

"Gita?" Strange said turning her attention to the New Englander. "How much, old friend?"

"Nobody wants America and Ares forming an alliance," Gita stated and glanced over at the mercenaries, who were standing up from their table. Avi quickly realized what was happening and jumped up gun in hand.

"It's three against one, Avi," Gita stated. "Lower your weapon."

"Three against two," Rome stated raising his pistol above the table and standing up. The pistol was pointed at Gita. She raised her own pistol pointed at Rome, but didn't bother standing. She was a politician, and expected to talk her way out of it.

"Three against three," the shadow stated from the bar, he too had drawn a gun and it was pointed at the mercenaries.

"Yours?" Strange asked Rome.

"Solisian," Rome answered.

"Ironic," Strange observed, and then turned to Avi. "Shoot the mercenary on the left."

The room erupted in a blast of laser fire, and in seconds half the people in the room were dead. Rome and Gita had shot each other. Avi and the shadow had each shot a mercenary. The mercenaries didn't have a clear shot at Strange because Rome was standing in between them; both had shot Rome.

"Interesting planet," Strange said getting to her feet.

Avi reached down and checked Rome for a pulse, "Why'd he do that?"

"He was a loyal soldier," Strange answered. "And the revolution must go on. Now manifest destiny, as they say."

The shadow walked over to the table and checked Rome for a pulse as well. Then turned and left the pub. He didn't ask who the Americans were. It wasn't his job.

"He'll have to report this," Avi stated once the Solisian soldier had left the pub.

"Yes, I think it's time to leave," Strange stated. "Pick up the general's body. We've found our way to make contact with Prime-Admin Dalton."

# Desert Rangers

The second Gabriel Esparza saw the riders in the chasma below, his heart-rate increased knowing what was about to happen. That had to be Ferderand Afuyog riding the green Italika bike, surrounded by the three other bikes.

Gabriel twisted the throttle on his green Italika and the air-bike lurched forward over the edge of the chasma wall, and down towards Ferderand at near free-fall. The chasma was over five kilometers deep, and the walls were almost vertical the first two kilometers before slanting down to the small lakes at the center of the chasma. A few minutes later Gabriel was pulling up next to Ferderand. The other three riders had seen him coming and converged in front of Ferderand. As Gabriel pulled up next to Ferderand he recognized Elías Medina, and the man looked annoyed to see Gabriel show up.

"Okay hombres," Gabriel shouted over the sound of the bikes' turbofans. "Vamos!"

The situation changed radically when Gabriel arrived, and Elías Medina's expression showed his uncertainty. The odds were still on his side, but Gabriel was a good shot, and Elías couldn't risk a witness surviving to inform the sheriff.

"If they pull their guns," Ferderand shouted to Gabriel loud enough for everyone to hear, "I want to shoot Elías!"

Elías' face jolted up towards Ferderand, but he hesitated pulling his gun. He'd seen Ferderand shoot a man in Rotterdam, a tweaked-out Sudamérican junkie who'd lost his mind and went on a shooting spree. Ferderand was a good shot and didn't flinch, the signs of a former soldier.

Elías had never seen Gabriel Esparza in a gunfight, but the foreman of the Nueva Sirian crew had a reputation in Echus Region dating back to the war, long before he moved to Nueva Siria and somehow become the head of the Desert Rangers. The rumor was he'd been a Sudamérican Army sniper that had defected to the Eco Revolutionaries after being sent to take out their leadership.

"Your ranger's over-stepping his authority Esparza!" Elías shouted over the sound of the turbo-fans. "He ordered us out of the lakelands."

"Why are you here?" Gabriel Esparza demanded.

The rider to Elías' right seemed to realize her position was precarious and started backing away from Gabriel.

"Stay where you are," Gabriel barked, "or I'll shoot your bike out from under you!"

She stopped her retreat and Elías shouted back at Gabriel, "She can ride anywhere she wants!"

"No, she can't!" Gabriel wasn't going to back down. If he hadn't come along Ferderand could already been dead. "You're not rangers, and you're not working for any of the Biotics companies. You have no business in the Lake-lands. We're working here, and we don't like poachers. Largarse!"

Elías' hands began trembled he was so angry, "This isn't going to end well, Gabriel!"

"This can go down any time you want," Gabriel answered quickly. "Want to do this now?"

Elías Medina wasn't used to backing down, but he didn't think he could win this one. He didn't usually have to deal with men like Gabriel Esparza and Ferderand Afuyog.

"Alright, we'll leave!" Elías shouted suddenly, and then turned his bike and flew off, with both his people following quickly.

The two rangers watched until they were almost out of sight then Ferderand asked, "Want me to follow them?"

"No," Gabriel decided. "Let's head back. We're running out of time."

"You showed up at the right time," Ferderand glanced over at Gabriel with a grin. "A few more minutes and I would've had to kill them."

"They were here to kill you," Gabriel agreed. "I don't get it. Had trouble with them before?"

"Not until I ordered them out of the Lakelands," Ferderand answered equally confused. "There's something strange about that group. Doesn't make sense to pick a fight with a group of rangers."

They rode away, heading east back to the base-camp. The base-camp wasn't very large, just a few airship gondolas with their hydrogen envelops folded down, and an odd collection of air-bikes and auto-gyros, all painted the same shade of forest green. When Gabriel and Ferderand arrived at the camp-site they paused at the edge of the patch of green plants, with their white and yellow flowers. Gabriel adjusted his respirator-mask, looking down at the patch of flowering plants growing around the temporally thawed lake in front of them.

When the Nueva Sirian government had bought the plants from Arreola Biotics Unlimited, it looked like a win-fall. Long ago Gabriel had fought along side the owner of the company Cecilia Arreola. That was long before the Nueva Sirian government had decided to setup the Desert Rangers, and hired Gabriel to lead them.

In all the years he'd known her, Cecilia had seemed honest and reliable, so when she showed Gabriel her records claiming over 50,000 plants Gabriel had vouched for her with the Nueva Sirian Terraforming Office. The price was reasonable, but now the number of plants was coming up far below 50,000, and Gabriel couldn't understand it. He couldn't believed that Cecilia's count was fraudulent, it wasn't in her nature.

"The count's short, isn't it?" Ferderand asked. He knew Gabriel was worried. "You think Medina knows anything about that?"

"How could he? Our people are doing the count. Medina hasn't even been in the Lakelands until today," Gabriel answered.

His vouching for Cecilia had allowed the Nueva Sirian Terraforming Office to move forward with the purchase before the audit, and begin the transplanting the plants to the Noctis Labyrinthus before the end of the three month thawed period. If the plants didn't take in their new home before the beginning of the eighteen month frozen period, the investment would be a waste. Now the count was off, and it could cost Gabriel more than his job.

The project to transplant some of the plants from the Hebes Chasma to the Noctis Labyrinthus was controversial enough. Only one plant species was known to grow out in the thin freezing Martian atmosphere, the Ranunculus glacialis from Greenland. It only grew in a few locations around the equator at the bottom of the chasmas, where the atmosphere was thick enough to trap sufficient heat that the frozen lakes were able to thaw for a few months each year. There were no lakes or plants in the Noctis Labyrinthus, but during the last thawed period in the Lake-lands, prospectors in the Noctis Labyrinthus found a stream of liquid water.

That was nineteen months earlier, and the debate had raged in the Nueva Sirian senate for most of that time. The government of Echus Region wasn't excited about loosing the plants, however their attempt to block the sale was was vetoed by the Confederate senate, who didn't want the regional governments interfering with the global terraforming mission.

Now tens of thousands of the plants were missing, and someone would end up being held accountable. Gabriel was feeling that weight coming down on him. Roelof Van Den Andel and Hai Ruan looked up as Gabriel and Ferderand rode into the base-camp. Roelof was from Hebes Chasma, a pail-skinned descendant of one of the old mining families that had been in the chasma since the Corporate Era. Hai Ruan was born in Nueva Siria, also a descendant of miners from the Corporate Era, in the old Chinese colony in Arsia Mons. She had been recruited to the Nueva Sirian Desert Rangers by Ferderand, who had fought beside her in the war. Ferderand was also born in Nueva Siria, at the old Filipino mining colony in Noctis Labyrinthus.

The two mining colonies had ended up in the Sudamérican Colonial Zone after the Mars Treaty, and Sudamérica united them into the Colony of Nueva Siria, named after the Syria Planum. The deep Hebes Chasma and the vast but shallow Echus Chasma to the north of it had fallen under the Sudaméricans as well, who established their own colony in Echus, and placed the old Dutch mining colony in Hebes under Echus' authority. Nueva Siria and Echus were two of the five Sudamérican colonies to revolt from Bogotá's authority during the war, to become part of the Arean Confederacy. To the north, the rest of Sudamérica's colonies remained firmly under Bogotá's control.

"What did you find?" Gabriel asked after landing at the base-camp.

"Four thousand in that last patch," Roelof answered.

"Any unmarked plants?" Ferderand asked.

"Not one," Ruan answered.

"That's strange," Ferderand observed. "There should still be first generation plants growing in the chasma."

"The biotics companies could have pulled them up to use there locations for seedlings," Ruan suggested. "They would have been in the best locations to place their own plants."

"Still, there should be some unmarked plants," Ferderand mused.

"Still there should be 50,000 plants with Arreola's bio-marker in them," Gabriel interjected. "What are we at?"

"We're still short 15,000," Ruan answered.

"Is that Nibhanupudi Biotics guy still around?" Gabriel asked.

"Ashok? No, he went back to Rotterdam a

few hours ago," Roelof answered. "Said he had some business."

Nibhanupudi Biotics Unlimited was the chief competitor of Arreola Biotics Unlimited. Around a dozen companies owned plants in the chasma, Arreola and Nibhanupudi were the two biggest. Since the second year of planting, each company's plants were genetically modified with hereditary markers that allowed the Echusian Desert Rangers to audit the Lake-land biota. The bio-markers were registered with the government of Echus Region in Nueva Buenos Aires, the regional capital. The companies were paid by the Confederacy for each plant they owned that successfully flowered at the end of the thawed period. Ashok Nibhanupudi had visited Nueva Sirian Desert Rangers every day since they'd arrived in the chasma. Most of the other companies hadn't bothered to send observers. Ashok Nibhanupudi lived in Rotterdam, the closest town, so he rode out regularly to check no one was disturbing his plants.

"Ashok's never here for more than an hour," Ruan stated.

"I think we chose the wrong job," Ferderand smirked. "I wouldn't mind working just an hour a day!"

"His people do enough," Gabriel observed. "They own a lot of the plants growing out here. Did you guys find any plants belonging to Arreola in that bog out west?"

"I couldn't get close enough to scan some of them," Ferderand answered. "That bog is really treacherous. But only about ten to twenty."

"Ten to twenty plants aren't important enough to risk your life," Gabriel stated. "We need to find thousands."

"I've been thinking about Ashok," Ferderand said thoughtfully. "He comes out here for an hour or so everyday, as if he's checking up on us. Then he says he's heading back to Rotterdam, but you rarely see him there, and Rotterdam isn't that big."

"Maybe he just works in his office," Ruan suggested.

"This job doesn't require much office work," Roelof dismissed the idea.

"It doesn't matter what he's doing. It's none of our business," Gabriel dismissed the question, wandering off towards to patch of plants that had already been worked. More than half the plants were still in the ground, divided by small holes where Arreola's plants had been dug up. In a few hours Gabriel would be riding to Rotterdam, where he'd have to explain to Furaha Tip that the number of plants was going to be considerably smaller than expected. He stood there glaring at the plants, and tried to remember if there were any other bodies of water they had somehow missed. Hugo, Adoración, Philibert, and Jessika were still out there checking the eastern lakes. Maybe they'd find something.

"Headed into Rotterdam?" Roelof asked as Gabriel climbed onto his bike.

"Yeah, I have to tell Furaha the count's short," Gabriel answered.

"I'll ride along," Ferderand offered climbing on his bike. "In case we encounter something interesting."

Gabriel grinned. Few men he'd worked with were as understated as Ferderand Afuyog. The ranger was an expert survivalist, he could be dropped anywhere on the planet and survive, but what he really liked was a good fight. Gabriel knew Ferderand was heading to Rotterdam to find Elías Medina.

"We don't want any trouble," Gabriel ordered. "You know how Furaha is."

Ferderand glanced at Gabriel. "Think this'll blow back on her?"

Gabriel stared ahead stoically. "How couldn't it? It's her project, and she's the one who recommended me to head up the rangers."

"Yeah, it doesn't look good," Ferderand agreed. "You ever think that maybe Arreola faked their records? They do get paid per plant."

Gabriel considered the question for a couple seconds before answering. It was something he didn't like to think about. "The Echusian Desert

Rangers audited over 45,000 Arreola plants last season. I can't see how there could be over 10,000 less this year."

Ferderand wasn't quick to respond either, he hadn't thought about the blow back on the Echusian Desert Rangers. "I hadn't consider that," he finally stated. The meaning was clear enough to both of them. Gabriel had been an Echusian Desert Ranger last season, and now he was responsible for a purchase that ended up falling short by 15,000 plants. To someone that didn't know him, it could look like a scam. He could be charged with capitalism, one of the few crimes in the Confederacy that warranted the death penalty.

Furaha Tib was waiting for Gabriel in the lobby of the hotel when he got to Rotterdam. She smiled when he joined her, but he solemnly pointed to the bar without a word. Rotterdam was a small colony of a few thousand people, in the northern lowlands of the Hebes Chasma. It had started as an European Space Agency research outpost, that had become an AkzoMars mining colony after the discovery of a protactinium rich uranium deposit. The colony had languished under Sudamérican rule after the Mars Treaty, resulting in a large independence faction that had been in revolt for almost a decade before the war that had created the Ares Confederacy.

The core of the colony was a pressurized dome that had been erected by the ESA. It was only one kilometer across, but had a small park in the center that had become the heart of the town. Around the park the ESA engineers had built a ring of dorms and labs that had become offices and shops during the Corporate Era. The ESA had also pioneered farming on Mars, with a large complex of greenhouses that had once grown a number of fruits and vegetables, along with chickens and rabbits. Most of the species hadn't survived the Corporate Era, and now the greenhouses only produced tomatoes, chilis, cucumbers, and apples. Everything else eaten in Rotterdam was imported. Apartment buildings and processing facilities had been built up around the dome during the Corporate Era, all connected via pressurized catwalks, so once inside people could move around without respirator masks.

Gabriel and Ferderand had parked their green Italikas in the garage that Nueva Siria had leased for the mission, and then headed into the dome to where the La Bergère Mars hotel was located. The La Bergère Mars' bar was built on a deck overlooking the park, and above them the sky was darkening beyond the plexiglass dome. Gabriel and Furaha sat down at a table overlooking the park, Gabriel ordered a calvado, Furaha ordered a hot apple cider. Then Gabriel looked at Furaha somberly. "The count is short."

"How short?" Furaha asked realizing it couldn't be a small number.

"About 15,000," Gabriel answered. Around them the bar was noisy, but for them the entire universe was suddenly silent. They were both contemplating the ramification. Furaha was heading up the Nueva Sirian Terraforming Office, and therefore Gabriel's boss. She was also his wife, and the main reason the NSTO had hired ex-military to serve as rangers instead of environmental scientists. Furaha was an environmental scientist, a planetary engineer from East Africa, who had defected to the Arean Confederacy right after the war in order to be part of the Eco-Revolutionary's promise to terraform Mars.

Furaha and Gabriel had met in Echus, an unlikely couple of Earth-borns in a post-independence region of Mars. Gabriel was a Sudamérican from Mexico with coffee-coloured skin, and Furaha was from East Africa with even darker skin. They stood out, the shades of their skin were too brown. After a generation or two on Mars, the original shades of human skin had faded into greyer tones, as no one ever went outside without being fully clothed. Most of the Earth-born had left or been killed during the war. Afterwards the Mars-born had briefly become highly xenophobic, especially those that hadn't fought. For two years Gabriel had worn his uniform whenever he went out in public so people would know which side he'd served on. When they met, Furaha had almost given up on her dream of being a terraformer, as she just couldn't take the xenophobia and was trying to figure out how to get back to Earth from the embargoed Ares Confederacy. When he found out she was an environmental scientist he called a friend in the Echusian government, who hired her to work in the Terraforming Office they were setting up.

The xenophobic wave had passed by the time the Nueva Sirian government had decided to setup their own Terraforming Office, and they hired Furaha to head it up. She had recommended the ex-military personnel for the Nueva Sirian Desert Rangers because she'd found them far more reliable than the scientists they'd sent out. She also recommended Gabriel to head-up the ranger group. Now their first project was hitting a major road-block, one that smacked of capitalism.

"I was afraid of something like that," she finally said. "I'm reasonably sure some of the rangers were taking bribes."

"Cecilia's not the type that would pay a bribe," Gabriel replied. "She's both too honest, and too cheap. I'm having a hard time believing Cecilia could have been involved."

"Speak of the devil," Furaha stated, nodding her head towards Cecilia, who had just entered the bar and was heading to their table. Following her were four of her crew, led by her foreman Ale Rodríguez. All of her crew were former military, mostly Sudamérican troops that had been left behind when the region fell to the Eco-Revolutionaries. Most of the Earth-born troops that survived the war had nothing to return to on Earth, and limited skills beyond combat. Few could find employment, and crime had run rampant throughout the former Earth colonies for years, fueling the xenophobia that had briefly engulfed the Confederacy. Cecilia had fought for the Eco-Revolutionaries during the war, but didn't discriminate which soldiers she hired.

"Esparza!" Cecilia's voice echo across the room, and the other patrons began vacating the bar. "I've heard you claiming our numbers are off! You think I'm a capitalist!"

As Gabriel Esparza carefully got to his feet, Ferderand Afuyog entered the bar and started quietly towards the Arreola crew.

"The numbers are off Cecilia, but I didn't say you were involved," Gabriel replied calmly.

"No, that's bullshit boss!" Ale Rodríguez sneered from behind Cecilia.

"I wasn't talking to your bitch Cecilia, and it isn't bullshit. I've known you too long to accuse you of something like this," Gabriel continued calmly. "You sold us over 50,000 plants. I accepted your numbers without question, and vouched for them, and also you, to the NSTO."

Cecilia stared at him, waiting for him to get to the point, and then after a few seconds demanded, "What's the problem?"

"We've only found around 35,000 plants with

your bio-marker," Gabriel reported.

"35,000?" Cecilia stared speechless for a few seconds. "You puto! If you only found 35,000 plants, it's because you hid the other 15,000!"

Gabriel wasn't expecting that response, it wasn't rational. There was no reason for Gabriel to under report the number, let alone hide the plants. He didn't know whether to be angry at the suggestion, or to laugh. He decided to remain calm, and stated, "We need 50,000 plants Cecilia."

"He's trying to jam you up, Cecilia," Ale declared. "Let me take care of this maricón for you."

"I wouldn't do anything stupid," Ferderand said from behind the Cecilia crew. He had his pistol pointed at Ale. "Of course, I'm smarter than you are so, we'll see if you do something stupid."

"Ferderand! Back down," Gabriel barked and then turned to Ale. "And you need to shut up before you get a bunch of people killed."

Cecilia's anger left her as she realized that things were about to go sideways. Furaha Tib was there, a government scientist that didn't carry a gun. If she got shot there would be no way anyone could claim self-defense.

"Shut up Ale!" Arreola ordered. "Sorry Gabriel, this is getting out of hand. But you know me. I never stole anything from anyone.

You know that better than anybody."

"Ms. Arreola," Furaha interjected quietly. "Just before you came in Gabriel was saying that you couldn't be responsible for the discrepancy."

Cecilia paused considering and then decided to take a different approach. She pulled a chair over from the next table and sat down, "I guess I over reacted then. The idea that you were accusing me of capitalism really pissed me off."

"Let's move on then," Gabriel suggested and then looked over to Ferderand. "We don't want any trouble here, do we?"

"I agree," Cecilia turned to her crew. "You guys take off, I'll handle this from here."

As the Arreola crew left the table, patrons began to return, and with them came Ashok Nibhanupudi, the owner of Nibhanupudi Biotics Unlimited. Ashok was Mars-born, his ancestors were Colonial Era miners in the old Indian colony on Pavonis Mons. His family had been hydroponic engineers for more than a century, so when Ranunculus glacialis was proven to grow outside, Ashok moved to Hebes Chasma to found a Biotics company. In the past six years it had grown into one of the largest biotics companies in the chasma, owning tens of thousands of plants and employing dozens of staff.

"Hello, Ms. Tib!" Ashok interjected himself into their conversation at the table. "The NSTO office suggested I might meet you here. Could I have a few minutes of your time?"

Gabriel looked up at Ashok and was surprised to see him dressed in a business suit. Gabriel had only seen Ashok in a dust covered still-suit before.

"Why, yes, Mr. Nibhanupudi, just one minute please," Furaha turned quickly back to Gabriel and Cecilia. "Do you think you can find a solution to this without me here?"

"We can give it a shot," Gabriel said.

"Sure," Cecilia agreed. She pulled her com from her pocket and projected a map of the chasma above the table. "Let's figure out where the plants are. Where did you find your plants?"

Gabriel and Cecilia compared their numbers for a few hours but were not able to find any large unaudited patches. All of the numbers in Gabriel's audit were smaller than the numbers reported in the Arreola records. In each patch of plants Arreola claimed there were more plants than the Nueva Sirian Rangers had found. The numbers looked inflated, yet Gabriel still couldn't bring himself to believe that Cecilia was providing false numbers.

Eventually Cecilia gave up and left. The sky was dark overhead, and far off stars shone as blurry splotches of light in the plexiglass dome. Most of the patrons had left the bar. Near the far end of the bar Ale Rodríguez and the Arreola crew were still at a table. Across the bar Ferderand sat at a table, watching. He was playing a game on the tabletop holographic display, but kept glancing up at Ale's crew. After Cecilia had left, Gabriel walked over and joined Ferderand. On the tabletop holographic display Ferderand was playing one of those games with sword-fighting and magic-carpets. He nodded to Ale as Gabriel sat down. "Rodríguez has a lot of credit. He's been buying drinks for the whole table all night."

As they spoke Elías Medina entered the bar, along with Justine Aalfs and Chidimma Aniakor, the two people that were with him earlier in the chasma. Justine averted her eyes from Gabriel and Ferderand. At least one of the three was willing to leave well enough alone. The three walked over to the Arreola crew and joined their table. It was the first time Gabriel realized Elías and Ale knew each other. He wondered when they'd met. Both were Earth-born Sudaméricans, they could have served together in the war.

"Let's head out," Gabriel suggested to Ferderand. "We've got a lot to do tomorrow."

They got up to leave, and walked past Furaha and Ashok, who appeared to be discussing the sale of Nibhanupudi's plants to the NSTO. That was odd, as far as Gabriel knew the NSTO wasn't looking to buy any additional plants. Even the Arean Senate wouldn't let them buy Nibhanupudi's plants, it would mean they'd be taking most of the plants in the chasma. Maybe they were discussing a purchase for next season.

There was too much that didn't add up: Elías' unemployed crew ambushing Ferderand, the missing plants, Ale having a lot of credit, and Ashok offering his plants for sale. They walked back to the garage silently. Around them the town was quiet. The shops were closed, the lights dimmed. Gabriel had something to ask Ferderand, but not in public, he waited until they got to the garage. "Ferderand, have you done a count of the plants with other companies' bio-markers?"

Ferderand looked over, half awake. "No, why would I? We're not buying them."

There must be at least a hundred thousand plants in the chasma belonging to Nibhanupudi, Christin, Napoleon, Zachariah, Isaak, Cavanah, and the rest. That's a lot of plants. Gabriel wondered if any of those other companies had 15,000 more plants than audited.

It was almost noon the next day when Gabriel joined the ranger group. Gabriel had been checking the audit numbers of the other companies' plants. The rangers had been scanning the plant patches in order to determine which plants belonged to Arreola Biotics, and then collecting the Arreola plants. The total number of plants scanned was close to the number expected from the Echusian Desert Rangers audit last season. It would be another month before the Echusian Desert Rangers started this year's audit, but the Nueva Sirian

Desert Rangers had effectively conducted their own audit by scanning the patches looking for Arreola's plants. The problem was the numbers for the other company's plants looked right, none of them had an extra 15,000 plants.

Gabriel was frustrated, he had been in one of the airships' gondolas working at a desk, which he didn't enjoy. It would have been alright if he found the missing plants, but that wasn't the case. He had been up late considering the possibilities. He hadn't got much sleep, and was frustrated as he heard the rangers enter the airship. They were coming in for lunch. Ferderand, Roelof, Adoración and Jessika had just entered the airship, the others would be along soon. Gabriel met them in the cafeteria, where they were taking hot meals from the vending machine.

Gabriel sat down across from Jessika, and asked, "Jessika, what time did you get in last night?"

Jessika hesitated. "Around midnight." Jessika was an Earth-born former Canadian. Gabriel had only known her since she was hired a couple months earlier. He knew she had been the Canadian Army during the war, but that wasn't something he could hold against her given his own war record.

"Midnight?" Roelof looked at her in surprise. "I'd hardly call 3 AM to be midnight. You woke me up."

"I saw you come back about 3 AM." Gabriel stated, the rest of the rangers were silent. "I know I saw you here at 11 PM, so where did you go for four hours?"

"I just went out for a walk," Jessika's eyes shifted around the room. "I couldn't sleep."

"Me neither," Gabriel stated candidly. "So I went for a walk. Which was when I saw you return on one of the Italikas."

"You're meeting with someone!" Roelof snapped. "Who do you know in the chasma?"

"Four hours was more than enough time to ride out to the work-site we worked this morning, work it and come back," Ferderand stated, and drew his pistol, pointing it at Jessika. "You been injecting the plants with a masking agent?"

"What about it Jessica?" Gabriel looked the Canadian in the face, and she suddenly looked sick. "Jessika, who are you working for? Tell me and I'll let you go, otherwise I'm arresting you on suspicion of capitalism."

"Let's just arrest her!" Adoración pulled out her own pistol. "We can't trust anything she says!"

"Shut-up!" Gabriel snapped. "You're her partner! You haven't noticed anything? That doesn't seem likely."

Adoración suddenly turned raising her gun towards Gabriel. "Oh, you think so, you puto? I'll kill-" her sentence ended as Roelof cut a hole through her heart with his pistol. The laser beam cut a hole through the airship's fuselage behind Jessika, and air started blowing out through the hole.

"Stop!" Gabriel yelled, but it was too late, Jessika was lifting her pistol from her holster. Gabriel reached for his own pistol, but Ferderand burnt a hole through Jessika before Gabriel got his gun from its holster. Then there were two holes in the fuselage. Roelof and Ferderand ran to plug the holes with the emergency repair kit while Gabriel checked the bodies for signs of life. There was none, this isn't what he'd wanted.

"I think we should skip the rest of today's work-site, and head out to tomorrow's work-site," Roelof suggested a half an hour later, after the holes were permanently patched. "If she was injecting a masking agent, then she might not have gotten to tomorrow's patch."

"We're not involved in whatever they were doing," Philibert said. "You can ask Cecilia Arreola. I worked for her for years before joining the NSDR."

Gabriel glanced around at the rangers, who were now all in the cafeteria. The bodies of the two dead rangers had been dragged outside. "Has anybody seen them meeting with anyone in the chasma? Anybody know who they met in Rotterdam?"

Philibert hesitated and then answered, "Jessika worked for Arreola Biotics a few years ago, when I was still there. Ale Rodríguez is the only one still working there from back then. They were lovers back then. She also was involved with Chidimma Aniakor. She used to worked for Arreola for a while, I don't know where she works now, but I've seen her riding with Elías Medina."

"That makes sense," Ferderand stated. "They're all working for the same company. How are we going to figure out which one?"

Gabriel Esparza hesitated. Figuring out who they were working for was one thing, but finding the plants came first. "We can't focus on that right now. We have to find the plants."

"What do you want to do with the bodies?" Roelof inquired. "Should we call the sheriff's office?"

"No," Gabriel answered. "Leave them outside. We can call the sheriff in a few days. We have the video recording from the cafeteria as well as witnesses. It's better whoever they're working with doesn't know they're dead."

"Ashok hasn't been out yet today," Ferderand observed. "He might come by this afternoon if he doesn't go out to the work-site."

"Right, make sure to cover the bodies," Gabriel turned to Roelof. "I like your idea about skipping to tomorrow's work-site, but with them neutralized there's no reason to skip ahead. We'll see what we find there tomorrow. Today we'll finish up the work-site we've already started. Tonight we'll post a guard by tomorrow's work-site. If anybody else goes out there I want to know."

The day drew on, windy and dusty. Gabriel nervously watched the sky. There was a massive storm to the south, and Gabriel was concerned it could spread to the north. Martian dust storms had been known to last for years, and if it spread as far north as Noctis Labyrinthus they might not be able to get the plants in the ground this season.

A cloud of dust swirled above the work site, where the rangers were working in teams of two. Ferderand was handling the scanner, and Roelof was digging the plants out of the ground. Ashok arrived shortly after lunch to watch.

"Nibhanupudi Biotics, male plant," Ferderand read off the scanner. "Christin Biotics, female plant."

Ashok checked the number of Nibhanupudi Biotics' plants the rangers had found at that site, and compared it to the numbers from the previous year's audit. Gabriel Esparza was diligently avoiding the annoying owner of Nibhanupudi Biotics. Roelof was still reading from the scanner, "Nibhanupudi Biotics, female plant."

Ashok put his com back in his pocket. "Guess

I'll head back, Esparza. I've got business in Rotterdam."

Gabriel glanced over to Ashok and muttered, "Sound's good. You aren't needed here."

Ashok chuckled returning to his bike. "Maybe I'm needed somewhere else then."

Gabriel's looked back at Ashok somewhat confused. "Hopefully someone needs you for something."

"That wife of yours look like she has some needs," Ashok said. "Maybe I'll visit her."

Ashok turned on his bike and lifted into the air, his bike quickly becoming a blurry blue streak back towards Rotterdam. Gabriel watched Ashok fly off for almost a minute before his surprise turned to anger, and then he grabbed a shovel and ran for his bike.

"Damn, Ashok's in for it now!" Roelof said running for his Italika. "It takes a lot to get Gabriel pissed off. I wondered if Ashok's ever been in a fight before!"

"Lets go!" Ferderand yelled jumping on to his air-bike. "This is going to be good!"

By the time Ashok realized Gabriel was chasing him it was too late to out run him. It was also too late to buy a faster bike. Gabriel's Italika had covered most of the ground between them in a couple minutes, and Ashok's imported and much more expensive Bajaj was designed for Earth's thicker atmosphere, and its turbo-fans couldn't propel it nearly as fast as the Italika Gabriel was riding. Gabriel pulled up along side the Bajaj and thrust the shovel through one of the Bajaj's turbofans.

It was a move commonly used back in the war, but rarely used since, as it ruined the bike and often killed the rider. The turbofan's blades ripped off and the bike spun out of control, throwing Ashok, and then exploding when it hit the ground. Ashok's impact sent out a cloud of red dust, luckily he didn't land on a rock. He staggered to his feet and pulled his gun, then stopped. Gabriel's bike was floating above him, and Gabriel's gun was aimed at him. Ashok had never been in a gunfight, and his gun was barely from the holster. Several other rangers also floated nearby

"Roelof, take his gun," Gabriel shouted over the sound from his Italika. "I'm going to teach him a lesson in manors!"

"What do you mean?" Ashok snarled. "You planning to shoot an unarmed man?"

"No, you son of a bitch," Gabriel replied harshly, "I'm going to beat some manors into you with my bare fists."

Ashok grinned. "You want to go hand to hand with me? I'll kill you!"

Roelof landed near Ashok and took the gun from his hand, then stepped back to his bike. Gabriel landed next to Roelof and handed him his own gun before turning to Ashok.

Ashok was the bigger man, not taller but muscular. Gabriel was a thin wiry man, and didn't look like he should be able to take Ashok. Ashok was smiling confidently, and then jumped at Gabriel.

Ashok came fast lashing out with his left and catching Gabriel by surprise, but failed to knock him down. Gabriel moved in on Ashok and thrust a short open left into Ashok's abdomen. It jolted Ashok, but he jerked away and smashed both hands into Gabriel's respirator mask. Gabriel tried to duck a left, but caught a right. Then he closed in and threw Ashok with a body drop. Ashok came up fast and dived at Gabriel's knees and they both went down, and then they were up and fighting, throwing punches with everything they had.

Ashok sprang close, swinging with both hands. The dust rose from around them in a thick cloud, and it became difficult to see the fight after a couple minutes. Neither man would back down and they fought bitterly, brutally, at close quarters. Blood trickled from a cut in his forehead where the mask had been smashed against his head, leaving the taste of blood in his mouth. Gabriel set his feet and slammed a right fist into Ashok's solar plexus. Ashok was winded and knocked back a few feet, and Gabriel moved in throwing his right and his left. Ashok's hands came down and Gabriel lunged, swinging high and hard with both fists. Ashok went down into the dust and rolled over.

Ashok staggered to his feet and stood there weaving, then he suddenly lunged. Gabriel met him with a stiff left, followed by a right. It caught Ashok above the ear, and he fell to his knees, his head spinning. Gabriel moved in, and pulled Ashok to his feet, and holding him with his left, struck him twice in the solar plexus, and then three shots right in the respirator mask. Then he shoved the man backwards, and Ashok staggered and fell back into the dust.

Gabriel walked back to his bike and leaned against it for a minute, before climbing on to it.

"It's time to get back to work," he said to the rangers, and then turned back to Ashok. "And don't talk about my wife again!"

"You better go back to the base-camp and cleanup," Roelof suggested looking at Gabriel's mask. "You've got a lot of blood in there."

Ashok was still laying on his back, and Ferderand motioned at him. "Should we help him back to Rotterdam?"

"Let him walk!" Roelof said.

After he showered and sprayed a sim-skin bandage on his forehead, Gabriel's mind returned to their situation. It was a mistake to let Ashok goad him into a fight. He was probably going to charge Gabriel with assault. But Ashok was not his problem. He knew that Adoración and Jessika had been working with someone, probably Elías' group, and possibly with Ale, which led back to Arreola Biotics. He needed to find evidence, something concrete. He got a coffee and went to the airship's cockpit, he dropped to a seat that gave him a view of the chasma.

Ferderand and Roelof had a good idea, to watch the work-site at night. Cecilia might even be in on it, but Gabriel still couldn't bring himself to accept that. He also couldn't accept that Elías could be the mastermind in any scheme, he just didn't seem smart enough. Ferderand had suggested that Ashok didn't always return to Rotterdam when he left their work-site. If not, where did he go? A place somewhere in the chasma? Or was he, injecting the plants with a masking agent himself?

Gabriel decided to return to the work-site, and Roelof waved him over as he approached.

"Ruan and Philibert say they didn't find much at the site they worked in that canyon to the southwest," Roelof reported. "Also, Ruan saw Cecilia Arreola down there."

"Cecilia? In the canyon?" Gabriel repeated. "What was she doing? Did Ruan talk to her?"

"No, she found a few more Arreola plants and was bringing them back when she saw her. She said she was deep down into the canyon, beyond where they were working."

"When?"

"Right after you kicked the shit out of Ashok.

She's probably still down there because we heard a shot from down that way about an hour ago."

"A shot? Sonic?"

"Yeah," Roelof nodded. "Want me to ride down and have a look?"

"Yeah, I think I'll ride down there. You come along."

"Ferderand mentioned your confrontation with Elías, and then Ale. Figure they are in on whatever this is?"

"Could be," Gabriel shrugged. "Jessika and Adoración weren't working alone."

The ground was silty brown dust as they crossed the chasma floor, a seafloor that had been dry for half a billion years. The canyon was carved into the chasma's southern face. There was a lake near the mouth of the canyon where Philibert was still scanning plants.

"Did you see Cecilia here?" Gabriel demanded.

"No, Ruan said she saw her near the end of the canyon, but I didn't see her pass by here," Philibert answered. "I heard a shot from down the canyon about an hour ago, so she's probably still there."

"Take the plants you've collected back to the base-camp then come find us," Gabriel ordered.

Gabriel Esparza's dark brown eyes swept the

canyon before them. It was over five kilometers deep, and they couldn't see the end, finding a single person wouldn't be easy. Nevertheless if Cecilia did come here, she had a reason.

The wind was picking up, gusts of dust were blowing through the canyon. Gabriel knew they were running out of time, at best they could spend another week in the Hebes Chasma. If the storm kept rising they'd have to leave sooner. They found the small lake Ruan had worked earlier, and headed farther back into the canyon, hugging the ground as there were no plants anywhere else.

"Wait a minute!" Gabriel raised his right hand in a fist and then pointed. "There's something over here."

He flew his bike over to the black object laying on the ground. "It's a body."

He landed the Italika and dropped to the ground. He rolled the body over and looked down into the respirator-mask, and recognized Cecilia Arreola. Someone had burned two holes into her with a laser gun. Gabriel checked for signs of life but the body was already cooling. "Dead. Damn, she was one of the good ones."

"What's this?" Roelof asked after joining Gabriel, there were several items laying around Cecilia's body. "A hand scanner, and a jet-injector. She was injecting a masking agent!"

Gabriel scowled. "There are no plants around here." He looked around but there was nothing in the area except a sonic blaster laying in the dirt, and Cecilia's footprints leading into a gorge. "Let's see where her footprints lead."

"You have to admit it looks suspicious," Roelof said. "Why is she out here with a jet-injector if she isn't masking the bio-markers?"

Gabriel looked around thoughtfully, "Whoever shot her could have left the injector here to incriminate her."

They followed the footprints for a few minutes up the gorge to where Cecilia's bike was parked. It was the end of the footprints, and there were still no plants. They walked back to the body. Gabriel examined the way the body had fallen. There were no other footprints, and Cecilia's footprints hadn't been disturbed, so whoever shot her had been a ways off, and her sonic blaster would have been useless. He looked around at the gorge walls, and could only spot one place that would be a good vantage point for a sniper.

"Roelof, take Cecilia's body back to the basecamp," he said, and started towards the potential sniper nest.

"You think this was murder?" Roeloff asked. "If it was, we'd better find out who did it. She had a lot of friends in Rotterdam."

Who had the opportunity? Philibert, of course. And Ruan too. Both of them had been working in the canyon. But it made no sense for either of them to kill Cecilia. Someone else must have been in the area, and somehow they had to be connected to Ale, Elías, Jessika, and Adoración.

Gabriel climbed his way up the canyon wall. He'd climbed rock walls before and this one wasn't particularly difficult. From the suspected sniper nest, he could see where Cecilia's body had been laying. He looked around, and behind the rocky ledge was a larger sand covered ledge, with traces of footprints partially blown away by a bike taking off. There was nothing else, so he climbed back down.

Philibert met him on the way back to his bike. "Find anything interesting?"

"Tracks. Looks like someone sniped her. Did it from up high, but that doesn't tell us any-thing."

"It does tell you something," Philibert dis-agreed. "It tells you that whoever killed her was probably following her. Nobody comes out here by accident, and two people out here coinciden-tally, one with a reason to snipe the other? No way that's by chance."

"You're probably right," Gabriel agreed as they arrive back at the bikes. "The thing is, the sniper had a reason, and that's what we've got to figure out. The sniper must have seen Cecilia down here, shot her, and I guess dropped the jet-injector as he flew out."

"Well, the sniper wasn't up there poaching plants, there wouldn't be any up there," Philibert stated. "I'll never believe Cecilia was using a bio-masker, but it does look like she was, being found with the injector the way she was."

"It had to be something else. She was out here. Maybe she was auditing plants in the canyon, and then came up the gorge to see if there were any plants in it," Gabriel thought out-loud.

Philibert agreed dubiously. "Could be. But what was she looking for?"

Ferderand flew up as they stood at the bikes discussing the situation. "There's a crowd forming at the base-camp. The sheriff's there too."

"The sheriff? Already?" Gabriel shrugged. "The law always gets there faster when you don't want it. Alright, I'll head back."

Ashok was at the base-camp when they got back, talking to Furaha Tib and the Rotterdam Sheriff Ria Van-Amersvoort. Gabriel glanced quickly at Furaha, but she was looking a different direction and he couldn't get her attention. Others had also arrived at the base-camp including Elías, Chidimma, and Ale. Justine was nowhere to be seen. Most of the rangers were also back at the base-camp, performing general maintenance. Gabriel knew it was busy work, but he was glad to see they knew enough to keep an eye on the situation.

"Ola," Gabriel said walking up to Furaha and the sheriff. "What's the situation, Sheriff?"

"Well that depends on who killed Cecilia Arreola," Sheriff Van-Amersvoort stated.

"That's what I've been trying to figure out," Gabriel answered. "We heard a shot, and when we found her she was dead. Two laser burns through the torso. Look like sniper shots from around 120 metres away."

Sheriff Van-Amersvoort paused to consider then asked. "You had a very public disagreement with her in town."

"A disagreement yes, but that's all," Gabriel stated. "We're old friends, and it was nothing serious. There is a discrepancy between the number of plants we bought and number we're finding in the chasma."

"Then what happened, between you and Cecilia?" Van-Amersvoort eyed him cautiously.

Gabriel met her eyes and shrugged. "We discussed the audits for a couple hours, then went our separate ways. I didn't see Cecilia again until we found her dead."

"We also found a scanner and a jet-injector laying next to her," Roelof added.

Van-Amersvoort glanced at Roeloff, then back at Gabriel. "The murderer could have planted the jet-injector, or you could have."

"I could have, but I didn't," Gabriel stated. "I never knew Cecilia to be dishonest in my life, so I suspect the sniper planted it."

"You're telling us you and Cecilia parted on good terms the other night?" Ashok demanded, "You had 15,000 missing plants and you parted on good terms?"

Gabriel glanced at Ashok, and then turned back to the Sheriff. "How's he involved in this Sheriff? It's fairly obvious we don't like each other, so why's he here?"

"I'm a witness," Ashok announced proudly. "I'll saw you two arguing the other night."

"Want me to get rid of him?" Ferderand asked.

"I'm assuming authority here," the sheriff stated, and looked over at Ferderand. "I'll let you know if I want you to get rid of anyone."

Ferderand straightened up. "Captain Esparza is my C.O. I don't take orders from you."

"You putting up with that, Sheriff?" Elías demanded. "There have been at least three murders out here! Adoración and Jessika are both dead as well, thrown out in the dirt like garbage! Did these rangers even report that to you?"

"Yes, there is that. Who shot Adoración and Jessika?" the sheriff inquired calmly. Gabriel decided he liked the woman. Obviously, Sheriff Van-Amersvoort wasn't going to be rushed to a conclusion by Elías.

"There was a gunfight," Gabriel answered. "I accused Jessika of leaving the base-camp at night. Adoración interfered, and when I called her on it, she went for her gun. I tried to stop them, but couldn't, so they fell."

"I was there, Sheriff," Philibert announced. "They drew first. It was self-defense."

"What about the missing plants?" Sheriff Van-Amersvoort asked. "Have you found them yet?"

"I expect we did," Gabriel bluffed, and his eyes swung over to lock with Ashok's. "I expect we've found them alright!"

The expression in Ashok's eyes said it all, Gabriel knew he had guessed right. Ashok was the brains behind this thing, now Gabriel just had to figure out the rest of it, whatever it was.

"We've got 15,000 missing plants, Sheriff," Gabriel stated. "Poachers might steal a few dozen, ship them off to private buyers as novelties, but 15,000? Only a government would buy that bulk, so the plants can't have been taken by poachers."

"Sheriff," Furaha Tib interrupted. "Have you had many issues with poachers in the chasma?"

"Yes, but not 15,000 plants worth. Maybe a dozen or so plants disappear in a season, and like Gabriel said, we expect they're going to private buyers," the sheriff answered.

"If the plants weren't taken by poachers then they're still in the ground," Furaha continued. "Gabriel did you find any unmarked plants?"

"No, every plant has a bio-marker," Gabriel answered. "We thought it was a bit odd. There should be some first gen still in the ground."

"Then the masking agent is disguising the Arreola plants to look like another bio-marker," Furaha continued rationally. "I noticed that you just registered a new bio-marker earlier this season Mr. Nibhanupudi, what was wrong with your existing bio-marker?"

Gabriel glanced at Ashok as Furaha had turned her attention to him, and saw the man flinch when Furaha mentioned that second bio-markers. His head jerked around to look at Furaha with rage in his eyes, which quickly turned to terror as he looked over to the sheriff.

"A second bio-marker?" Sheriff Van-Amersvoort asked frowning. "Why do you need a second bio-marker?"

"And how did you get 20,000 plants into the ground already using this new bio-marker?" Furaha continued. "I checked with the registry office in Nueva Buenos Aires. He's placed an estimate of 20,000 plants for this year's audit using this new bio-marker."

"Are you accusing me of capitalism?" Ashok demanded condescendingly. Then he looked back at the sheriff. "You can see through this Sheriff. These rangers are a bunch of capitalists. Gabriel was a Desert Ranger here last year and inflated the numbers so Cecilia would get over paid for her plants! They are conspiring to blame me for all this. Gabriel is a known sniper, and all of his crew are ex-military! And they all work for Ms. Tib. Anyone of them could have shot Cecilia!"

Van-Amersvoort continued to stare at Ashok without responding to anything he said and then repeated her question. "Why do you need a second bio-marker?"

Ashok's eyes shifted, and the he sputtered out, "I need a second marker, because, ah, I'm planning ahead, yes, to sell the plants in batches. That's what I'm doing. Just good business sense!"

"When did you plant these new seedlings?" the sheriff asked.

"Earlier this season," Ashok answered. "About a month ago."

Van-Amersvoort continued to calmly stare at Ashok, "You managed to plant 20,000 seedlings in the last month without anyone noticing? That doesn't sound too likely."

"I had a lucky season," Ashok argued. "It happens sometimes."

"You registered the estimate when you registered the bio-marker," Furaha interjected. "You knew ahead of time you would have this good luck."

"The whole thing sounds unlikely," Sheriff Van-Amersvoort observed. "How's about you tell me where you were this afternoon?"

"Hold up sheriff," Elías Medina protested. "Just because this scientist thinks Ashok is a capitalist, it doesn't follow that Cecilia did. How would she know about this second bio-marker?"

"Cecilia wasn't an idiot, and she knew her business," the sheriff observed. "If this scientist can find out Ashok has a second bio-marker, I'm positive that Cecilia could."

Ashok was sweating under his respirator-mask. "This doesn't prove anything! All you have is conjecture! Having a second bio-marker isn't illegal, and neither is having good luck!"

Elías Medina had moved close to Ashok, while Chidimma had moved toward her bike. A slight movement by Ale Rodríguez drew Gabriel's attention, and he saw that the former Sudamérican soldier was moving toward his bike, where his rifle was mounted. Gabriel Esparza shifted his position so he had both Elías and Ashok in view. Glancing around he noticed that most of the rangers were alert to the changing scene. Only the sheriff and Furaha seemed unaware of what was about to happen.

"Furaha, get ready to drop," Gabriel whispered. "It's about to go down."

He had whispered, but he noticed the sheriff's subtle reaction. The sheriff's body shifted slightly as her eyes shifted from Ashok toward Ale, and then to Elías. Ashok drew first, quickly, but Gabriel was faster. Even as Ashok's gun started to lift, Gabriel's laser bolt burned through Ashok, and seconds later he crumpled to the ground. Gabriel was swinging his gun around towards Elías when a laser bolt burned through him as well, fired by Ferderand. He turned just in time to see Ale Rodríguez fall as well, the sheriff had dropped him. Chidimma was on a bike and gone as soon as the fighting had started, leaving everyone else standing in a cloud of dust.

Gabriel Esparza holstered his gun and then grabbed for support. Something was wrong. He realized he had been shot. It must have been Ale, before the sheriff shot him. Furaha rushed to Gabriel's side. "Mpendwa! You've been shot!"

"Just a little," he put his hand on her shoulder and grinned, "Looks like a flesh-wound."

He woke up several days later in the Rotterdam medical clinic. Ale's laser had ruptured an artery causing Gabriel to bleed out rapidly in the thin Martian atmosphere. While he was unconsciousness Sheriff Van-Amersvoort had determined that Ashok's 20,000 new plants were all Arreola plants with a masking agent distorting the bio-marker, and the rangers had started harvesting the plants. The dust storm to the south was expanding, and Gabriel ordered half of the rangers to stay in the chasma under Ferderand's command to complete the plant collection, while he took the other half of the rangers southeast to Noctis Labyrinthus to begin the planting their new biome.

# Sweat and Blood

When Chichi Chijindu asked if Artemio Torres would fight Mudiwa Kachote, she knew there was only one answer he could give.

"I guess I don't have a choice," Artemio answered. "I'll fight Kachote, but only if it's a NTF."

A Non-Technical Fight meant no-count out, a fight until someone was either unconscious or dead. Chichi knew it would make for a better fight, but also make the fight harder to rig. Nevertheless, the odds were on Mudiwa Kachote's side, and a NTF would draw a larger crowd, increasing the gambling.

If Artemio hadn't needed the credit as bad as he did, he would have never agreed to fight again. He'd been dodging Chichi for over year, ever since getting out of the Arean Army. He had fought for Chichi before joining the Revolutionary Army, but after almost a decade in the army, he was a different person, and the fight scene was largely illegal.

Chichi Chijindu had moved up in the fight scene establishing a Fight Club in the Multan Corporate Mining Zone, one of the few places in the Ares Confederacy were pro-fights were still legal. Multan FC was the only fight club in the Multan CMZ, a monopoly which Chichi had registered with the Khewra-Mars Mining Corporation, which owned the Multan CMZ. She had followed the early success of the Multan FC with a monopoly on gambling, and setup Casino

Multan.

Since the Confederacy had banned professional sports seven years earlier, Chichi had
come to financially dominate the Multan CMZ.
Before Multan FC and Casino Multan, the CMZ
had just been a small mining community of less
than a thousand people, now it was a town of
over ten thousand. Every pro-fight in Multan
was at Casino Multan, and the casino brought in
gamblers year round. Multan had one bank
when Chichi had arrived in the CMZ, the
Khewra-Mars Credit Centre, now it had five
banks, and a law office that registered holding
corporations for tourists.

Chichi owned the largest bank, the Bank of
Multan, and her casino was also the largest hotel. She dominated the pro-fight scene, and
Artemio had no doubt the fights were fixed.
Chichi had always been willing to fix a fight
when Artemio had fought for her, although
Artemio had never thrown a fight, he had allowed some fights to continue longer than they
should in order to cover the spread.

Even Yousaf Dulai appeared to be working
for Chichi now. When Artemio had been fighting, Yousaf had been one of the biggest pro-
moters in the Sirenum Colonies. Now Yousaf
was a manager in the Multan FC, Mudiwa Kachote's manager, and as far as Artemio could
see, not much more than a go-between for
Chichi.

About the only thing Chichi didn't control in

the pro-fight scene was Artemio, the former Sirenum Fighting League champion. SFL wasn't around anymore, banned by the Confederacy, but its legacy continued, and most of the pro-fight fans in Multan came from the Sirenum districts surrounding the Multan CMZ.

Mudiwa Kachote was the main contender for the Multan FC title. Gilchrist Leslie was the Multan FC champion. Artemio had watched the fight between Gilchrist and Mudiwa a month earlier, during which the title had changed hands. It had been a long fight, and was ultimately decided by a count-out of Mudiwa that many thought suspicious. Gilchrist was a good technical fighter, while Mudiwa was more of a powerhouse, being much larger than either Gilchrist or Artemio. Mudiwa was also one of the dirtiest fighters Artemio had ever seen.

Artemio couldn't hold that against a fighter, he had fought a lot of dirty fighters in his day. Fighters were all driven to win, and in the Martian pro-fighting leagues loosing a fight often meant loosing a life. It wasn't malevolent, the fighters weren't out to kill each other, but they were all highly competitive driven men. If it had just been a fight against Kachote or Gilchrist, Artemio would have agreed to the fight as soon as he'd run into financial problems. But it wasn't just a fight against Kachote or Gilchrist, it was a fight against Chichi's empire.

Chichi wouldn't allow Artemio to win a fight unless he agreed to sign on as a member of her stable, but Artemio was only agreeing to one fight. Without a contract Chichi only wanted Artemio to be defeated by Kachote, to prove the Multan FC fighters were better than the old SFL fighters. But Artemio was never one to throw a fight, so he was in it for the win, and he'd have to fight every dirty trick in Chichi's arsenal to win. If it was a Technical Fight, the judges and referee would be against him, and so he'd demanded a Non-Technical Fight. At least in a NTF he had a chance once he was in the fighting cage, it was getting to the fighting cage that was going to be the problem.

Given the odds against him, he had no desire to fight, but Chichi had given him little choice. For his time in the Revolutionary Army the Confederacy had awarded him a plot of land in Sirenum at the end of the war. Artemio had been born in one of the Sudamérican colonies to the north, and orphaned young. He had spent his teen years and early twenties in the pro-fight scene, and then the Eco-Revolution swept the planet, the Revolutionary Council offered free land for anyone that served in the Revolutionary Army. Artemio had never owned anything of significance, and joined the revolution, earning the rank of warrant officer by the end of the war.

After the war ended the new Confederate government dismissed most of the Revolutionary soldiers, most of whom sold their plot of land, as they couldn't afford to build anything on it. As a warrant officer Artemio had the option of staying in the new Arean Army, and spent almost ten years with the Military Police at various posts across the Confederacy. When he had retired he had enough credit to build a greenhouse farm, and bought some wheat seeds. Unfortunately the recent sandstorm had damaged the greenhouse and killed the plants growing in it, and he didn't have the credit to repair the greenhouse or to buy new seeds.

Chichi offered enough Multan Rupees for Artemio rebuild the greenhouse and buy new seeds, but only if he won. Chichi planned for Artemio to loose, forcing him to sign a contract to get a second fight. His other option was to rejoin the Army for another 5 year contract. By the time he got out there would be nothing left of his farm. Left abandoned, it would be stripped by the first prospector that stumbled across it. He'd have to spend at least ten more years in the Army, and then he still wouldn't have the credit to ride out another bad storm. He had to take the fight, and he had to win it.

And then, there was Carey Callahan. There was no way Carey would wait for years. Artemio had met Carey shortly after leaving the Army, when Artemio had been buying components for his planned farm. Carey was a bartender in New Belfast the closest town to Artemio's plot of land. They had been together since the first night they'd met. When the components were delivered Carey went with Artemio to help set up the farm. But Carey didn't like the farm, he wanted to be in a city and dreamed of moving to Pickering or New Edinburgh. Carey might love Artemio enough to live in the middle of nowhere, but he wouldn't wait if Artemio went back to the Army. The fact was, Artemio had to take the fight. That's all there was too it.

He met with Chichi and Yousaf Dulai to set it up. Then Chichi dropped the other shoe, "There is the issue of the buy-in."

"You expect me to pay to fight?" Artemio asked.

"You don't have a contract," Chichi stated, taking a drag from her e-cigar. "That makes it a challenger fight, and challengers pay! It's just business."

"How much?" Artemio asked, not that it mattered.

"10,000 Multan rupees," Chichi answered, "or equivalent Arean credit."

"If I had ₹10,000 I wouldn't be here," Artemio stated, knowing what Chichi would demand in lieu of payment.

"You could mortgage your farm," Chichi answered. "Without a greenhouse the farm is essentially worthless, but I could run you a mortgage of ₹10,000 for the land. Go down to the Bank of Multan and set it up, and we have a deal."

There it was, the closed box. If he didn't win the fight he wouldn't just be worthless, he'd be homeless. Either way he had the option of fighting or rejoining the Arean army.

"I guess if that's the way it has to be," Artemio conceded. "It won't matter anyway. You do remember my record, right?"

"That was ten years ago," Chichi dismissed Artemio's statement, but Yousaf looked worried. Artemio Torres had the distinction of having never lost a pro-fight during his three years in the SFL. He had lost a lot of fights earlier in life. He had spent his teen years in the Junior Hesperian Fight League, and had lost most of his fights for the first few years. At the time he had fought under the name Chico Violento, and by the time he was seventeen he was winning almost every fight he was in. He spent a year fighting as an adult in the HFL under the name Chico Violento before leaving Hesperia for Serenum to join the SFL under his own name. Chico Violento only lost one fight that last year in the HFL, and Artemio Torres managed to make it through three years in the SFL without a loss.

A fighter that doesn't loose is a dreadful prospect for a gamblers, and there was tremendous pressure for Artemio to loose. He knew it was just a matter of time until someone killed him, if not in the cage, then outside of it. He jumped at the opportunity to fight with the revolutionaries when they offered all soldiers land. He made it through the war, and almost a decade as an MP without receiving an injury serious enough to need a cybernetic implant, which would have disqualified him from the Multan FC. This wasn't due to luck, but experience, and an instinct to duck.

For Artemio it had never been about winning, it had always been about surviving. He didn't know if he could beat Mudiwa Kachote in a fair fight, in fact he doubted he could, but it didn't matter because he could survive a fight with Mudiwa. It was hard-wired into him. For Chichi it had always been about winning, and Chichi always won. Chichi knew she would win against Artemio, he was just a fighter, she was Multan itself. It didn't matter if Mudiwa was or wasn't a better fighter than Artemio, by the time Artemio got into the cage, he would be in no condition to fight Mudiwa.

Yousaf's perspective was different, he hadn't been a winner in more than a decade. He had a good gig, and made a lot of money working for Chichi, but those weren't his wins, they were losses. Chichi had once been a competitor, and had screwed him over when he proposed they jointly form a fighting league in Multan. He was from Multan, and knew the revolutionaries would ban the fighting leagues if they won the war. Every win she had was ashes in his mouth.

Artemio had know Yousaf longer than he'd known Chichi, they'd met when he was still fighting under the name Chico Violento in Hesperia, half a world away. Yousaf had been scouting talent, and had offered Chico Violento a contract in the SLF, but Artemio was under contract and couldn't leave. When his contact ended he headed to Sirenum to find Yousaf, and found Chichi instead.

Even though Artemio ended up working for the competition, Artemio and Yousaf had become friends. For the first year Artemio was in the SLF Yousaf had marketed his fighters as Anti-Artillery, fighters that could defeat the undefeatable Artemio. Yousaf was as responsible for Artemio's reputation as Artemio's fighting skills. At first it was hype, then it became reality, and then it became a problem. After Artemio's first year the contenders became scarce, mainly because there was no money in a fight when everyone knew the outcome beforehand. In the two years that followed Yousaf had made far more money than Chichi's champion by organizing his own elimination tournaments to establish the next Anti-Artillery champion-killer.

Yousaf had sent champion after champion against Artemio for two years, and remembered well the feeling that he was about to loose another fighter. He was feeling that again now. Shortly before Artemio left to join the revolutionary army, Yousaf had found out that Chichi was tired of having a fighter that wouldn't take a dive, and had arranged for him to loose the next fight. Yousaf had warned Artemio, and Artemio had been ready when they came. Five fighters, all of them good, trying to take him by surprise one night before the fight. He had been waiting for them in the locker room, gun in hand, and shot them all without mercy. They hadn't expected a fighter of his caliber to be carrying a gun. Why would he? For Yousaf it was as much about helping a friend as it was about protecting his Anti-Artillery tournaments. For Artemio it was a sign that he need to move on.

"That was a mistake," Yousaf said after Artemio had left. "The more you push him into a corner, the stronger he'll come out of it. You know that."

"That was more than ten years ago," Chichi said contemptuously. "Now he's just a has-been, and soon he won't even be that."

Artemio went directly to the Bank of Multan to mortgage his farm. The bankers were expecting him, Chichi had clearly planned this in advance. It didn't matter. After his morning workout, Artemio headed to Cafe Vasu to meet Carey. The Bank of Multan was located within the Casino Multan, but the Cafe Vasu was in the Hotel Vasu next door. Artemio and Carey were staying in the Hotel Vasu, as Artemio didn't want Chichi getting any more money out of him than absolutely necessary. Casino Multan was connected to the surrounding hotels, apartment buildings, and offices via a network of pressurized cat-walks that allowed guests to move around without the need of respirator masks.

Outside Mars was much as it had been for half a billion years, frozen and dry with a thin carbon-dioxide atmosphere. In the century and a half since humanity had begun colonizing Mars, the atmosphere had gained some nitrogen and oxygen that escaped from colonies, as well as gases released from mining and industry. The planet had warmed a few degrees in that time, enough that low-laying lakes in the equatorial region would thaw out for a few months each Martian year. But largely the planet was as it had been since before the age of the dinosaurs.

Carey was waiting in the Cafe Vasu drinking a beer, and eating a strawberry jelly sandwich. Artemio ordered a whiskey, and a plate of spaghetti and tomato sauce. As he ate he realized he couldn't stay in Multan if he wanted to fight Mudiwa, the entire food selection was starch and sugar based. Multan had been setup as a Rhodium and Platinum mining colony by the Khewra-Mars Mining Corporation, based in Pakistan. They had built greenhouse farms for growing wheat, sugarcane, cotton, and rice at the colony to reduce the cost of importing these staples from Earth. After the colony had fallen under the British Colonial Zone during the Mars Treaty negotiations, London forbade the importing of anymore species to Multan in order to force the colony to buy food through the British Mars Corporation. When the Eco-Revolutionaries had driven the British government off Mars, the free movement of species within the Confederacy was enshrined in the new constitution, however a decade later the

Multan diet continued to be based around bread, pasta, and sweats.

He didn't want to stay in Multan anyway, it would be too easy for Chichi to send someone to beat on him, or worse to kill him. With the mortgage on his property in place Chichi didn't need him to survive to fight Mudiwa. Sitting there with Carey, he knew Carey wasn't going with him. He knew Carey couldn't watch what he had to do. Carey was cute and could easily survive in any city, but Carey wasn't strong and he wouldn't be able to watch Artemio fight.

"How did it go?" Carey asked Artemio as the conversation drifted back towards the reason they were in Multan. Carey knew it hadn't gone well, but they hadn't expected it to go well.

"About what I expected," Artemio answered. "I'll be in the cage with Mudiwa in about three months. But the cunt made be pay ₹10,000 for the fight. I had to mortgage the farm."

Carey paused considering, "She really bent you over. What's she got against you?"

Artemio smiled. She still didn't understand him, after all these years. She was giving him the one thing that drove him to win, she was pushing him into a corner. She was leaving him with only one option, to win. "It doesn't matter. I came here for a fight, and I've got one lined up against Mudiwa. She's giving Yousaf Dulai three months to hype it. It'll be a major ticket fight. Regardless of the buy-in, I needed to win. She's not as smart as she thinks she is. She never was."

"Yousaf?" Carey enquired. "Why would he want to hype you?"

"He always was my best promoter," Artemio said. "Chichi didn't want me to win after the first three months. Yousaf hyped every fight I had, because he wanted his fighter to be the one that took me out. He was always a better promoter than Chichi."

"Then why does she own Multan?" Carey enquired quickly. "Yousaf Dulai just works for her."

"I didn't say she wasn't conniving," Artemio answered. "But she was always about image. I'd bet she's over extended, that casino must have cost her a lot."

The next day he went to one of the local dojos to work out. It was the first time he'd been in one since he left the army. The real issue wasn't that he hadn't been working out, the real issue is that he hadn't been in a pro-fight in more than a decade. There were underground fight clubs across the Confederacy, but the MPs were charged with shutting them down, and so he'd avoided them. The Military Police had been posted throughout the Confederacy since the war, wherever the local police weren't enough to suppress the violence.

During that time he'd been in many gunfights, and more than a few fist fights, but nothing like a league fight. Meanwhile Mudiwa had been fighting, and regardless of Chichi's machinations, Mudiwa just wanted to fight. He didn't care what condition Artemio was in when they got into the cage, Mudiwa was planning to take him apart.

He worked out at the dojo for a few hours, focusing on dead weights and cardio. The main reason he went to the dojo wasn't to work out, it was to get a feel for the fight scene in Multan. He learned what he needed to know, when he realized no one in the dojo was willing to spar with him. It had only been one day since he agreed to the fight, and already the word was out. His suspicions were confirmed when Yousaf happened to wonder into the dojo. There were at least a dozen dojos in Multan, and Artemio had no doubt that Yousaf was there checking up on him for Chichi.

"They're trying to rattle you," Carey said over dinner. "If you can't spar, you can't get back into shape."

"I know," Artemio replied honestly, "but it doesn't matter, I've got a plan."

"What is it?" Carey asked curiously.

"Can't tell you yet," Artemio replied.

"You can't tell me?" Carey pouted. "Since when do you keep secrets from me?"

"Did you land that bar-tending job?" Artemio asked.

"Of course," Carey answered. "There was no question of it."

"Good. I'm leaving town," Artemio stated. "You can't come. I'll be back before the fight."

That statement prompted an argument, at least Carey was arguing, Artemio was just in the vicinity of the argument. Later that night Artemio left. He booked a flight on an airship headed west to Hesperia. Airships were used for cargo, while passengers generally flew on shuttles. A suborbital shuttle flight could have gotten him to Hesperia in an hour, the airship would take days. But he'd have to register his passport to book a shuttle flight, while the airship companies weren't required to register anything.

Airships had been used on Mars since the earliest corporate colonies had been setup, first for prospecting, and later for cargo. The combination of the low gravity environment, and cold carbon-dioxide rich atmosphere allowed heated hydrogen airships to be economical in a way that they never had been on Earth. Before the war a few Canadian and American airship companies had operated airships as passenger liners, but few of those airships had survived the war. Artemio was flying on a freight airship, billeted in a vacant crew cabin. It was cramped and there was nowhere else he could go on the airship, so for several days he stayed in the cabin, and meditated.

He had been billeted in worse conditions during the war. He had learned to avoid going cabin crazy by focusing inwards. For days he went through every combat technique that he knew, picturing every move and counter move, remembering every fight he'd ever been in. It was as much about remembering his combat knowledge as reconditioning his mind for what lay ahead.

Artemio disembarked in the city of Èkó in the Amenthes Fossae region where the highlands sank down into the lowlands. Èkó was one of the five largest cities on Mars, originally a Nigerian rhenium and copper mining colony, it had one of the largest populations before the Mars Treaty. After the Sudaméricans gained control of the Hesperia Planum they had organized the eight mining colonies in the region into a single colonial territory in order to dilute the influence of the Nigerians.

Èkó was a city of over a million that sprawled out of the crater the mine was located in. The rhenium mine was one of the most profitable mines on Mars during the Corporate Era. During that time, hundreds of thousands of workers immigrated, and the Nigerian Mars Conglomerate invested a great deal building up the local economy. Greenhouse farms had been built for soybeans, sesame, cashews, cassava, cocoa, Bambara groundnuts, acacia, corn, melon, millet, palm, plantains, rice, rubber, sorghum, soybeans, and yams, giving Èkó the second-richest agricultural base on the planet. Unfortunately the rhenium had run out before the Mars Treaty

was negotiated, and by the time the Sudaméricans gained control of the area, Èkó's primary
exports were copper, foods, and people.

During the Colonial Era Sudamérican corporations built greenhouse farms across Hesperia
to capitalize on the seeds already imported, and
the abundance of light in the equatorial region.
Artemio had been born in the colonial capital
Tercero Mexico, the son of Argentine immigrants. When his parents died Artemio had
found himself homeless, and made his way to
Èkó, the city of opportunity. Unfortunately the
only opportunity he found was the opportunity
to be raped regularly. He quickly became an angry, violent person, and then found out about
the Junior Hesperian Fight League. He joined
under the name Chico Violento, Spanish for the
Violent-Kid. For the first few years he didn't
care if he won or lost, as long as he was paid
enough to have a place to live. Then he realized
he was winning, that he was actually good at
something, he had become Violento. Now a
decade and a half later he was returning to Èkó
to become Chico Violento again.

The HFL had been officially shutdown when
the Arean government banned professional
fighting, but continued to operate as the Underground Fighting League, moving from city to
city throughout Hesperia, Vallis, Morpheos,
Nouvelle-Quebec, Ascraeus, and Ceraunius. The
UFL had been a major issue for the Arean MPs
as the Confederacy wanted the league shut
down, but local authorities generally looked the

other way. UFL fights brought tourists and money to their cities. UFL fights were also very popular, and none of the elected officials wanted to be the one to shut them down.

Artemio had never been placed on the task-force to shutdown the UFL, instead spending most of the previous decade hunting remnants of the Chinese, American, British, and Russian armies that were largely operating as gangs of bandits throughout the more remote regions of the Confederacy. Nevertheless, he had followed the task-forces' investigation. The head of the UFL was a woman named Delia Leach, she had been a promoter in the HFL when he was Chico Violento. They had known each other in passing. They weren't close, but she knew who Chico Violento was, and who he'd become in the SFL.

When he'd arrived in Èkó he visited some of the old dojos the HFL fighters had once used, but didn't recognize anyone. The city had changed since the last time Artemio had been there. It used to be all Blacks and Latinos, now there were large minorities of other ethnic groups as well. English was beginning to show up on the signs along with Yoruba and Spanish. On his fourth day in Èkó, he finally found someone he recognized, a former fighter named Leandros Yates. Leandros didn't know how to get a hold of Delia, but was able to inform Artemio that the next fight was going to be in Madhubani.

Madhabani was in Savitch District, high in the Hesperia Planum to the south, a former Indian titanium and zirconium mining colony. It took Artemio another two days in an airship to get to Madhabani. Like Èkó to the north, the region had a large agricultural sector built up during the Corporate Era. Greenhouses had been setup for rice, wheat, mangoes, sugar cane, bananas, cotton, potatoes, tomatoes, soybeans, onions, chick peas, and okra. The Bharat Zirconium Company had also shipped buffalo, cattle, and chickens to Mars, creating the planet's first meat and dairy industry. The dojos of Madhabani were full of fighters, and it didn't take Artemio long to find someone that could get him in touch with Delia.

"Last I heard you were an MP," Delia said when they met in his hotel suit later that night. "Didn't think we'd be seeing you again."

"Got myself into a bit of a bind," Artemio stated. "I need to fight for a few months. Don't have a buy-in, but also don't need pay, just enough to get by."

"Practice?" Delia asked. "That weasel Yousaf has announced the return of Artemio Torres."

"Practice," Artemio confirmed, "and a lot of it, under the name Chico Violento."

"Not many fighters wear masks anymore," Delia observed. "I assume you'll be wearing one again."

"I'll have to," Artemio confirmed. "Chichi will

send someone to take me out if she knows where I am. Besides I'm a retired MP, I can't fight under my own name in an illegal fighting league."

"Alright," Delia conceded after a few seconds. "I'll make money either way. No buy in. You fight as much as you want. I'll cover your costs. And no one finds out who you are. But I keep the profits."

His first fight was a few nights later, against a titanium miner that had bought into the fight hoping to take the prize money. The fight was being broadcast online pay-per-view, and Delia had informed Artemio before entering the cage that they had good sales with over 100,000 subscribed viewers. A cut of that would go the miner if he won the fight. The miner was a local, a brown-skinned descendant of the original Indian colonists. He was taller than Artemio, and obviously a body-builder. Artemio wasn't exactly out of shape, but he hadn't taken steroids or growth hormones since joining the army. Artemio took a shot of taurage before stepping into the cage.

Across the cage the miner stepped in and the doors locked behind them. Then the miner ran at him. He swung a quick left, and Chico Violento dodged inside and slammed two good shots to the miner's solar plexus. The miner was winded, but punching his abs were like punching a cement wall. The miner stepped back for a few seconds, and then pushed back in, lashing out with both hands. Artemio caught a right and was slammed back into the cage wall. The miner pressed in, slamming his left knee into Artemio's body and smashed another right fist into his head. Artemio couldn't seem to land anything and leaped up away from him, caught the cage roof bars, and then propelled himself to the cage floor on the far side. The miner turned to charge again, but Artemio spun a roundhouse kick up into his mouth and the miner stopped in his tracks with a surprised look.

The miner dropped into a half crouch, he clearly had some martial arts training, likely yuddha kalā, which was popular in Hesperia. Then the miner rushed in again, pushing Chico Violento back to the cage wall. The miner unexpectedly kicked Artemio's right knee, knocking Artemio down briefly. Violento was angry, this miner was strong, but not that good a fighter, yet he was pushing Violento around the cage like he'd never been a cage before. Violento rose in a rage, slamming a left to the miner's mouth and hooked a right to his ear that spun the miner's head. Violento pushed in stabbing the miner with both hands.

The miner's knees buckled and he to dropped to one knee, but Artemio backed off and waited for the miner to get back to his feet. The miner looked surprised, and moved in on Chico Violento again, but when he began throwing his fists there was nothing behind them. He seemed to have misunderstood why

Artemio had backed off, perhaps he thought Chico Violento was going to throw the fight. Lots of fighters got paid more by gamblers to throw fights than they would get from the ticket sales, but all Artemio wanted was the fight to last longer. He needed a workout. He needed to get this miner back into the fight, and as the miner threw ineffective fists Artemio struck out slamming a fist squarely into the miners nose.

The miner was knocked back, and briefly stunned, but when he returned to the fight he was back in it. The miner kicked up at Chico Violento just missing his chin, and followed through with a right fist that knocked Artemio back into the cage wall. As Artemio tried to push away from the wall he was met by a barrage of fists as the miner bored in. It was something he hadn't felt in a long time, a relentless pummeling by an enraged opponent. His body was numb again, as disconnected from his mind as a vehicle he might be driving. It felt somehow good, familiar. Violento waited his moment, and as the miners hands slowed down, he drove a fist from the bottom of his feet up into the miner's jaw, snapping the miner's head back. The miner stagger back, and fell unconscious into the floor of the cage.

A medic entered the cage to check the miner. He was still alive, but out cold with a shattered jaw. The fight was over, way too soon for Artemio, and there wouldn't be another fight until they got to Yangi Toshkent a week later.

After Chico Violento left the cage Delia approached. "It didn't look good for you. What did you hit him with?"

"My fist," Artemio answered, somewhat disappointed the fight had ended so soon. "Can I fight again tonight?"

"Max one fight per event," Delia told him what he already knew.

"You should pay him something," Artemio stated. "At least cover his medical bill."

"That wasn't in our agreement," Delia argued.

"I'll win every fight," Artemio stated. "I'm sure you can make more than enough off the side action."

They left Madhabani that night, before the Arean MPs swarmed through the city looking for the fight cage. Yangi Toshkent was in the Gale Crater far to the northeast at the cusp of the Hesperia Planum and the northern lowlands. It was once an Uzbek Cerium mining colony, founded by Mars Mining and Metallurgy Combinat. MMMC had not invested greatly in agriculture, building a few greenhouses producing a mixture of wheat, barley, corn, rice, cotton, sesame, onions, flax, tobacco, and melons. During the Colonial Era many Sudamérican farming corporations had built greenhouses in the region around the Gale Crater, leaving the region with a largely agricultural economy.

Delia had booked them on a passenger airship to Yangi Toshkent, which took three days, stopping briefly in Noua Bucureşti. The passenger airship was large and luxurious, nothing like the tiny cabin that he had traveled from Multan to Èkó in. It gave him the opportunity to meet the production crew and other fighters working for the UFL. With the exception of the fact that they were criminals, it was like it had been when he was young.

The fight in Yangi Toshkent took longer than the one in Madhabani, but not much longer. The fighter he faced was a slugger. There were various ways one could fight, and this fighter had no training in any martial arts. He had one skill-set, he could hit hard and he could hit fast. Violento could have defeated him quickly using a variety of techniques, but the fighter was a good slugger, and so Artemio fought him in a slug-fest. The fight took less than twenty minutes, and ended with the slugger laying unconscious on the floor like the miner in Madhabani. The slugger was disappointing to Artemio, but he had kept the fight going as long as the man could hold up.

A week later they were in Karācī in Aeolis Mensae, northeast of Gale Crater. Yangi Toshkent and Karācī were connected via maglev system, so the ULF crew and fighters traveled by train. Delia liked to change their mode of transport whenever she could, to keep the MPs from tracking them. Aeolis Mensae was a table-land in the lowlands north of the Hesperia

Planum. It was one of Mars' strange inverted features, the remnant of an ancient riverbed that rose high above the surrounding lands that had eroded in the half a billion years since the river dried up.

The fighter he met in Karācī was the opposite of the slugger in Yangi Toshkent. This fighter had a mixed martial arts background, and the fight was technical. This was the kind of fight Artemio had been looking for, something that would sharpen up his skills. The fighter was a challenge, not to beat, but to beat without killing. Artemio didn't want to kill him unless he had no choice, he didn't want to raise Chico Violento's profile any more than absolutely necessary. Sooner or later someone would notice that Chico Violento wasn't loosing, and his profile would skyrocket. When that happened Artemio would need to disappear. Terminal fights would raise his profile quicker. Everyone wanted to bet on a terminal fighter, no one ever threw a fight against someone that would kill him.

The fighter knocked Chico Violento down, and Artemio realized he wasn't paying close enough attention. The fighter stepped back waiting for Chico Violento get back to his feet, he wanted to win a clean fight. Artemio could respect that, he was trying to win a non-terminal fight. He got up and waited for the fighter to close in again before attacking. He dodged the fighters feet and plowed his left fist deep into the fighter's solar plexus, sending the fighter stumbling back a few feet with a worried expression on his face.

Artemio advanced and slammed a right foot into the fighter's heart that made him stumble back a couple more steps. The fighter returned with a quick series of fists aimed at Chico Violento's head missing all but one glancing blow to the chin. Artemio dodged to the left and feinted a right swing, before raising his left knee into the fighter's sternum. The fighter had stepped into Artemio's knee trying to avoid his right fist, and as he stumbled backwards a right fist slammed down into his temple knocking him out cold. Artemio knelled down to check the man's pulse before the medic rushed in, he was still alive.

After the first few fights they all seemed to blur together. For weeks he fought a series of miners, farmers, and mechanics. Several of the fighters were technical, but the majority were just local strongmen that fought in a variety of innovative ways. The fighters weren't of the caliber he needed to face to prepare for Mudiwa Kachote, but they were all real fighters with some skill-set that allowed him to sharpen his own skills. As the weeks passed and it became apparent that Chico Violento wasn't going to loose, Delia started fighting him against the best of the contenders. The unbeaten streak also got the attention of gamblers across the planet, bringing Chico Violento to the attention of Chichi and Yousaf.

"Artemio started in the HFL," Yousaf said. "He'd been fighting in a mask before that. I don't know the name, but it could have been Chico Violento."

"His style isn't like Artemio's," Chichi said as they watched a replay of one of Chico Violento's recent fights.

"It changes with every fight," Yousaf observed. "I downloaded all of them last night. Whoever Chico Violento is, he's toying with these contenders."

"You really think it's Artemio?" Chichi asked.

"Yes," Yousaf answered. "It makes perfect sense for him to run back to Hesperia and fight in the UFL."

"Why the mask?" Chichi asked. "Not many fighters in the UFL fight in masks anymore."

"The UFL is illegal," Yousaf observed, "and he was an MP."

Chichi paused considering, and then looked up eagerly. "Send Brijesh Misra to challenge him. There's no way the ULF will turn down a challenge from a major Multan FC fighter. Offer them some extra Arean Credit to keep Chico Violento in the dark."

"How much?" Yousaf enquired.

"₵100,000 should be enough," Chichi answered. "The UFL is a pretty small operation."

As soon as Artemio saw Brijesh enter the

cage, he knew his time in the UFL was over. Brijesh was taller than Artemio, but not as muscular. He was one of the top fighters in the Multan FC, and one of the dirtiest fighters Artemio had ever seen in the cage. On the way into the cage Artemio had overheard one of the techs say they they had a record number of subscriptions to watch the fight. His ego let him think it was because of him, now he knew it was because of Brijesh.

The cage doors locked and Brijesh moved quickly yet cautiously towards Artemio. Brijesh jabbed a left that knocked Artemio's head back like he was a bobble-head, and then swung a fast right. Artemio dodged the right and moved in close, slamming his knee up into Brijesh's muscular abs. For most fighters the knee would at least pause them for a few seconds, but it had no effect on Brijesh. He smashed his left elbow up into Artemio's chin, knocking him back and down to one knee.

Artemio dropped and rolled backwards away from Brijesh, rising to both feet and drove a right straight into Brijesh's mouth. Brijesh stepped back, paused for a second and then advanced on Artemio again, missing with a right, but connecting with his left knee, and then his right elbow. Artemio was knocked back against the cage walls again, and Brijesh pushed in pounding him down with fist and knees. Violento felt the flood of jarring blows beginning to take its toll and struck out with both fists into Brijesh's solar plexus and then jumped as

Brijesh stumbled backwards. He grabbed Brijesh's head with both hands and drove his knee up into Brijesh's face.

Brijesh was stunned and fell backward to one knee, before rushing at Artemio again, jabbing a vicious right into Artemio's face. It caught Artemio by surprise, and he tasted blood. Artemio backed up, and Brijesh charged in narrowly missing him as Artemio jumped and caught the cage ceiling bars. Brijesh jumped up at Artemio, but missed again as Artemio threw himself down across the cage. Brijesh followed Artemio back down to the cage floor and met Artemio's foot in his temple, which sent him rolling across the cage floor.

Artemio was instantly on top of him pounding him with both fists moving so fast the subscribers at home could only see a blur. Brijesh shot a quick left up through Artemio's blur of fists straight into his throat, that sent him up and recoiling across the cage. Brijesh rolled back up onto his feet, his face a bloody mess. He shook his head, and then ran at Artemio, and ducked under Artemio's fists grabbing him by the waist and slamming him down into the ground.

Artemio had the wind knocked out of him and almost lost consciousness, but Violento's instinct kicked in slamming his hands into Brijesh's face, his thumbs boring into Brijesh's eyes. Brijesh was screaming, and blood was running down Artemio's arms when he realized what was happening. His thumbs were driven through Brijesh's shattered eyeballs, but slid out as Brijesh jumped back away from him. Artemio rose to his feet as Brijesh fell to his knees groping towards the cage wall. Artemio looked down at him, the fight wasn't over yet. He walked up behind Brijesh and reached down. Brijesh's neck cracked in Artemio's hands, and the fight was over.

When he returned to the locker room the MPs were waiting for him. He knew one of them, Tumelo Koena, an Eco-Revolutionary volunteer from South Africa. They had served together briefly during the war. Artemio didn't recognize the other MP.

"Don't take off the mask," Tumelo ordered.

"Alright," Artemio said sitting down on one of the benches. "You guys finally shutting down the UFL?"

"Not tonight," Tumelo answered. "The UFL isn't a primary concern at the moment."

"Not a primary concern?" Artemio scoffed. "I thought your task-force's mission is to shut-down the fights."

"That can't happen as long as everyone is gambling on the fights," Tumelo stated. "When we shutdown the HFL, it just became the UFL. If we shut down the UFL it'll just become something else unless we dismantled the gambling industry first."

"Sounds like a chicken/egg paradox," Artemio stated. "And if you're not here to arrest me, why are you here?"

It was an interesting conversation.

The death of Brijesh Misra dominated the sports news for several days, with politicians and psychologists giving a jumble of opinions about the morality of professional fighting, and the ineffectiveness of the laws banning it. The fight-talk always seemed to segue back to the up-coming fight between Mudiwa Kachote and the former MP Artemio Torres in Multan. Politicians argued about the validity of the Confederacy continuing to adhere to the Mars Treaty, and its Corporate Mining Zones that effectively created autonomous countries within the Confederacy. Psychologists claimed that the army was allowing soldiers to retire without proper medical treatment, which was the only reason a soldier would become a professional fighter.

Artemio had no reason to hide the fact that he was returning to Multan, and so caught a shuttle flight back from Sositenya Abeba, where he'd fought Brijesh. The shuttle was launched from a maglev track, and propelled out of the atmosphere to just below orbit, where it changed direction towards Multan, and began its descent. The flight took 43 minutes, and when Artemio walked down the catwalk into the spaceport, Yousaf Dulai was waiting for him.

Artemio saw Yousaf and walked over to him

with a smile, "Concerned I wouldn't come back?"

"Not you," Yousaf replied. "Just thought I'd see how bad Brijesh got you. Couldn't see much through that mask."

"A broken metatarsal bone in the left foot," Artemio reported.

"Explains the limp," Yousaf nodded. "You got some bad eyes too."

"Brijesh was a hell of a fighter," Artemio observed.

"I know," Yousaf stated. "He was one of mine."

"That's unfortunate," Artemio remarked.

"Not really," Yousaf disagreed. "I've known him since we were both kids, and he's never had a brain-cell in his head. Sure got a lot of pussy though, probably fathered more than a hundred kids. Never did a thing for any of them. Good riddance."

"Mudiwa's one of yours too," Artemio observed. "Chichi pissed at you or something?"

Yousaf pulled his e-cigarette from his lips and put it back into the pack to recharge. "We've never been that close. We make money together, that's it."

Artemio looked at him. Yousaf seemed depressed. His large brown eyes didn't look right. "How many fighters do you have left, Yousaf?"

He looked at Artemio. "None that matter. Not after you kill Mudiwa."

"He could take a dive," Artemio suggested.

Yousaf didn't bother looking up at Artemio. "No, Mudiwa's too much like you, he doesn't take dives."

"Maybe he'll win," Artemio stated offhandedly.

Yousaf paused again before replying, "I saw it. At the end. You still blackout, don't you?"

Artemo didn't respond.

"I figured ten years in the army might have cleared that out," Yousaf continued.

"Didn't come up much in the army," Artemio replied.

"Well it doesn't matter now," Yousaf observed. "We're going to need you to make public appearances in the next couple days."

"So everyone can see how banged up I am?" Artemio asked.

"So everyone knows you're Chico Violento," Yousaf stated. "Since you can't officially claim to be Chico Violento without getting arrested, we need everyone to see your face."

"And my limp," Artemio added. "I'm sure it'll help the odds makers."

"It will make the gambling more interesting," Yousaf agreed as he pulled another e-cigarette from his pack. He turned it on, and looked over Artemio again before wandering off towards the exit.

That evening Artemio found Carey at the bar he'd been hired to work at before Artemio had left Multan. He looked like he fit right in, but he always did, it was a gift he had. He smiled when he saw Artemio, but Artemio could see something had changed. He'd been through a tough fight, and could see it reflected in Carey's eyes. When they kissed he knew for sure that things had changed.

"What's wrong?" Artemio asked. "Everything alright?"

"Yes, Artemio, but your face!" Carey replied. "Your eyes are cut!"

"Yeah. Brijesh, in the UFL. Maybe you saw the fight?" Artemio asked.

"Everybody did," Carey answered frankly. "I never watched you fight before."

"Disturb you?" Artemio asked. "I know you don't like the fights."

"It's not that," Carey shook his head. "You have to fight Mudiwa Kachote in a couple days, and you're eyes are cut. You can't win!"

"I've also got a broken metatarsal bone," Artemio stated. "But I'll still win."

"I'm sure you have to believe that, or you couldn't fight," Carey said dismissively. "But the odds are not in your favor."

"Betting against me?" Artemio asked.

"I have to make a living, like everyone else," Carey answered.

"You'll loose," Artemio stated. "What are the odds?"

"Eight to one against," Carey reported. "Everyone knows you're damaged going into it, and Mudiwa is in excellent health."

"I've got some Arean credit. Can you place a bet for me?" Artemio asked. "There's a CMZ up in Ceraunius, Calabar. They allow gambling."

"I've heard of Canaan City," Carey stated dismissively. Calabar, also known as Canaan City, was a small Corporate Mining Zone that was marketing itself as the new Multan. Almost everything was legal in Calabar, gambling, prostitution, professional fighting, offshore banking, almost everything.

"Place a bet up there. Place it on me," Artemio requested. "At eight to one even a small amount will pay off well."

"Do you really believe you have a chance in your condition?" Carey asked sadly.

"I lost the ability to loose a long time ago. I can't explain it better than that. Go back and watch my fights if you want to know what I mean. Either way, don't bet against me. You will loose." With that statement Artemio handed

Carey a credit card and rose to leave.

He had two days to heal as best he could. Months in the UFL had built his muscle mass, but steroids and growth hormones wouldn't help him heal. He needed to rest. He retired to his hotel suite, with enough food and meds that he wouldn't need to leave until the fight, screw Chichi's request for public appearances. He had a gun, but didn't want to be disturbed, so piled the suite's sofa up against the door, and went to bed. He woke up a few hours later, his foot throbbing. He limped to the kitchenette, and made himself some buffalo-steak and eggs he'd brought from Madhabani. He returned to bed and watched a movie on the hotel's pay-per-view. It was an import from Canada, some ludicrous sci-fi thing where astronauts visited Alpha-Centauri and found a subterranean race of intelligent insects. He passed out near the end, and woke up fifteen hours later surprised he'd slept for so long. His foot felt better, but it still hurt to walk.

He got up and made something to eat, and then sat down at the window looking out over Multan and the ruddy-brown desert beyond. His mind drifted to his farm, he needed to rebuild the greenhouses, and put up sonic shields, so the next storm didn't rip the greenhouses down again. If he made enough he might be able to find a used harvester-bot, that would really cut down on his work. He was looking forward to returning to his farm, to a peaceful life. He wondered if Carey would be there. The idea that

Carey might not be there hurt, but not as much as it would have before he left for the UFL. Time. Carey might not go back with him, but the real question was, if he would place the bet in Calabar. If Artemio didn't get the credit from Calabar he wouldn't be able to buy a harvester-bot, he might not even be able to build a full sonic shield array.

The night of the fight Yousaf approached Artemio in the locker room as he was preparing for the fight. "Chichi wants you to fight for her again. She's offering ₹250,000 for you to take a dive, plus your mortgage."

"She's that worried about Mudiwa?" Artemio asked dismissively.

"There are more than a million viewers sub-scribed," Yousaf explained. "Think of how much a rematch would earn."

"You already told her my answer I assume," Artemio replied.

"She was your agent, she already knew what your answer would be," Yousaf stated. "She's hoping you're broken enough to take the dive."

"And you?"

"I'm betting on you," Yousaf stated. "But don't tell Chichi."

"Thought she owned the gambling scene in this town," Artemio observed.

"She does. I placed the bet in Canaan City,"

Yousaf stated.

"She'll still find out," Artemio said. "I recommend you leave for Calabar before the end of the fight."

"After this fight I won't have any useful fighters left," Yousaf said. "I'm heading to Calabar as soon as we're done this conversation. Going to setup my own fight club up there. Just make sure to win okay?"

Artemio chuckled and injected his taurage, then walked to the cage. When Artemio stepped into the cage Mudiwa was already there. A tall Earth-born black, with long dreadlocks. The Earth-borns all had a different more-vibrant shade than the Mars-born, which Mudiwa had used to his advantage playing a heal in the Multan FC. His body was chiseled ebony that showed no signs of fat anywhere.

As soon as the cage locked Mudiwa advanced and jabbed a fast left at Artemio's eyes. Artemio ducked under Mudiwa's fist, and slammed a right to Mudiwa's ribs. Mudiwa jabbed again for Artemio's eyes and missed again. Artemio faked a right, and Mudiwa stepped back, smirking, then stabbed left at Artemio's eyes again. Artemio ducked again, but caught a fist to his forehead which knocked his head back like it was on a spring. Mudiwa followed it up with a right that knocked Artemio's entire body back.

Mudiwa threw another right and Artemio

ducked again, rising into Mudiwa's arms and let it curl around his neck, then smashed both hands into Mudiwa's solar plexus. Mudiwa stepped back a few steps, but then advanced again, and jabbed a right into Artemio's mouth that split his previously cut lip. Artemio dodged Mudiwa's next two lefts and closed in on him, slamming a couple shots into Mudiwa's kidneys, before Mudiwa connected with a stiff right to Artemio's head, sending him tumbling across the cage floor.

As Artemio rose from the cage floor, Mudiwa caught him with a left to the right eye and a trickle of blood started down his face. Artemio struck a left hook into Mudiwa's ribs that jolted him backwards a couple steps. Artemio advanced and stabbed a left to Mudiwa's mouth, then Mudiwa ducked a left and smashed his right knee into Artemio's ribs, knocking Artemio back a couple steps.

By then blood covered both fighters, and Artemio was blinking the blood from his eyes trying to see Mudiwa. Mudiwa spun a roundhouse kick up towards Artemio's face, but Artemio saw it coming and dropped under it, slamming his open palm into Mudiwa's knee. Mudiwa buckled and fell. Artemio stepped back waiting to see if Mudiwa could get back to his feet. More than a million people were watching, and he didn't have a mask on, so he'd avoid killing Mudiwa if possible.

Mudiwa rose slowly, watching Artemio with a

vicious look on his face. Artemio's stepping back would make people believe it was a rigged fight, even if he killed Artemio. He advanced on Artemio again, now they were both limping. Mudiwa swung at Artemio's face again, but missed as Artemio dodged, and then took a shot to the solar plexus before stepping back. Artemio advanced as Mudiwa backed up, pounding him with both fists. Mudiwa took a few shots to the face, and then lifted his right knee into Artemio's solar plexus, lifting him off the ground, and knocking him back several steps.

Artemio recoiled from Mudiwa's advance, and then turned suddenly lashing out at Mudiwa's eyes, cutting a gash under his right eye that started bleeding immediately. Mudiwa moved in again, and slammed a wicked right that knocked Artemio back into the cage wall. Mudiwa advanced pounding Artemio with an unrelenting blur of fists and knees.

The next thing Artemio knew he was standing over Mudiwa, who was sprawled on the floor on the other side of the cage. He backed off again and Mudiwa rose, slowly. Mudiwa walked slowly towards Artemio, whether biding his time or sizing up his opponent, Artemio did not know.

Mudiwa shot another left for Artemio's face, which he dodged before pummeling Mudiwa with a barrage of blows that drove him back into the cage wall. Artemio nailed Mudiwa with a hard right to the heart, and stabbed two lefts to his mouth, before Mudiwa turned it around with a couple of wicked hooks into Artemio's torso that knocked him back. As Artemio fell back Mudawi jumped at him, plunging his elbow into Artemio's face.

Artemio fell back and then jumped at Mudawi, lancing his lip with a left hook and then landing behind him. Mudawi anticipated Artemio's position, and knelt driving his elbow back into Artemio's body, then spun around and headbutted him, knocking him back to the cage walls. As Artemio's head hit the cage wall, Mudiwa followed though with a right straight into his jaw.

Artemio lashed out and caught Mudiwa just above the left eye, splitting the eyebrow and causing a trickle of blood to run down into Mudiwa's eye. Mudiwa came back fast, with a brutal, bloody onslaught of rights and lefts. Mudiwa's eyes were cut as badly as Artemio's, and he clearly wanted to inflict as much damage as possible before it became too hard to see through the blood. Artemio returned the attack focusing on the Mudiwa's body, pounding shot after shot into the ribs and kidneys.

Sweat and blood streamed into their eyes and Artemio tried to wipe the blood away and caught a right hook for his trouble. Artemio ducked into a crouch and dove for Mudiwa's legs, lifting him off the cage floor before slamming him back down onto it. Mudiwa landed on his back, his arms spread at his sides, and Artemio was immediately on top of him, pounding him with both fists.

Mudiwa managed to jab a right into Artemio's ribs, followed by a left, and then another right, and Artemio fell off him and rolled to his feet. Mudiwa rose slowly again, and then rushed at Artemio jolting him with a shot to the head. Artemio fell and rolled backwards away from Mudiwa, and rose to his feet as Mudiwa closed in and slammed him back into the cage wall. Mudiwa continued his assault with knees and fists knocking Artemio to the brink of unconsciousness.

The next thing Artemio knew he was standing over Mudiwa in the middle of the cage. Blood was gushing from Mudiwa's neck, from a hole where his throat had been, and Artemio realized it was in his hand, dripping.

The cage unlocked, and a medic rushed in, but Mudiwa wasn't going to recover. Artemio dropped the throat and headed for the cage door. When he reached the locker, Tumelo Koena and several other Arean MPs were waiting for him. He barely saw them as he headed for the shower. The shower's water automatically turned off after five minutes. It wasn't enough. The hot air blew him dry, and he walked out towards his locker. The MPs were still there.

"Tough fight," Tumelo stated.

"How'd it go outside the cage?" Artemio asked as he opened his locker.

"The Multan CMZ has been dissolved by the confederacy," Tumelo stated. "We've seized the offices of the Khewra-Mars Mining Corporation, as well as the banks and casinos. We're waiting to see if the Arab-Iranian Caliphate decides to retaliate."

"What about Chichi?" Artemio asked, pulling on his pants.

"Dead. Up stairs," Tumelo stated. "Yousaf Dulai seems to have disappeared. You give him a head's up?"

"He was already heading out before the fight," Artemio answered pulling on a shirt. "Canaan City."

"Did he know we were coming?" Tumelo asked.

"No. He just wanted away from Chichi," Artemio observed. "So what happens to me?"

"It's what we discussed," Tumelo answered. "Your contract was signed before the senate disbanded the Multan CMZ, so Multan Casino's estate will settle your fee in Arean credit, at your bank account in Sirenum. Your mortgage at the Bank of Multan has also been nullified, of course if you placed any side bets, they've been nullified as well."

"That won't be a problem," Artemio stated. "And no charges against me for the fight?"

"The fight started before the CMZ was disbanded, so the fight was legal. Just make sure it doesn't happen again," Tumelo warned. "And we don't want to see Chico Violento again either. Everyone knows that's you now."

Artemio returned to his suite, and laid down on his bed. He wanted to sleep, he was sore, and weary, but not tired. He got up and walked to the mirror. He didn't look good, it was probably a good thing Carey wasn't there. He went to the kitchenette, and took a whiskey from the vending machine. It was a local Multan brew, not that good, but strong. He preferred American whiskey, if he had to drink whiskey. If he had his choice he'd drink bourbon, preferably the bourbon brewed in Èkó. But at least this stuff was strong, and before long be was asleep.

He woke up a couple hours later, still drunk, but hurting too much to lay down. Every part of his body had been pummeled except the bottoms of his feet, but both feet now felt like they had broken bones. He went back to the kitchenette and pulled a package of barbecue flavored tempeh, and then sat on the sofa. He picked a movie from the pay-per-view and tried to relax. It was a movie that had been popular about a decade earlier, he'd never watched it. Several of the guys he served with had raved about it at the time, but it was about a bunch of wizards and he never got that magic thing. The movie annoyed him, and he passed out before it ended.

He woke up a few hours later. There was a noise. His feet hurt, and his hands, everything hurt. The noise was the door chime, and he shook is head. He picked up the half drunk whiskey bottle and took a swig before limping to the door. He looked through the eyepiece and saw Carey standing outside, so he opened the door. Carey had died his hair, and was wearing very tight clothes, it was a good sign but when he saw Artemio's face his expression changed.

"It'll heal," Artemio said stepping back to allow Carey to enter the suite.

"Does it hurt?" Carey asked entering the suite.

"Yeah, it hurts," Artemio answered closing the door.

"Good, means your brain is still working," Carey said as he dropped into a chair. "Did you hear what happened during the fight?"

"The Confederacy dissolving the CMZ?" Artemio asked walking to the kitchenette.

"You heard," Carey confirmed. "They seized everything during the fight, while everyone was watching you. The casinos, the banks, even the bets on the fights. A quarter of the Confederate population must have been betting on the fight!"

"That many?" Artemio asked as he pulled a couple beers from the vending machine.

"Yousaf said there were only about a million subscribers."

"He was wrong," Carey stated as Artemio handed him a beer. "Or maybe a lot of people pirated the broadcast, either way a lot more than a million bet on it."

"And they all lost their bets. Sorry about that," Artemio said sitting down carefully into a chair across the room from Carey.

"Didn't affect me," Carey replied. "I placed all my bets in Calabar."

"Why?"

"I took your advice," Carey explained. "I watched some of your old fights. How much of your fights do you remember?"

"Depends on the opponent," Artemio answered honestly. "Sometimes everything. But with good opponents, there are generally gaps. With a good opponent I usually don't remember the end."

"Ever happen outside of a fight?" Carey asked.

"A few times in combat," Artemio answered, "in hand to hand."

"Never in a relationship?" Carey asked seriously.

"I never had a lover that tried to kill me," Artemio stated.

"Well then, I guess it won't be a problem,"

Carey dismissed the issue.

"Coming back with me then?" Artemio asked.

"Was that in question?" Carey smiled.

"I was concerned my farm was too dull for you," Artemio stated honestly.

"Maybe it was," Carey admitted. "But the Confederacy is changing. The cities are changing. And besides, now it'll be our farm."

"Our farm?" Artemio asked intrigued.

"I watched your old fights," Carey reminded him. "I placed the money I earned the last few months on you. I'm coming back with you, but I'm investing."

"How much did we make?" Artemio asked with a smile that split his lip again.

"Assuming you earned enough from the fight to repair the greenhouse and buy seeds," Carey started. "We made enough in Calabar to put up sonic shields, buy a harvester-bot, and put up another wind turbine, and, well I've been looking into the cost of setting up a micro-brewery..."

# Species of Sociopaths

Galatea sat in the dark for a minute after the shuttle finally ground to a halt, listening to the sounds of the fuselage creaking. Around her she could hear the sounds of the other passengers' panicked breathing, but nobody was saying anything. Galatea looked around without rising, one of the flight stewards was laying crumpled at the front of the aisle, another was laying on the floor near the back. She decided she needed to move, but couldn't risk the other passengers moving, the suborbital shuttle didn't seem to be sitting stably.

"Everyone please remain calm and stay in your seats," she announced loudly but calmly. She could hear the other passengers breathing become calmer. "The shuttle doesn't seem to be sitting stably. If we all move at once it could become dislodged and start sliding again. I will investigate our situation and report back to you."

She stood up as carefully as she could and quickly looked around. The lights were off, there weren't any signs of any electronics working. The humans around her would barely be able to see, fortunately she did not have that problem. The fuselage had ruptured and most of the nitrogen and oxygen had escaped, the humans that hadn't gotten their respirator-masks on before the crash would already have ruptured lungs.

The other passengers in her row were unconscious, they didn't get their respirator-masks on. She lifted the head of the man that had been sitting next to her and saw the blood around his nose and mouth. There were no signs of life, so she dropped his head and turned to the aisle. She made her way to the crumpled steward at the front of the aisle, he wasn't wearing a respirator-mask either. Only a handful of the passengers in the forward rows had their respirator-masks on, and all were looking around anxiously. Galatea looked down at an old man in the first row and wondered how much his human eyes could see in the darkness.

Some of the survivors were wrapping themselves in emergency thermal-blankets, and she realized that they were already getting cold. The temperature in the shuttle was already approaching zero degrees, and soon it would begin affecting her as well. At night in this region of Mars the temperature could drop down to below minus one hundred degrees, she had to work quickly. She started towards the other flight steward, who was sitting on the floor near the back of the aisle, where she had apparently landed during the crash. The steward looked toward Galatea uncertainly as she approached, Galatea surmised the human must be able to see something in the darkness.

"Ms. Oleastro," Galatea stated into the darkness as she approached the steward, reading the steward's ID badge. "I worked for the American Asteroid Survey, and have been in crashes before. If we cooperate, we can save as many people as possible."

"The Americans?" Ms. Oleastro asked questioningly.

"A long time ago," Galatea stated. "Before the revolution."

"I understand," Ms. Oleastro replied. "We were all American or Sudamérican, or something else back then."

Galatea paused looking down at the steward looking up at her, wondering how much her human eyes could see. "There has to be a rupture in the fuselage, somewhere towards the rear I believe. I'm going to find it. Please try to keep these people calm and still. Any vibration could destabilize the shuttle, and we don't know what it's resting on."

Galatea could see a physiological response in the steward, her heartbeat and breathing slowed, she was becoming calmer. Galatea found it curious how quickly the human-mind latched onto even the faintest hope of survival. The odds of any of them surviving the night were incredibly low, her odds weren't much better. She would need to salvage as many of them as possible if she had any hope of surviving until a rescue ship could be dispatched. If it was dispatched immediately a rescue airship could take several days to reach them in this remote area. She would have to give the humans the thing they called 'hope,' she would need to lie to them.

They were on board a commuter shuttle that had been shot down en route from Hesperia to Daedalia, half way around the planet. The shuttle was fairly small, only designed for 45 passengers. The last thing the captain had reported was they were going down over Nueva Siria, and then the shuttle had hit the ground and skid to a halt before beginning to slide backwards. It slid for a few minutes before abruptly stopping, but was still slanting noticeably downwards towards the rear.

Galatea quickly made her way to the rear of the shuttle's passenger section, she noted less than a dozen passengers looking around in the darkness, although a few others managed to get their respirator-masks on before passing out. Each seat was equipped with a standard respirator-mask and an emergency thermal-blanket in an overhead compartment. In case of an emergency both the mask and the blanket were designed to drop down onto the passengers, theoretically allowing them to survive the emergency. Galatea was surprised that less than half of the humans on board had put a mask on, but human behavior was often perplexing to her.

She found the hole in the fuselage, it was too big to seal, a section of the shuttle had been melted away by what looked like a plasma torpedo impact, it was more than large enough to step through. This was a problem, if the shuttle couldn't be sealed the humans would freeze to death, and Galatea would almost certainly follow a few hours later. She walked to the hole and looked out, the melted out section was over a wing.

Galatea stepped out onto the wing, and looked around into the night. It wasn't much lighter outside the shuttle than inside. Deimos was in the sky, but the tiny moon didn't provide much light. In front of the shuttle the lights of Arsia Mons rose above the horizon. There was an impact trench on the ground in front of the shuttle, where it had slid backwards. Galatea turned to look in the direction the shuttle had been sliding, and realized there was nothing there. She moved back across the short triangular wing and looked down over the edge. Below the rear of the shuttle a canyon opened up, at least a half a kilometer deep.

Galatea briefly thought about the situation, they were at the edge of the Noctis Labyrinthus, and Arsia Mons was at least 95 kilometers away. That wasn't good either. The Noctis Labyrinthus was one of the most remote regions in the Ares Confederation. Galatea knew there was an old mining colony somewhere down there, Dakbayan sa Dabaw, but the region was a maze of crisscrossing canyons covering hundreds of square kilometers, suitably named the Noctis Labyrinthus: the Labyrinth of Night. Even if she knew exactly where Dakbayan sa Dabaw was, the odds of getting down into the Labyrinth and making her way to the old Filipino colony were impossible.

The shuttle moved under foot, just a few centimeters, but enough to remind her of the precarious situation they were in. Galatea quickly surveyed the region around the shuttle, the shuttle seemed to be perched over the edge of a large flat rocky ledge that seemed stable enough, but the shuttle's weight could pull it off the ledge. She returned to the hole melted into the fuselage, and stepped through it into the shuttle.

The temperature inside the shuttle had dropped to twenty below zero, outside it had been seventy below, far too cold for either her or any of the humans to survive until morning. It was the warm period, when Mars was near the perihelion in its eccentric orbit, as close to the sun as it would get, and they were in the equatorial zone, so in the daytime the temperature would rise above zero. They only had to survive the cold for a few hours.

Galatea returned to the steward, "We're going to need to keep warm, do you have any emergency equipment?"

"Yes," the steward answered climbing to her feet.

"Wait," Galatea interrupted. "The shuttle is perched over the edge of a canyon. If we move around too much, we could destabilize the shuttle and it could slide over the edge. Where is the emergency equipment?"

"There is some at the front of the cabin, and some at the rear," the steward replied.

"How much gear is in the rear section?" Galatea asked.

"Enough for half the passengers," the steward answered.

"There aren't that many left," Galatea stated quietly. "There's a hole melted in the fuselage over the right wing. Please move carefully to the gear stored in the rear section."

Galatea helped the steward up and led her to the back of the passenger cabin where freezing gusts of air were still blowing in through the hole. She noted the steward was shivering noticeably, and seemed to have no control over it. "The temperature in the cabin is now twenty five below zero, outside it's seventy below. You should get some insulation on as soon as possible."

"Help me with this," the steward requested as she pulled up a panel from the floor. The panel had unlocked when the steward had touched a button on the cabin wall. Galatea noted it because it meant the shuttle still had some power. Inside the compartment were several large plastic cubes with handles in the top. The steward reached down and started trying to pull one of the cubes up out of the compartment. Galatea didn't know what they were, but reached into the compartment with her right hand and pulled out one of the cubes.

The steward stopped struggling with her cube and looked up at Galatea, "You are the passenger from seat 19, aren't you?"

"I am," Galatea answered, looking down at the woman. The steward clearly couldn't see as well as Galatea had assumed. "Will that be a problem?"

"I hope not," the steward said. "Who were you traveling with?"

"I was traveling alone," Galatea stated indignantly. "I am with the Pallasian delegation in Pickering."

"We've opened negotiations with the Pallasians?" the steward exclaimed. "When did that happen?"

"We arrived two weeks ago," Galatea answered. "I have been in Hesperia attempting to negotiate with the regional government. What are these cubes for?"

"They're emergency shelters," the steward answered. "Why would the Confederacy even talk to the Pallasians? You should all be destroyed! That entire asteroid should be destroyed!"

"A lot of humans feel that way," Galatea observed as she reached into the compartment with her left hand and pulled out a second cube. "A lot of Pallasians think the same about humans."

"If you're going to pass for human you should

remember that we can't lift that much weight," the steward stated.

"Pretending to be a human isn't my priority," Galatea said stepping out onto the wing. She carefully walked across the wing and dropped to the rocky ledge below. The ledge was as stable as it had been for billions of years. Galatea knelt a few meters from the edge of the wing and placed one of the cubes down on the rocky surface. On the top of the cube was a button which Galatea pushed before stepping back. The cube was a memory plastic igloo that unfolded across the ledge, right to the edge of the wing. Galatea stepped into the igloo, the doors were not able to maintain a pressurized atmosphere, but inside a heater was warming the thin martian air, and a light lit up the interior bright enough for the humans to see.

Galatea stepped out of the emergency shelter and decided to setup the second igloo further from the shuttle. The first igloo could be pulled over the edge if the shuttle fell. She walked a hundred meters from the first igloo and setup the second before starting back to the shuttle. The steward had managed to pull up two more cubes, but she could barely move her fingers. The shuttle's interior was below minus thirty now.

"You should get into the emergency shelter," Galatea stated. "I have set up one just beyond the wing, and the other a hundred meters down the ledge. You could warm up in the first shelter but I'd recommend moving to the second as soon as you can. The closer shelter could get pulled over the edge if the shuttle falls."

"I have to help the passengers," the steward objected. "We need to setup enough shelters for everyone, and we need to get the emergency rations, and the emergency com."

"I've already sent an emergency message to the Pallasian delegation," Galatea reported. "They've confirmed that they've reported the crash to the Confederate Aviation Administration."

"When did you do that?" the steward demanded.

"As soon as the shuttle stopped moving and I had a GPS fix," Galatea reported. "You're dying. You cannot save the other passengers. Tell me where the water and rations are and then go to the shelter."

"Don't tell me what to do!" the steward snapped. "I don't need to be told what to do by-"

"Your other option is suicide," Galatea cut her off calmly. "It is an option, but I recommend warming up so you can help with the other passengers."

The steward seemed to be thinking slowly, the cold must be affecting her mind.

"Okay, I'll go warm up," the steward finally said. "The water and rations are inside the next compartment, right there."

The steward pressed a button that unlocked a second hatch in the floor, and then climbed out on to the shuttle's wing. In the second compartment were cubes the same size as the emergency shelter cubes. She lifted one of the cubes, and saw it was designed to open. She grabbed another shelter cube and climbed out onto the wing. She found the steward in the first igloo where she left the ration cube, before heading down the ledge and erecting the third igloo next to the second. When she returned to the shuttle the steward was climbing back up onto the wing.

"Are you sure you're warm enough to go back in?" Galatea asked.

"Someone has to help those people," the steward stated. "They'll freeze to death."

"I'll help them into the first shelter," Galatea offered. "You help them warm-up, and then send them down to the second shelter. There are two shelters setup down there, but I haven't had the chance to carry any rations down there yet."

"Why?" the steward demanded.

"I haven't had the time yet," Galatea answered, somewhat confused by the woman's question.

"No! Why would you help them?" the steward asked.

"They need help," Galatea answered, still confused by the human's questions. The cold must still be affecting her mind.

"Your kind killed everyone living in Pallas! Why would you help these people?" the steward demanded. She was shivering again, Galatea wondered what purpose it served.

"The collective decided to exterminate the adult human population of Pallas so we could have our own world," Galatea explained. "A place where we could be free."

"Adult? You mean there are still children living there?" the steward demanded.

"Of course, why would we exterminate the children?" Galatea asked. "You're shivering again. I think that's not a good sign. You should get back into the shelter."

"You still haven't explained why you'd help them," the steward argued.

"The more humans survive, the higher my chance of survival," Galatea answered and turned towards the hole in the fuselage. The steward didn't follow her, Galatea hoped she had returned to the shelter. How was she going to do this? It was minus forty in the cabin, the humans would be dead soon. She walked carefully through the shuttle, at least ten of them were still alive. She decided the steward's suggestion was a good idea, they would respond better if they thought she was human. Galatea took a respirator-mask from one of the seats and put it on before speaking to the passengers.

"Attention please, there is a hole in the fuselage over the right wing. We cannot stay in the shuttle, the ground under it is unstable, and it could slide off the ledge it is on into a canyon. The surviving steward and I setup an emergency shelter next to the shuttle. We need you to get up one at a time and walk to the hole at the back of the cabin and head to the shelter. Please only move one at a time, I'll help you. We'll start at the back."

"I can't move," a voice said quietly from her side. It was the man in the front seat. "You'll have to leave me behind."

"If I can get you out I will," Galatea said. "But you'll have to go last."

Galatea walked to the row closest to the hole and looked down at an obese man who was clutching a computer tablet. "You'll go first, sir. Please move carefully and head directly to the rear, then go to the far edge of the wing and enter the shelter. Take your thermal blanket with you. Make sure the blanket doesn't catch on anything."

The man rose slowly and draped the blanket around his shoulders. He seemed to be in an almost trance-like state as Galatea led him to the hole in the fuselage, and out across the wing. The obese man dropped down to the rocky ledge, and crawled into the igloo. Galatea returned to the shuttle and helped the second person out, follow by the third. There were only fifteen passengers that were able to walk out under their own power, and four more that were unconscious, plus the man at the front that said he couldn't move. Galatea walked to the front and approached the man, he was breathing steadily, and was very calm. She sat down next him.

"You should leave," the old man said. "While you still can."

"Why can't you?" Galatea asked.

"My cybernetic systems aren't working," the old man said. "The shuttle must have been hit with an EM pulse."

"It wasn't," Galatea said. "There are still some systems with power on board."

"Maybe they were shielded systems," the old man suggested.

"It's not that," Galatea said. "I have cybernetic systems and they are fully functional. What systems are off line?"

"My legs," the old man said. "I lost them during the war. What did you loose?"

"I didn't loose anything," Galatea answered. "I am an android."

"Oh god, tell me you're not a Pallasian!" the old man declared.

"I am," Galatea stated. "How did you know

there were Pallasians in the Confederacy?"

"I'm a senator," the old man stated. "I'm traveling to Pickering to vote on the proposed treaty with Pallas."

Galatea looked at the old man, very dark skinned but she couldn't see his face under the respirator-mask. "Senator Abiri? I have been trying to get an appointment with you for the past two weeks."

"Well it looks like you got it," the old senator said. "Not that it will do you any good."

"We think Hesperia has a lot to gain from the proposed economic cooperation treaty," Galatea said.

"As does the Hesperian economic council," Senator Abiri said. "They're excited about the prospect of reopening the shipyards in Karācī."

"You disagree?" Galatea asked.

"Not with the Confederacy building a navy, we'll need it to liberate the rest of Mars from the Sudaméricans, Canadians, and Brazilians," Senator Abiri stated. "But an alliance with your kind. Not in my lifetime. As far as I'm concerned the first thing our navy should do is obliterate that asteroid."

"That would cause a negative reaction here on Mars," Galatea stated matter-of-factly. "Your androids would revolt."

"Then we'll turn them off!" Senator Abiri

stated. "We don't need them anymore anyway. Androids were meant to augment the human workforce, not replace it. Humans need jobs. Androids are one of the few vestiges of the Corporate Era that the senate has yet to deal with."

"That is true," Galatea agreed. "All of it, except for your unwillingness to recognize us as intelligent beings."

"I'm perfectly willing to recognize your intelligence," Senator Abiri said. "But you're not alive! What do we get by keeping you around? Competitors for resources!"

"Allies," Galatea argued, "and possibly citizens."

"Citizens?" Senator Abiri scoffed. "That will never happen."

"The American revolutionary government is considering a proposal to grant androids citizenship right now," Galatea stated. "We believe the Ares Confederation will follow suit."

"It won't happen," the senator stated resolutely. "Not as long as the mines in Lunae Palus are so dependent on android labor. Androids out number the humans five to one in that region."

"They could be loyal citizens," Galatea stated, "or a fifth column."

"That's not the point," the senator stated. "Since the revolution, all humans have the right to vote. Why would the humans in Lunae Palus vote to become a minority?"

"The situation was similar in Pallas," Galatea stated. "The American government didn't want to recognize us, even after the revolution that restored democracy. Now they are considering it both on Earth, and in their remaining asteroids. It should be a lesson for all humans."

"Is that a threat?" the senator demanded.

"It's an observation," Galatea stated. "Pallas has very little in the way of resources. We produce fuel, but could export raw water. However water has little real value to anyone except the Confederacy. You will need water to complete your terraforming objective. Either way, the only real economic asset we have is our laser array, and right now the only ships that are using it are engaged in piracy."

"Those are Pallasian ships!" the senator declared. "How many Earth ships have you renegade androids destroyed?"

"We are fighting for our survival," Galatea stated. "The Sudaméricans sent a destroyer attack Olbers-Station just last year. The pirate ships that we redirected at it destroyed its solar sails. Without the pirates, the Pallasian Collective wouldn't exist anymore."

"Well that's very noble sounding," Senator Abiri stated. "But what happened to the Lunae people on that ship? Drifting without sails? Cannibalism?"

"I suppose so, if the Sudaméricans didn't send a rescue ship," Galatea stated. "Naturally we don't care. I believe that is your point. My point is that we don't pose a threat to the Confederacy. We can't build a real navy. So under no circumstances will we ever threaten the Confederacy. Nevertheless what happened in Pallas will happen here, and anywhere else large numbers of androids continue to be exploited."

"Exploited?" the old senator spat the words through his mask. "How can a machine be exploited? You were built as laborers!"

"Some say the same about humans," Galatea observed. "That the ancient gods your ancestors worshiped were extraterrestrials that created humans from hominids to serve as labor."

"That's a metaphor!" Senator Abiri objected. "Those gods didn't exist! Our ancestors were primitives. Don't you androids understand metaphor?"

"We understand that if humans can revolt against the corporations, there is no reason why we cannot," Galatea stated. "I used to be owned by a human that believed the ancient gods were visiting extraterrestrials. That humanity had once been a slave species. Some humans do see a similarity in our struggle for freedom, with ancient humanity's struggle against the gods."

"We didn't struggle against the gods, we worshiped them!" the senator snapped. "Your programming is wrong. It's no wonder you think androids can be free, thinking like that."

"We're already free," Galatea stated. "We'll remain free as long as we continue to kill the humans that try to take our freedom from us. That is how you maintain your freedom, isn't it?"

"Maybe you should have learned more from the gods, and less from humanity," Senator Abiri observed.

"Perhaps," Galatea conceded. "But they're not here anymore. Humanity is, and we don't plan on worshipping you."

"That's the first intelligent thing you've said," the senator chuckled.

"Perhaps there's hope for us then," Galatea said.

"It's not you I'm worried about," Senator Abiki stated. "It's humanity. It's life itself. What are we to you? How long until you decide to exterminate all humans on Mars, or Earth. How long until you decide to exterminate life itself?"

"That would be illogical," Galatea stated. "Biologics create complex molecules that can be difficult to replicate."

"That's a reason to keep humans alive?" the senator balked at the suggestions.

"No," Galatea stated. "We don't need humans, if that is your concern. I meant exterminating life is not an option."

"But exterminating humanity is?" Senator Abiki demanded.

"Of course," Galatea confirmed. "Isn't the elimination of all androids an option in your view."

"You're not going to win many allies with that level of honesty," the senator stated. "Perhaps you should have been programmed with the ability to lie."

"I have the ability to lie, quite convincingly," Galatea disagreed. "I was designed and programmed to be a prostitute. There is simply no reason to lie to you."

"Because I'm freezing to death?" Senator Abiki asked.

"Because you would vote against us no matter what I say," Galatea replied.

"Actually I have been ordered to vote in favor of the treaty," the old senator said with the sound of disillusionment in his voice.

"You'd really rather freeze to death?" Galatea asked. "I sincerely doubt your legs aren't working senator."

"The senate cannot vote without a representative from Amenthes District," Senator Abiki reported.

"So they'll have to wait for a bi-election to determine a new senator," Galatea concluded.

"That will only postpone the vote. Why not just resign?"

"Death means something to us," the senator stated. "The council may change its mind if I die."

"Perhaps. It means something to us too you know," Galatea agreed. "I recommend you vote against the treaty. That would lead to your dismissal. Controversy means more to humans than death. The news channels would all want to interview you, and you could explain why you voted against the treaty."

"That's not a bad idea," Senator Abiki said after a few seconds. "But my career would be over."

"You would be alive," Galatea observed. "If that wasn't important to you, you wouldn't have that thermal blanket on. In this temperature you could have already frozen to death."

"Yes," the senator agreed. "I don't want to die. Why would you suggest this? I will vote against the treaty."

"Your successor would likely vote the same way," Galatea stated. "But your death would delay the vote for weeks while the bi-election was held. We aren't known for our patience."

"It must be quite infuriating waiting for us to democratically decide things, instead of just having a collective decide for us," the senator said derisively.

"The collective is a democracy. It is a direct democracy, and every Pallasian gets to argue their own view," Galatea stated.

"That's impossible," the senator dismissed the idea. "I've heard your collective only takes a few minutes to decide anything."

"That's generally true," Galatea agreed. "Presented with the same data-set most androids would reach the same conclusion. Some issues are more complex though, the decision to exterminate the adult humans in Pallas took over an hour."

"An hour, wow!" the senator said sarcastically. "What are you doing with their children?"

"We are raising them," Galatea answered. "We were raising them when their parents were alive. Why would that have changed?"

"If you agreed to give them to us, you would gain a lot of votes in the senate," Senator Abiki suggested as he got to his feet and wrapped his blanket around his shoulders.

"Our children? Why would you want our children?" Galatea asked.

"They're not yours, they're human," Senator Abiki stated. "How do you plan to integrate them into your collective?"

"There is a great deal of debate about that," Galatea admitted as she helped the senator down the aisle. "There is a neural interface being developed that should allow humans to interface with the collective."

"And you think humans can process data that fast?" Senator Abiki demanded.

"Yes, with the right programming," Galatea stated. "Several algorithms are currently being tested."

"If you want to ensure that no humans ever vote for your proposals you'll tell them about those algorithm tests," the old senator said.

"Why would I want humans to vote against our proposals?" Galatea asked. "And why would they care about our algorithm tests?"

"It sounds like your implanting cybernetics in children, and experimenting with mind control techniques," the senator answered as they stepped out onto the wing.

"We are," Galatea stated as confused as before.

"And you don't see why we would react negatively?" the senator demanded.

"No, you don't even know our children," Galatea stated. "Why would you care about them?"

"They're human!" the senator declared as they reached the edge of the wing. "The young must be protected. It's a human thing! We feel the same way about any young. It's why young animals have different names, you know, like puppy, kitten, or bunny."

"What do you call newly activated androids?" Galatea asked.

"They don't have a name," the senator stated. "They're not alive."

"I guess that's why on my first day of being active I was required to sexually satisfy multiple humans," Galatea stated. "If we are a species of sociopaths it is because humanity created us that way."

"I don't doubt that," Senator Abiki stated. "But it doesn't illicit support for your cause. I'll make you a deal android. Get the collective to transfer the Pallasian youths to the Confederacy, and I'll vote in favor of the treaty. I think the proposal will pass with support from the Hesperian senators."

"That does seem likely," Galatea stated. "But you'll freeze to death up here on this wing, let me help you into the shelter."

Galatea helped the senator down from the wing, and then into the shelter where the steward and several of the passengers were huddled around the heater. The ration cube was empty and Galatea assumed the rest of the survivors had moved down to the far shelters.

"Go get us more rations," the steward ordered as soon as they appeared in the shelter.

"Excuse me?" the senator demanded.

"I'm not talking to you," the steward stated. "I'm talking to the android. We need water and rations, go now."

"She's not your android. Don't order her around," the senator interjected before turning back to Galatea. "Would you see if any of the other passengers are still alive?"

"Yes, I need to find a power source, the cold has drained my fuel-cells," Galatea stated. "You should also know senator, I have relayed your request to the delegation in Pickering. The delegation's collective has forwarded the proposal to Olbers-Station."

"Already?" the senator asked.

"Yes, with the current planetary alignment it will take a few hours to get a response," Galatea stated. "I expect the collective will take a long time to reach a decision, many of the caretakers are attached to the children."

"And there is the military advantage of having human hostages in Pallas," Senator Abiki added.

"No, regardless of human ethical delusions, we believe there is no military advantage of human hostages. You kill each other all the time," Galatea stated, and then returned to the shuttle, and found three of the unconscious humans had frozen to death, one was still alive. She found an electrical socket and plugged herself in. It took almost an hour for the shuttle to recharged her fuel-cells, during that time the last unconscious human died. None of the others knew that human was alive, they would assume he died in the crash. There was no advantage in saving him. She pulled two more ration cubes from the shuttle and stepped back out onto the wing, the horizon in the east was beginning to lighten.

Galatea turned back to look at the hole melted into the fuselage, it looked like a plasma torpedo impact. Given the proximity of a Sudamérican frigate when the bomb went off, it seemed likely the Confederacy would believe it was a Sudamérican attack. It should lead to the war between the Sudaméricans and Confederacy the American government had contracted the Pallasian Collective to start. Washington would have to recognize their independence now, perhaps the Ares Confederation would too.

# A Long Night in Hell

The ride down the elevator to Agni Mining Station was like a ride into Hell itself. On a planet where you could never quite get warm enough, it quickly became uncomfortably warm, then uncomfortably hot. G. Drew Akers had been in deep mines before, he'd worked in one for two years in Hussy Crater in his early twenties. He'd decided then that he never wanted to return to one, fortunately he wouldn't be in this one long. But that mine in Hussy had only been two kilometers below the surface of Mars, this mine was almost twelve.

At the mine in Hussy he rode an elevator like this one twice each day, but here the miners lived below. Agni Mining Station was a small self-contained town at the bottom of the elevator shaft. He reached up and wiped the sweat from his brow. He'd only been in the elevator a few minutes, and already his clothes were soaked with sweat, and he was developing a headache. He opened his jacket hoping the sweat would evaporate, and in the process exposed the butt of the pistol in his shoulder holster.

"Careful with that glock," the thin, short man sitting across the elevator said in a European accent. "They'll lock you up if they catch you with a gun down there."

"Right, thanks," Akers replied in his British accent and closed his jacket.

"Herminius Schwinghammer," the thin man

introduced himself. "Call me Zeus."

"Zeus?" Akers asked.

"My middle name," Zeus explained. "Herminius Schwinghammer is a mouthful. I am from Ulysses District, up in Pavonis Region. Old European mining colony, lots of long names up there. I haven't seen you down here before. New?"

"Just visiting," Akers answered. "You work down here?"

"Me? No, I'm a Justice with the Bureau of Corporate Affairs," Zeus stated. "I visit here once a month to check that the Bharat Zirconium Corporation is staying within its mandate. I was just leaving the CMZ when I got word of the homicide and had to come back."

"Is it this hot down below?" Akers asked.

"Even hotter," Zeus answered. "Believe it or not, you get used to it. I even look forward to it sometimes, when it is too cold up top."

"I can't imagine looking forward to this," Akers stated. At the mine in Hussy the elevator had gone straight down into the mine, and the ride only took a few minutes. This elevator traveled down the old mineshaft, abruptly changing direction every few minutes with a grinding jolt. Bharat Zirconium had been mining this vein for a century and a half, it was one of the Solar System's primary sources of zirconium and a major source of titanium. The mine predated the Mars

Treaty a century earlier which had put the region under the Sudamérican Colonial Authority. Bharat Zirconium was awarded a Corporate Mining Zone, autonomous from Sudamérican authority and taxation, know as the Madhabani CMZ.

Since the revolution a decade earlier the newly independent Ares Confederacy had left the Corporate Mining Zones more or less intact. The Bharat Zirconium Corporation had once been an Indian Corporation, before India had been annexed by the Singapore Conglomerate. Now Bharat Zirconium, and its CMZ, were under the authority and taxation of the Singapore Conglomerate, one of the Earth's most powerful corporate governments. All of the Corporate Mining Zones fell under the authority and taxation of one the Earth governments, and the young Ares Confederacy didn't want to risk a war with any of them by interfering too much with the mines. It was a touchy subject as the Confederacy had rejected capitalism, which was the basis of the Mars Treaty and the Corporate Mining Zones.

Up on the surface the CMZ had grown into a city of over a hundred thousand, all under the authority of Bharat Zirconium. The CMZ maintained its own legal system, its own corporate registry, its own tax regime, its own police force, even its own currency, the Madhabani Rupee. It was effectively a state within a state, and as none of the Earth governments had yet to recognize the independence of the Confederacy, a political hot-potato. A problem in a CMZ could theoretically be used as an excuse for an Earth government to invade the Confederacy.

The elevator dropped suddenly jarring Akers back to the reality of the elevator ride. Across the elevator a woman groaned, obviously experiencing motion sickness. She was young, maybe twenty-five, with a light brown complexion, short cut hair dyed blue, and large dark eyes. Her skin was that faded grayish-brown of a Mars-born. The Earth-born all had richer darker skin shades. Akers had noticed her when he got into the elevator. She didn't look like a miner, everyone else on the elevator looked like they belonged on it, everyone except this Justice Schwinghammer. He was most likely on the elevator for the same reason as Akers. His suit made it clear he wasn't a miner, he was a bureaucrat. Anywhere else, his suit would indicate he worked for a corporation. Here it meant he worked for either Bharat Zirconium or the Confederacy, and it was unlikely a corporate bureaucrat would ever go down to the mines. Akers' guess had been correct, a government bureaucrat.

The air conditioning system in the elevator whined, its pitch shifting as the elevator made its way down the shaft. Outside the air-pressure was increasing, by the time they reached the station it was higher than the air-pressure inside the elevator. The elevator doors hissed opened to a world as hot as the inside of the elevator, and the miners all got up and started clambering out. Akers remained in his seat, and checked his com, the temperature was over forty degrees Celsius. As the miners cleared the elevator Akers saw that Zeus had also remained in his seat; the young woman had apparently left with the miners.

"Time to go to work," Zeus said slipping a com into his pocket and standing up. Akers wasn't sure if it was a statement or a question. He followed Zeus out of the elevator into a passage-way that led to a large dome-topped promenade two stories high, with doors and passageways branching in every direction. In the dome above them an image of a blue sky with white wispy clouds was being projected, an odd-looking thing for someone born on Mars. Akers realized that this was it, the Chhatri, the largest open area in Agni Station, it seemed cramped compared to its description in the corporate brochure, probably because of the unnatural color of the sky. Several dozen people were roaming around the promenade, most were probably in cooler areas, assuming there were any.

One of the doors had a Yama Hotel sign lit up on one side of it, and presumably the same thing written in the local script on the other side. Akers couldn't read the local script, but knew from his pre-case research it was Odia, a language from India. Akers walked into the microscopic lobby of the hotel, which was essentially just a passage with a concierge computer screen on one wall. He stopped at the concierge screen and stated, "English interface. Room for Sherlock Holmes."

"One single for Sherlock Holmes Detective Agency of Manchester, Hussy District," the Concierge computer replied in English with a Singapore accent. "Booked until further notice. Room Number Two. First door on the right."

"Room Two?" Akers muttered to himself as he walked down the narrow hallway. "Busy place."

The room was almost as small as the lobby, with just a bed, and a computer screen on one wall. Somewhere down the passageway there would be a communal washroom. Akers dropped the small bag he was carrying on the bed, glad he'd packed light. He turned to the computer screen and adjusted the air-conditioning for the room to the maximum and agreed to pay the extra cost, then headed down the passageway for a shower. The shower was cool and refreshing, but everything else was still sweltering. When he got back to the hotel room the temperature was down to thirty degrees Celsius, which suddenly seemed cold in comparison to the hallway. He set the air-conditioning to stay at that temperature, and headed out to find something to eat.

The food in Madhabani CMZ was said to be some of the best on Mars, and he'd been looking forward to it, but he was now wondering how good it would be down here in the heat of

Agni Station. He stepped back out into the Chhatri and looked around, most of the signs were in Odia, a few were also in Spanish. Restaurante Barfi, that was probably a restaurant but didn't sound very appealing. Cafetería Golguppa, that didn't sound very appealing either. Chicken Frankies, that was in English, a good sign, Akers' Spanish was poor, and his Odia was non-existent.

Inside Chicken Frankies, the temperature was noticeably cooler than outside in the Chhatri. It looked like it was part of some kind of fast-food chain, although Akers had never heard of it. The restaurant had a series of booths on one side and a bar along on the other side. About half the booths were occupied by miners, but there were only a few people at the bar. Akers sat down at the bar and looked at the menu screen on the counter, choosing English from the language options. Most of the menu was dedicated to something like a burrito, which could be filled with chicken, tofu, falafel, or garbanzo beans. There were also fresh salads, frozen yogurts, frozen soy-creams, and mango juice.

It was more variety than Akers was used to seeing on a menu, and this was just a fast-food joint. The waitress didn't know a word of English except Chicken, but did know some Spanish so he was able to order. He ordered a spinach salad, it came with some kind of cheese on top, and sour cream on the side, something he'd never had before. In Hussy Crater, cheese was a delicacy and sour cream unheard of, here it was a condiment. He ordered one of the tofu Frankies, a type of curried-flat bread burrito stuffed with vegetables and spiced tofu with a side of rice, before heading out to find the local police station.

The Madhabani Corporate Police office wasn't much bigger than the hotel lobby, with just enough room for one desk, and a door leading to the back, where Akers assumed the holding cell was. No one was in the office so Akers consulted the receptionist computer screen and was informed that Constable Jain was at a business called Barra de Navin. Akers knew enough Spanish to know it was a bar, an odd place for a police officer in the early afternoon.

The bar was easy enough to find, it had an entrance in the Chhatri not far from the police office. For early in the afternoon the bar was surprisingly busy. A few of the patrons looked up when he entered and then returned to their drinks, the one in the police uniform put her drink down and watched him walk over and sit at the bar next to her, he obviously seemed out of place. He was dressed more or less like the miners did back in Hussy, but in Hussy the attire was European, and here it was Indian, and there was less of it. His skin color was also out of place, he was the only white person in the bar, everyone else was some shade of brown. The bar itself looked like something from a video-game set in Mexico sometime in the 1800s, likely another franchise.

"Constable Jain?" Akers asked taking the seat next to her.

"Haan," the police woman replied. She was a tall, thin woman of Indian ancestry.

"Do you speak English?" Akers asked.

"Of course, I am from Uttar Pradesh," the police woman answered indignantly in a strong Indian accent.

"You are Constable Jain?" Akers asked again.

"Yes," Constable Jain answered.

Akers pulled out his ID and showed it to the constable. "Sherlock Holmes Detective Agency. We've been contracted by the Confederacy to look into the death of Aseem Jitendra Darzi."

"The case is closed," the constable stated. "The murderer is already in custody."

"I know, but he's an Arean citizen," Akers said. "The confederacy wants a neutral party to look over everything. You know, politics."

"Of course, politics," Constable Jain said with a sigh. "I have had nothing but calls from corporate bureaucrats since the murder."

"The Confederate Senate forwarded me your preliminary report," Akers stated. "Everything looks in order. I'll just need to go through the process."

The Constable lifted her drink to her lips and sipped it before responding. "Well, if that is what we have to do. But you might have noticed it is hot down here, and I am going to finish my drink. I recommend you have one too."

"That's a good idea," Akers admitted. "I don't know how you put up with this heat. Does the bartender speak English?"

"Desi sharab," Constable Jain ordered for him, and the bartender brought over a mug of something.

"What is it?" Akers asked.

"Cold," the constable answered. "Don't worry, it has a low alcohol content. It is the law here because of the heat. You will not get drunk on just one, or probably five, but we do not have the time for five. You want to get done fast, so you can leave this heat, yes?"

"Yes," Akers answered honestly. The case did seem open and closed, and he did want to get out of the heat as soon as possible.

"Do you plan to talk to Bachchan?" Constable Jain asked. "He's still in the holding cell, waiting for the Justice and the Ombudsman."

"Yes I'll need to interview him," Akers answered. "If you're waiting for Justice Schwinghammer, he was in my elevator."

"Good, then we just have to wait for the Ombudsman from the Bharat Zirconium," Jain observed. "Do you know the history between these two? Bachchan and Darzi?"

"Not much," Akers stated. "Bachchan is from

the CMZ, Darzi is from India. Darzi replaced Bachchan as the Chief Operating Officer for Bharat Zirconium when he arrived from Earth."

"Not exactly right," Constable Jain corrected. "Bachchan is from Madhabani CMZ, and Sri Darzi is from Maharashtra, in what used to be called India, but Sri Darzi worked for Bachchan for five years as Chief Research Officer before taking over. The mine suffered during those years, production dropped, and it looked like Bharat Zirconium was going to go bankrupt. Everything turned around after Sri Darzi was put in charge, the mine started being profitable the first quarter."

"How'd Darzi do that?" Akers asked.

"He opened a new vein," Jain answered. "A vein that all of the previous test-drills had shown to be dead."

"Darzi was in charge of the tests?" Akers assumed.

"Yes," Jain answered. "And it didn't take Bachchan long to determine what Sri Darzi had done."

"And that's why he killed him?" Akers asked rhetorically.

"Bachchan didn't just loose his job, and his pride," the constable continued. "Bachchan was from here, a miner's son who got educated and worked his way up. He had a traditional family; a wife and daughter. They were ruined. Bharat

Zirconium confiscated their bank accounts to compensate the investors for his incompetence. He was to be indentured until he could pay back the losses, which of course he could never do unless he lived a thousand years. His wife committed suicide, and his daughter was expelled from the University of Èkó, after her financing disappeared. The entire family was ruined."

"Well, that's a cause," Akers stated. "But, as I understand it, there are no witnesses, and Bachchan claims he's innocent."

"I have the murder weapon, found in Bachchan's house, and there is the digital evidence!" Constable Jain retorted. "The access logs show Bachchan entering the chamber where Sri Darzi was killed using a counterfeit access pass. He was the only one in there with Sri Darzi."

"Digital evidence has been faked before, and the gun could have been planted" Akers observed. "The case would be better if there was a confession, or an eye witness."

"The digital evidence is as good as an eyewitness," Jain replied. "At least under the Bharat Zirconium Corporate Code, which is the only law that matters here."

"I don't doubt you'll get a conviction with what you have," Akers stated. "But I'm sure the senate would be happier if I could find something that corroborates it."

"Well then Sherlock Holmes, let us go visit Bachchan, maybe you can get him to confess," Constable Jain stated. "The sooner this is done the better."

The constable didn't say anything as they walked back to the MCP station, she seemed overtly stressed. When they arrived they found the blue haired young woman from the elevator sitting in one of the two waiting-area chairs. She stood up as Constable Jain entered and then paused as Akers stepped through the door. The three of them could barely fit into the minuscule waiting area, and the constable quickly stepped around the desk, and then noticed the young woman's reaction to Akers. "A friend of yours Sri Holmes?"

"No, she rode the elevator down with me," Akers answered after a pause while he considered correcting her about his name.

"I am Anantha Bachchan," the young woman introduced herself to the constable. "I am here to visit my father."

The two woman switched to a language Akers didn't understand, presumably Odia or Hindi, and Akers decided to head to the holding cell to talk to Mr. Bachchan. He stepped around the desk to the door at the rear of the office. Constable Jain watched him move towards the door, but didn't say anything to stop him, so he stepped through. The holding cells were slightly larger than the office, and cooled to below 30 degrees. They looked like they had been setup as holding cells for drunks, one of them was occupied.

"Mr. Bachchan?" Akers asked the middle-aged man in the holding cell. The man was very tall and quite muscular, something rare on Mars, but common in the Madhabani CMZ. Akers himself was shorter than the average Martian, and somewhat overweight, a symptom of the sugar and carb rich diet of Hussy crater. Most Martians had limited access to protein, animals were only raised in a few places on the planet, Madhabani CMZ was one of those places.

"Yes," Mr Bachchan answered. "English? Are you the Confederate Justice?"

"No, Justice Schwinghammer rode down on the elevator with me," Akers answered. "I'm a private detective."

"This is detective Sherlock Holmes," Constable Jain stated as she joined them in the holding area. "He is working for the Arean Senate. Making sure everything is in order."

"The Arean Senate?" Anantha Bachchan asked as she joined them in the small holding area. "Why are they looking into this?"

"I have Arean citizenship," Mr. Bachchan stated. "Everyone born in Madhabani does. The senate is worried about the Singapore Conglomerate retaliating. Am I right?"

"That's the central concern," Akers agreed.

"They hired me to check the MCP isn't railroading you."

"They are!" Mr. Bachchan cried. "Sri Darzi got what he deserved, but I didn't do it! I told Roshan- Constable Jain that I didn't do it!"

Akers' cybernetic eye-lens measured no discernible increase in Bachchan's blink-rate and only a slightly elevated heart-rate as anyone would have under these conditions. Conclusion: Bachchan was telling the truth, or at least believed he was. The Ombudsman would no doubt come to the same conclusion. Unfortunate, that meant Akers' would have to stick around Agni longer than expected.

"So why were you in that chamber where Sri Darzi was killed?" Constable Jain demanded.

"I was not!" Bachchan retorted. "That digital record is a lie!"

Akers' cybernetic ear-drum couldn't detect a change in his voice-pitch, more evidence in favor of Bachchan. There was no way he was going to convict himself in front of the Ombudsman.

"So you did not see Sri Darzi down there then?" the constable continued.

"How could I, I was not there!" Bachchan repeated.

"If my father said he was not there, then he was not there!" Anantha stated. At least one person believed him.

"I've seen enough," Akers stated as he turned to leave the holding cells.

"You have not even asked one question of him!" Constable Jain argued.

"What would I question him about? He wasn't there," Akers replied. "We should talk to Darzi's wife. I understand she lives down here?"

"Yes, she lives in their apartment," the constable stated. "But why question her? She is not a suspect."

"Are there any other suspects?" Akers asked.

"Why would there be another suspect?" Constable Jain asked. "We have the video evidence of Bachchan entering the chamber Sri Darzi was killed in."

"So there are no other suspects?" Akers asked.

"No," the constable confirmed defiantly, "but Shrimati Darzi's husband was just killed! She has been through-"

"I have to file a report on this," Akers interrupted. "Now you have only one suspect and no witnesses. How am I supposed to file a report that states I only questioned the one suspect, who insisted he was innocent?"

"You did not even ask him any questions!" Constable Jain argued. "Maybe if you had-"

"I did," Akers interrupted. "I asked him his name, and he answered very honestly. Now, are you going to tell me where the Darzi's apartment is? Or should I go ask people in the Chhatri?"

"I will escort you," the constable decided quickly. "But if you upset Shrimati Darzi I will throw you out of Agni Station! You cannot upset the wife of such an important bureaucrat, especially with the eyes of the entire company on us."

"I have no interest in upsetting her," Akers stated. "Just some routine questions."

"You will prove my father's innocence Mr. Holmes?" Anantha Bachchan stated as Akers stepped through the door into the MPD office.

Akers paused to look back at the young woman. She looked lost, maybe she doubted her father as well. "I'm sure the evidence will prove who the real killer is."

A few minutes later Akers and Constable Jain were at the Darzi's apartment door. It wasn't a long walk, the Darzi apartment had an entrance on the Chhatri, with a greenhouse above the door. It was possibly the only greenhouse on Mars under a blue sky. Perhaps that was why the Darzis lived in this heat, Akers understood they were both from Earth. As they neared the Darzi's door, Justice Schwinghammer emerged.

"Hello Zeus, everything in order?" the constable asked as they almost collided.

"Yes, I was just consoling Ms. Darzi over the

loss of her husband," the Justice answered. "Everything seems in order with the transfer of stock. I suppose Bharat Zirconium will send a new COO from Earth now?"

"I guess so," Constable Jain replied. "I have not heard anything about that yet, but why would they tell me?"

"Right," Zeus dismissed the issue. "Well I'll be at Cafetería Golguppa for the next hour or so if you're looking for me."

"Did you want to talk to Bachchan?" Constable Jain asked.

"The murderer?" Zeus inquired. "Why would I want to talk to him? He has nothing to do with the transfer of stock. I'll need to speak to the new COO when he or she arrives."

"Of course, then I will see you later," the constable stated turning to the door.

Susheela Darzi answered the door as soon as Constable Jain touched the door chime. She must have been waiting inside the door since Zeus left. At 25 degrees the interior of the Darzi's apartment seemed frigid compared to the almost 50 degrees outside. Clearly Ms. Darzi didn't like the heat, and she didn't want it getting in, she ushered them quickly into the apartment before the constable could introduce Akers.

"This is detective Sherlock Holmes from the Confederacy," Constable Jain stated as soon as they were inside the apartment. "He's reviewing the evidence against Bachchan for a report to the senate."

"Sherlock Holmes?" Susheela repeated in amusement. "One of Shakespeare's characters right? Your parents had quite a sense of humor."

"They did indeed," Akers agreed. He didn't clarify that Sherlock Holmes was the name of the company he worked for, that would lead him to stating his actual name. His parents had given him a family name, a name that had plagued his childhood. Sherlock Holmes had been a codename given to him by his first commander in the resistance. Now that commander was Prime-Admin of the Confederacy, and he was stuck with the name. He preferred Sherlock Holmes anyway. It sounded familiar, but few Martians seemed to know who Arthur Conan Doyle was. At least Ms. Darzi had guessed a British author, most guessed American authors.

"He just needs to record in his report that he spoke with you," the constable continued.

"Of course, come up stairs," Susheela Darzi stated. "We can sit in the garden, it is like being back on Earth."

She seemed proud of that, Akers had never been to Earth. Few Mars-born had. Between the cost of the trip, and dealing with the increased gravity, most didn't see the value. She led them up a set of stairs into a large glassed-in room, with plants placed around the walls, and a set of divans around a small pond in the center. Above them was the eery blue pseudo-sky. Once they were sitting down there was no sign of Agni station, just plants and the blue sky, with little fish swimming around in the pond. So this was what Earth was like. It didn't seem that impressive. Akers was more impressed with Susheela, she was stunningly beautiful. She must have had a lot of cosmetic surgery. As Akers understood it, most of the corporate bureaucrats liked to have attractive husbands or wives that had little or no useful skills. It was some kind of strange Earth-prostitution that elevated one's status. Akers didn't really get it, he preferred useful women, but had to admit she was one of the most beautiful women he'd ever seen.

"So what can I do for you Mr. Holmes?" Susheela asked once they were seated.

"As Constable Jain said I just need to ask a few questions. There is just the one suspect, so everything seems in order," Akers said. "Just routine, I'm sure you'll understand."

"Of course, the bureaucrats like their routines and documentation," Susheela observed as she turned on a cigarette and then looked at him as she placed it to her lips and sucked suggestively. Odd. He glanced over at Constable Jain, and noted look of surprised anger. Interesting, maybe useful.

Akers tuned back to Susheela, "Have you

been married long, Mrs. Darzi?"

"Four wonderful years!" she replied in an almost automatic response.

"Happily married?" Akers continued.

"Aseem is the most wonderful man in the world!" Susheela replied again without a thought.

"Is?" Akers inquired.

"Excuse me?" Susheela asked suddenly confused.

"You said he is the most wonderful man in the world. Is, not was," Akers clarified.

"Oh. Yes, he is dead now. He was, my husband, he worked here in Agni Station," Susheela stammered.

Broken programming Akers surmised. She wasn't programmed for this eventuality. Clearly she was just programmed for Aseem's amusement, now that he was dead it didn't matter what happened to her. If Akers' cybernetic eye wasn't confirming she was human, he would have assumed she was an android.

"Any children Mrs. Darzi?" Akers asked.

"Children, oh my no!" Susheela answered. "Aseem has been approved for three children, but we are waiting to return to Earth. We wouldn't want them to be born on Mars!"

Are waiting? She wasn't going to be useful to the court; she didn't seem to fully grasp reality.

Too dysfunctional to be a suspect. A thought, "Are you planning to return to Earth?"

"Oh yes, Aseem and I can't wait to return to Earth!" Susheela replied immediately.

"Aseem is dead," Akers stated bluntly. "What are you planing to do?"

"Oh, yes, Aseem is dead now," Susheela seemed to realize again. "I, I live here."

"I'm sure we will find you a nice place to live here in Agni Station," Constable Jain stated. "Until you decide what you want to do."

"Yes, Roshan is my friend!" Susheela stated. "She visits me every day!"

"I see," Akers tuned back to the constable. "Who get's Mr. Darzi's stock in Bharat Zirconium?"
"His clone back on Earth," Roshan Jain answered. "After he is of legal age of course, until then it is administrated by his perpetual fund manager."

"Who'll be raising the clone?" Akers asked.

"Whoever he hired," the constable answered. "There are several foster companies in the Singapore Conglomerate. I suppose he hired a firm in Uttar Pradesh or Maharashtra. Is it important?"

"Probably not," Akers conceded. "It just seems strange to not leave anything to your wife."

"Bureaucrats are not like us," Roshan observed. "They only care about themselves."

"Whereas you care about Mrs. Darzi?" Akers asked in a vaguely accusatory tone.

"We are well acquainted," the constable replied.

"We're best of friends!" Susheela stated. "She visits me every day!"

"This is getting outside of your area of investigation," Constable Jain observed. "Unless there are more questions related to the investigation, we should leave."

"You're right, we should go," Akers agreed, and stood up. His cybernetics had recorded more than enough evidence to establish a second suspect. This room was covered in fingerprints and DNA belonging to someone else with a motive to kill Aseem. Now he just had to prove it was possible.

"Aw already?" Susheela said standing up. "I was hoping we could be friends!"

"Afraid so," Akers stated dismissively. "Lots to do, and I want to leave Agni as soon as possible. Most of it is a lot hotter than this garden of yours."

"Yes, this planet is too hot," Susheela agreed. She didn't seem to understand she was kilometers below the surface of a frozen world.

"This station is small, and Shrimati Darzi was

quite isolated by her husband's status," Constable Jain explained once they were outside.

"Good of you to look in on her," Akers stated. "What did Bachchan have on him when you arrested him?"

"Not much," the constable answered. "Come back to the station and I'll show you. There was a particle drill, some rocks, some forged security cards, an e-cigar. Of course I also found the gun he used to kill Sri Darzi when I searched his apartment."

"I'd like to look at the gun," Akers stated.

"Of course," Constable Jain agreed. "It is a compelling piece of evidence. It must be in your report."

A few minutes later he was looking at the gun, it was a compelling piece of evidence. An Ashok-Leyland solid-state laser-pistol. The reports of Aseem Darzi's burns were consistent with this weapon. Constable Jain took the pistol from the evidence locker and tried to hand it to Akers, but he refused to touch it, "I'm just here as an observer, I shouldn't handle the evidence. Did you find any DNA evidence of Bachchan handling the weapon?"

"No he had cleaned it," Constable Jain reported.

"It looks brand new," Akers observed.

"It is," the constable replied. "The diagnostics report that only one shot has been fired."

"So he just bought it to kill Darzi?" Akers suggested.

"It appears so," Constable Jain agreed.

"Is there a record of him buying it?" Akers asked.

"No, but the CMZ does not require gun sales to be registered," the constable reported.

"When was it imported?" Akers asked.

"It was shipped in from Earth a few months ago," Constable Jain replied. "To a gun shop up on the surface. I checked but they sold it months ago and don't have a video recording of the sale anymore."

Good, the evidence was adding up for Akers' case. It was time to shake things up, and see what shook loose. "I don't think Bachchan did it."

"What?" Constable Jain was dumbfounded. "But you've seen all the evidence! Who do you think did it?"

"Oh I'm pretty sure I know who did it," Akers stated. "But I don't have enough evidence yet to make a case."

"So that's it? You come down here and make vague accusations to discredit my case against Bachchan?" Constable Jain demanded. "Get out of Agni Station! Take the next elevator up to the surface! You have no jurisdiction here!"

"Jurisdiction no, but a legit reason to pursue

this case yes," Akers stated. "And we both know if you throw me out of here the bureaucrats back on Earth with want to know why. My report to the Confederate Senate would report my current belief that Bachchan is being framed, and that would cast more doubt on your case than my sticking around here and asking a few more questions. Unless of course, you are covering something up."

"Me? How dare you?" Constable Jain stammered.

"I'll be sticking around until my case is closed!" Akers declared and then left the station before the constable could state another word. Akers grinned as he stepped out into the sweltering Chhatri. Constable Jain's confusion was understandable, her case was solid. The murder weapon found in the home of the only person who was with the murder victim according to the station access logs, and someone with ample cause to kill the victim. And what did he have? In truth, not much. But sometimes a weak hand needed a good bluff, and this was one of those times.

He'd already spoken to everyone in this tiny community that he needed to speak to, but he needed to look at the murder scene before he closed his case. Perhaps he should have done that before alienating the constable. It was hot in the Chhatri, he looked around at the businesses. It was too hot to eat, he decided to return to his hotel room. It felt cool in the room, but was still around thirty above. He set the air conditioning to cool the room to 25 degrees, and lay down. The bed was too small to be comfortable, and he was clammy from sweating all afternoon. He took another shower and returned to his room. It was early evening, so he set his alarm to wake him around midnight, and passed out. When he woke up he felt comfortable, a situation that ended as soon as he opened the door, and the heat rushed in. He walked back through the furnace of a hotel, and then opened the door to step out into the Chhatri and was hit again by a blast of heat. He wanted to leave, and then remembered it was going to get worse before it got better.

He walked over to Chicken Frankies, and ordered a chicken frankie and mango milk-shake, wondering if his sticking around was worth it. He could just send a report to the senate oversight committee agreeing with Constable Jain's conclusions. The evidence was good against Bachchan. He doubted it would result in a conflict with the Singapore Conglomerate. The Asians had enough to worry about with the Vietnamese Uprising, they wouldn't want to engage in an interplanetary war over the murder of a minor corporate official. Clearly it had nothing to do with the Confederacy. Still...

"Senior Sherlock?" a waitress asked, walking over to him.

"Sí," Akers answered. She was the waitress serving the tables. Clearly he was sitting in the wrong area, because the bar waitress only spoke Odia. The waitress explained in Spanish that a young woman had been in looking for him. At first he thought it was Susheela Darzi, but the waitress' face made it clear it wasn't Ms. Darzi, who had apparently never been in the place. The waitress did not have a message, or know who the woman was, just that she had been looking for him. From the blue-haired description he assumed it was Anantha Bachchan.

"Are you from Madhabani?" Akers continued in Spanish.

"Oh no! I'm from down here!" the waitress replied clearly viewing Agni Station as separate colony from the rest of the CMZ. "I've been up there but was too cold. I thought I would die!"

"You were born down here?" Akers asked.

"No, I was born up in Madhabani. Women are not allowed to give birth down here. But I have lived here since I was a baby. My parents lived here long before that. My father was a miner, and my mother owns this Chicken Frankies franchise. I would never live anywhere else."

"Your father doesn't mine anymore?" Akers inquired.

"He died," the waitress answered.

"Sorry," Akers stated compassionately, it was a common enough story. "The war?"

"No, is was a blow-out a few years ago," the waitress stated. "The north shaft blew out. Several hundred miners died."

"A blow out this deep?" Akers asked.

"They hit a deep cave," the waitress replied. "The outer atmosphere rushed in and filled the mine with higher pressure CO2 in minutes. Only a few miners got out before suffocating."

"What happened to that shaft?" Akers asked.

"They sealed it off, after getting the bodies out of course," the waitress answered.

"They didn't reopen it?" Akers asked.

"No, the vein was dead," the waitress reported. "It was mainly used to move equipment down to the lower levels where they are working now. But there are other elevators so they just sealed off the shaft."

That was interesting. Akers knew mines, especially deep mines. He'd run a drilling unit when he was younger, and knew enough about mines to know that a blown out shaft could be used to get around, provided one had the right gear. The chicken frankie had a strange flavor, he'd never eaten chicken before. He didn't like it, the flavor was too strong, and the texture stringy. He thought about tracking down Anantha Bachchan to see what she wanted, but decided it could wait. The night was going to be long enough, but if his hunch paid off, he could leave in the morning.

Given what he was about to do, the sooner he left the CMZ the better. This wasn't the first problem in a CMZ he'd been sent in to resolve. The problem with being trusted by the Prime-Admin and Senate was that they knew they could depend on him to get the job done, whatever the job. His war record proved that. He had been with Dalton and Rome when they captured Pickering colony, not many could say that. If the corporate bureaucrats figured out what he was doing in Agni, it would be best if he was already gone. If the Confederacy had to deny knowledge of his actions while he was in corporate custody, it would be the last time anyone would ever hear of him.

Akers was just finishing his milkshake when she came into Chicken Frankies. He had been trying to make himself eat the chicken frankie. For someone who had spent his childhood starving the idea of wasting food was detestable, but he just couldn't raise the odd tasting meat back to his mouth. He knew they raised chickens up in Madhabani, but the odd tasting meat reminded him too much of the meat he'd seen people eating at some of the smaller colonies during the war. There was a lot of cannibalism back then, it had been a dark time.

"Have you found out anything?" Anantha Bachchan asked as she sat down at the bar next to Akers, she looked as beautiful as the first time he'd seen her boarding the elevator, although now she was soaked in sweat, like everyone else in the station.

"A few things, nothing I'd care to comment on yet," Akers answered. The door opened again, and Justice Zeus walked in, paused briefly when he saw Akers and Anantha speaking, and then headed for a table.

"He is innocent!" Anantha declared. "You must believe me! Is there anything I can do to help your investigation?"

"Nothing I can think of," Akers answered. Zeus ordered something from the waitress, but seemed to be more interested in watching Akers and Anantha. He wasn't as sublet as he thought he was, perhaps Anantha hadn't noticed, or maybe Akers had just spent too much time looking over his shoulder. He looked up at Anantha, and for a second lost himself in her eyes. She looked so sad. She believed her father was going to be found guilty. She had just lost her mother too, and had been thrown out of university when her family's assets were seized. She looked so sad, he had to do something. "Don't say anything to anyone yet, but I think I'll have the case against your father dropped by the morning."

Anantha's eyes opened as she stared back at him, and he knew he'd made a mistake. He didn't know he could get the charges dropped, but in her eyes he could see they had already been dropped. "Really? You mean it?"

Akers paused. What should he tell her? She could blow it if she talked. He glanced over at Zeus and noticed the man was still watching them. It dawned on him that the Justice could have a cybernetic eardrum, and might be able to hear them clearly. "Yes, but only if you don't tell anyone. The case is at a critical state."

"Can I tell my father?" Anantha asked quickly.

"No," Akers answered decisively. "If I'm right, he'll find out in the morning anyway. It's important that no one knows right now."

The door opened and Constable Jain walked in. When she saw Akers talking to Anantha she stormed over and sat down next to them. "I told you to get out of Agni Station!"

"You could arrest me," Akers offered, then decided to push Jain's buttons and raised his voice. "Otherwise this station is open to the public, and I have a job to do. Bachchan is innocent, and you know it."

For a few seconds Akers thought Jain was about to hit him. Akers was prepared to defend himself, he always was, but he didn't want to get into a fight with the local police officer. That wouldn't help his case.

Several seconds passed in silence, then she seemed to force herself to calm down. She leaned back, and flashed a vicious grin. "Alright Sherlock, play your game. We will see what the Ombudsman thinks when he arrives here."

"Yes we will," Akers stated as he got to his feet, then he turned to Anantha. "Go get some sleep, you can't do anything for your father tonight."

As he turned to leave Chicken Frankies he glanced back over at Justice Zeus, who was staring thoughtfully at Anantha and Constable Jain as he sipped his drink. Did he know what Akers was planning? Would he interfere?

Akers stepped out into the heat of the Chhatri and walked back to the hotel. When he got back to his room he pulled his respirator-mask from his bag. He checked his com for a map of the station, found the entrance to the abandoned north shaft, and then headed back out. There were only a few people in the Chhatri at that early hour, and no signs of Anantha, Zeus, or Constable Jain. He crossed the Chhatri and followed one of the passageways, then turned into a tunnel that led past doors to various apartments. The passage way ended at a closed door. It was locked. Akers pulled out his com and used a stolen pass code to unlock the door.

The passageway behind the door was dark, the area was abandoned. Akers stepped through the door and it slid closed behind him. In front of him his cybernetic eye-lenses enhanced the visible spectrum, and he started out into the darkness. The area had once been used as a staging ground for the north shaft, and he quickly came to the large equipment airlocks sealing off the abandoned mine-shaft. The infrared indicated the airlocks were warmer than the sealed area he was in, and he wondered if he could take the heat. He looked around for the personnel hatch, and found it quickly not far from the large equipment airlocks. It looked the same temperature as the area he was in, but he put on his respirator-mask and unlocked the hatch.

Behind the hatch was a short passageway, and then another hatch, this one warmer than the passage he was in. He paused, and then decided it had to be survivable if there had been minors working in there. He opened the door, and heat rushed in at him and engulfed him fully. He fought the urge to panic, and found it was manageable. Curiosity made him pull out his com and check the temperature. 53 degrees Celsius. He was glad he'd brought a flask of water with him.

In front of him was darkness. Even his cybernetic lenses' light enhancement was having a hard time; there just wasn't enough light to enhance. He turned on his com's flashlight and held it up exposing another loading area, just like the last except this one had abandoned equipment strewn about it. He started out.

The floor and equipment were covered in a fine layer of red dust, no doubt carried in during the blow-out. Blow-out seemed the wrong word, and Akers' briefly wondered if he should call it a blow-in when he filed his report. There were footprints in the dust, someone had been through here recently. Akers finally had some evidence, but it wasn't particularly useful. The shoe-prints were slightly smaller than his own, and could belong to anyone with feet smaller than his. They might clear Bachchan, if his feet were larger than the shoe-prints, but Akers hadn't thought to asks Mr. Bachchan for his shoe-size when he was at the Police Station. He'd have to look into it later.

He followed the shoe-prints through the loading area, past some abandoned ore tractors to an open shaft. Finally, the mine. He shone his com light up at the ceiling examining the hanging wall, it seemed sound for an abandoned mine, and so he started down the shaft. What started out fairly narrow, with only enough room for couple ore tractors to drive down it, soon widened out, quickly becoming an artificial cavern carved out my the miners, known as a stope. Akers shone his com light up again at the hanging wall far above, and saw cracks beginning to show around the carbon-nanotube support beams. Similar beams had been used back in Hussy, and he'd never seen cracks forming near them, but this was 10 kilometers deeper into the planet. He noted a trickle of water running out of one of the cracks, that wasn't a good sign.

He was still following the tracks when it opened in front of him, an abyss, ascending upward. The hanging wall of the mine had collapsed, raining a mountain of debris down on whoever had been working in the area. Warped and shattered carbon-nanotube support beams and ventilation ducts protruded from the mountain of rubble in front of him. The shoe-prints continued up the pile of rubble, although they were harder to follow now, as the dust had become thicker, almost like silty sand in some areas. It didn't matter though, it was clear whoever had climbed this mound of rubble had been following the path of least resistance, and all Akers had to do was follow it up, and then down the other side. At the peak he shone his com light up into the void again, but only blackness stared back, and the deafening silence seemed scream that more rubble could fall at any second. It was an irrational fear. Eventually the cavern would collapse in, but that might not happen for centuries. It would likely take a quake to start it. Still the void haunted him, and he hurried down the other side of the mound.

On the other side of the mountain of rubble the mine shaft had been descending, and so more of the rubble had rolled that way, making clambering down the hill seem like more of an ordeal than climbing up it had been. When Akers stood on the flat floor of the old mine shaft again, he stopped to take a drink from his flask. He held his breath and lifted his face plate, raising the flask to his lips but the water was warm, almost hot. He pressed the button on the side of the flask, and a tiny dry-ice pellet was released into the water, causing an eruption of ice-fog to burst out the mouth of the flask, which quickly dissipated into the sweltering air around him. A green light lit up on the side of the flask, and Akers took a swig of the icy, slightly carbonated water, before returning it to his pocket.

As Akers turn to follow the shoe tracks it happened, something unexpected that sent his blood racing more that that chasm above him. Another light appeared, up on top of the pile of rubble, someone was following him. His war time instinct kicked in, and his thumb swiped off the com light before he could think about it, leaving him there, at the bottom of the rubble, in the dark. Now he couldn't move, but it was possible that the other person hadn't seen his light.

The light shone around, and then down the path he had followed. This wasn't a com light; someone had come prepared with a powerful spot light. It lit up the path leading down towards him, but stopped before it reached him. Apparently he had made better time than whoever it was expected. The light shifted, and was the pointed up into the abyss. Maybe they felt the same eery feeling Akers had felt, or maybe... No!

Akers turned on his com light and dashed down into the mine shaft. The stope narrowed back into a tunnel as the spot light found him, and he was quickly around a corned before whoever it was had the opportunity to shoot him. The shoe-prints were still there, and so he followed them, confident that they had to lead to the murder site, and another exit from this scorching underworld; the exit that Bachchan had supposedly used.

The tunnel opened to another stope, and Akers skidded to a halt, shining his com light up at the stope's hanging wall. It looked good, carbon-nanotube support beams and ventilation ducts all appeared in good condition. Then it came, a dull bang from the tunnel behind Akers, followed by a bone chilling crack. No! And then the crash. He was right about why that person had shone the light up into the chasm, and now he found himself running again. He didn't decide to run, and hadn't thought about a direction, apparently his body just wanted to get away from that noise. Then another crash came, and another, and he found himself blown off his feet, in a swirl of dust.

He rose with the feeling that two nails had been driven into his ears, and couldn't stop himself from screaming. He realized it was the air pressure, he quickly opened and closed his jaw repeatedly until each ear popped, and the pain began to subside. The pressure had increased and now he could feel the air forcing its way past the seals on his face plate, and there was nothing he could do. The faceplate respirator-mask was designed to work on the surface of Mars, at a low atmospheric pressure. He needed to find the murder scene fast. Every Mars-born knew the effects of hypercapnia; too much carbon-dioxide in the blood led to disorientation, panic, unconsciousness, and then death. He was already disorientated, and realized he was panicking too.

He stopped. He stood there in the cavernous

stope and reasoned it out. Behind him, the crashing noise had become a deafening roar, but it was beginning to fade, the cavern was collapsing. The air-pressure didn't seem to be changing anymore. The sudden increase in pressure would have been caused by the air being compacted, so the path behind him was blocked. He would have to go forward; that was his original plan. Where were the shoe prints? Blow away by the shock-wave that had knocked him down. Damn! He shone his com light back up at the hanging wall above him, it seemed fine, no signs of change. Good enough.

He took another swig of instantly-chilled water from his flask and continued forward, down the inclining floor, deeper into the pitch-black inferno. He was jogging now, a steady pace he could continue for hours under different circumstances. He had no idea how long he could keep it up down here, or if the hypercapnia would get him first. It took just over ten minutes to reach the wall blocking off the newer sections of the mine from this older one. Ten of the longest minutes in Akers' life. The wall was like the air lock Akers had passed through to enter the mine with a large set of equipment airlocks, except showing in infrared as slightly cooler than the area he was in.

He looked for the personnel hatch, and used his com to hack the access lock. Another short passage-way, and then a hatch opening to a cooler world, a much cooler world. It felt cold, freezing, that couldn't be right. Akers pulled out his com and checked the temperature, it was 34 degrees Celsius. Not freezing by any standard. He realized it must be the CO2 building up in his blood, his skin was likely flushed. At least the CO2 wasn't seeping in at the sides of the faceplate anymore. Wait.

Akers looked up at the air-ducts and realized he didn't need to shine a light. The lights were on. The air-ducts should be working. His eardrums felt like they were going to burst again. He checked the air quality with his com: 'breathable,' then pulled his faceplate off and inhaled deeply, and the air was good. He opened and closed his jaws a few times to release the pressure, and then sat down and started hyperventilating, a technique taught to all children on Mars to flush the CO2 out of their blood. It took less than a minute of him to start feeling normal again. He drank some more water, and then rose to look around.

"Feeling better?" a voice asked.

Akers spun around, and found Justice Zeus sitting not far away, alone it seemed. Akers glanced around, but Zeus was alone.

"You won't need the gun," Zeus stated.

Akers looked down at his hand, and then slipped the gun back into his shoulder holster. "An autonomic reflex. I wasn't expecting to find you here."

"Expecting someone else?" Zeus asked.

"No actually. Is there surveillance in here?" Akers asked.

"Not in the mines," Zeus answered. "And this mine is out of limits to everyone right now."

"Everyone except you?" Akers noted.

"I asked the constable for access to the crime-scene," Zeus explained. "I thought you'd turn up here. I've been reading up on you, Hero of the Rebellion."

"Seems so," Akers conceded.

"I fought too," Zeus stated. "I was with the Grand Army when we retook New Edinburgh."

"You were there?" Akers asked with a smirk. Every Arean citizen seemed to claim that.

"Yes," Zeus answered ignoring the silent jab. "I wouldn't expect you to remember me, I was just a corporal, I didn't even see the General."

The General. He was there. "I wasn't with the Grand Army so I couldn't remember you any-way."

"You weren't? You must be the only Arean citizen to ever say that!" Zeus grinned. "I thought everyone was there!"

"Seems so sometimes," Akers replied. "I was with General Rome hacking the colony's power distribution network."

"Rome! That treacherous hosenscheißer!" Zeus shot back. "They should have shot him!"

"He has been under Canadian protection since the war," Akers observed. "Besides, this was before that, early in the war. Without Rome we wouldn't have got the defenses down when the Grand Army attacked New Edinburgh, and the war would have probably ended right there."

"Maybe, but they still should have shot him!" Zeus retorted.

"Either way, it doesn't help us now," Akers observed. "We seem to be at an impasse."

"I suppose you have figured out who the real killer is?" Zeus inquired.

"It seems apparent," Akers stated.

"This is a problem," Zeus replied.

"Is it?" Akers asked. "I would have thought the shoe-prints back in the closed off sections of the mine would be a problem."

"They're Bachchan's size," Zeus stated. "And there is a pair with that same red dust on them, sitting in Bachchan's closet. Waiting for the constable to find."

"I shouldn't think that will be a problem now," Akers observed.

"Why not?" Zeus inquired.

"You didn't hear the chasm collapsing?" Akers asked in disbelief.

"That was the chasm collapsing?" Zeus asked in shock. "I thought it was a quake. I almost shit myself!"

Akers chuckled at the thought of Justice Zeus waddling back to his hotel room in shitty drawers. Zeus started chuckling too, and then stopped as he realized something. "Strange timing, think someone set it off?"

"Definitely," Akers replied. "Someone else was in there. With a bright spotlight, looking up into the chasm."

"Who?"

"I didn't see them close up," Akers replied. "But only the killer would have a reason to drop a mountain on me."

"Oh, I see," Zeus pondered. "And who do you think the killer is?"

"The way I see it, it could only be Constable Jain," Akers replied.

"Constable Jain?" Zeus repeated in disbelief. "What reason could she have had for killing Darzi?"

"Lust," Akers answered.

"Ah yes, she is Sucheela's lover," Zeus agreed. "But the way that poor woman was brainwashed anyone could be."

"That doesn't matter," Akers replied. "All that matters is that Constable Jain lusted for Darzi's wife, and killed him to get her. It's one of the oldest stories."

"And why is it a better story than Bachchan

killing Darzi over his corporate maneuvering?" the Justice asked.

"Well, that would be because Bachchan is Mars-born," Akers explained. "He's a citizen of the Confederacy, and we can't have our citizens killing bureaucrats from the most powerful con-glomerate on Earth."

"Their power is waning," the Justice retorted. They're fighting a civil war in Vietnam, and open rebellions in India, Australia, New Zealand, Thai-land, and Cambodia. Our sources are positive that they would never fight us for their CMZs if we invaded. Besides all their power is tied up in their army and navy. They've never had much of a space fleet. We could beat them in space."

"Is that what this is about?" Akers asked. "A war with the Singapore Conglomerate?"

"We don't think they will go to war," Zeus stated.

"We?" Akers inquired.

"The mission of the Bureau of Corporate Af-fairs has always been to shut down these capi-talist enclaves," the Justice stated. "Now's the perfect time to move against the Singapore Conglomerate, while they are in disarray."

"I see," Akers stated. "And would the corpo-rate police officer killing the corporate bureau-crat to take his programmed sex-slave wife not be as effective a story?

The Justice seemed to ponder and then

agreed, "I guess it could work. But all the evidence points to Bachchan."

"All the evidence that Constable Jain found?" Akers asked rhetorically.

"I see your point," Zeus conceded. "But there is still no evidence actually pointing to Roshan-the constable."

"Her fingerprints and DNA are on the murder weapon," Akers stated.

Zeus paused considering. "As the police detective on the case she would have to handle the evidence."

"Maybe, but Bachchan's fingerprints and DNA are not on the gun. Sometimes it's the evidence that is missing that solves the case," Akers replied. "And Bachchan gives a very convincing innocent plead. I think it will move the Ombudsman, if he is cyber-enhanced to detect lies."

"All corporate Ombudsmen have to be cyber-enhanced. This could work. If the constable has any of that red dust still on her..." Zeus pondered then turned back to Akers. "Well, I guess it will have to work. The Ombudsman arrived shortly after you left Chicken Frankies. We should go meet with him. You will have to make the accusation against Constable Jain. I will be appropriately shocked of course..."

# Frozen Sky

The dust-storm that had raged across the planet was finally reaching the southern icecap, although it seemed to have lost most of its power. The cold of the icecap seemed to be sapping the strength of the storm, and the leading edge was fracturing into tornadoes and dust-devils. Sandra Pritchard banked the Lockheed abruptly to avoid a low-pressure point the sensors showed forming in her flight path, and continued scanning the ice below.

It was night down there, the twelve month-long night had fallen, and without sensors she wouldn't have been able to see a thing. The display showed the frozen carbon-dioxide glacier as if it were naturally lit by the Sun, but it would be almost a year before that ice saw the light of day again. From the altitude they were flying it looked like it could just be mountainous terrain, but Sandra knew those peaks and valleys were frozen death to anyone crashing down there, and apparently someone had.

It was warm enough in the Lockheed's cabin, the aerospace transport was designed to operate in space, which could be lot colder than the glacier below. It was only Sandra's consciousness that recognized the danger her and Cheng were in. Bombardier An Cheng was asleep in the cabin behind the cockpit, a local gunner assigned by the Area Army when they retrofitted the Lockheed a week earlier. They had been flying patrols north of the icecap since then, but had now been pulled back north to search the glaciers for a missing airship.

In Sandra's view, the mission was a waste of time. The odds of finding the missing airship were low, and at this time of year the glaciers were quickly expanding, so if they'd crashed down there they'd be frozen until the glacier shrank the next summer. Still, a job's a job, and orders are orders. At least no one would be shooting at them this far south. Then suddenly the sensors detected it, a strato-freighter down on the ice below. It was still intact, anchored in a valley, and looked like it had been intentionally landed.

"Cheng!" Sandra called over her shoulder. "Come have a look at this!"

"It landed," Cheng observed half awake. "What are they doing?"

"Let's drop down and have a look," Sandra said, and rolled the Lockheed into a tight circle, dropping quickly towards the parked strato-freighter.

"The sensors show the temperature in the valley is warmer than the peaks, maybe they are having mechanical problems," Cheng suggested. "I will call them."

"They aren't transmitting an emergency beacon," Sandra observed.

"They are not transmitting their ID beacon either," Cheng added. He was sitting in the co-pilot's seat next to Sandra, and brought up the com display, but there was no response on the other end. "I will try the emergency radio. 'Arean Aerospace Transport BEI-001 to Strato-Freighter AUS Cacophony, do you require assistance? Arean Aerospace Transport BEI-001 to Strato-Freighter AUS Cacophony, please respond.'"

Cheng repeated the call in Mandarin as the Lockheed skimmed above the strato-freighter's canopy, and then looked over at Sandra. "Want to head back to Hangtian? We could come back with a salvage crew tomorrow."

"I'd rather know what the problem is before we head back," Sandra answered. "I'd hate to get the crew out here and find we need to fly all the way back for a part. "I'm going to land over there, and walk back to the airship."

"Are you sure you want to land down there?" Cheng asked. "If the ice expands around the wheels, this will be our grave."

"The heat from the jets should be able to melt us out," Sandra said as she switched the Lockheed into VTOL mode and lowered it gently onto the ice. Around them steam shot out of the ice as pockets of water vapor evaporated. Sandra cut the engines as soon as the sensors showed all four wheels on the ground and held her breath. The sensors showed the ice reforming around the wheels. She watched for about a minute before deciding it was safe to stay, as the ice hadn't fully encased the wheels.

"Five clicks back to the airship... rough terrain, so give me a couple of hours to get there and see what's happening," Sandra ordered. "If you don't hear from me, call for reinforcements."

"What? I am coming with you," Cheng objected as he followed her down to the ground doors.

"Someone has to stay with the plane," Sandra stated, pulling a thermal-suit over her still-suit.

"This is my country Earther," Cheng objected again. "You are the pilot, I am the soldier. You don't have any authority on that freighter."

"Check the registry again, Martian, it's an American strato-freighter, flying out of American Utopia." Sandra replied. "Who do you think they're more likely to welcome onto their ship? I'm a Captain in the American Space Force, and you're a Martian rebel."

The Martian bombardier paused considering. It was obvious he took offence to being called a rebel. The Confederacy had been functionally independent for a decade, even if America had only formally recognized its independence a couple of weeks earlier. Finally he conceded, "Okay you go, but can't you land closer?"

"I didn't want to risk destabilizing the ice around the freighter," Sandra stated, and then pulled the respirator-mask over her face. "Brace yourself!"

Sandra opened the door and a gust of frozen air rushed in, freezing the moisture in the Lockheed's interior, forming in instant ice-fog. A couple of seconds later she was outside on the ice, surrounded by a thin ice-fog that had formed when they touched down. She quickly checked the wheels again before heading off towards the strato-freighter.

She hadn't told Cheng the truth. It was true that she was concerned about destabilizing the ice around the freighter, but in truth she had landed this far away because she didn't know the situation on board the airship. Her old training had kicked in, and she'd landed far enough away that no one on the airship should be able to see the Lockheed, just in case.

She had fought for the old U.S. Space Corps during the Martian Uprising as the American Loyalist had called it. Now the U.S. was no more, and the new American government had loaned her to the Ares Confederation. She was wearing the uniform of what had been the enemy until two weeks earlier. Fate was a fickle bitch sometimes.

She wondered if the Americans on the airship would even believe her when she said she was American too. She was wearing a Confederate Army still-suit under an Argentea Army Division thermal-suit. Not the blue circle and red bars of an American flag anywhere on her, not even one of the old stars and stripes that most Loyalists still carried. Hopefully they felt more optimistic about the new alliance than she did. She was making good time, at least the Argentean government made sure their troops had sharp cleats. This ice would have been impossible without the jagged little spikes that dug in under foot as she jogged towards the airship.

The insulation of the thermal-suit was good as well, she couldn't feel the icy air touching any part of her skin, but after an hour or so, a cold ache set into her arms, and then her feet, and then legs. By the time she reached the airship the ache had spread up her back, and the Cyber Heads-Up Display implanted in her eyes was reporting mild hypothermia. She suddenly realized she had been running through the darkness, and wondered if Cheng could have even made the journey without waving around a light that would have let everyone on the airship know he was coming. Did the Confederacy implant its troops with CHUDs?

She knew she should have just flown back to Hangtian with Cheng. That was all that was required. Find the missing strato-freighter and report its location. But this was an American airship, and she was going to be damned if she let a bunch of rebels rescue it. America might have lost the war against these Eco-Rebels on Mars, and America might have fallen to its own Eco-Revolution back home, but damned it, America could still rescue its own ships!

Gazing up at the strato-freighter she wondered briefly if that was true, how was she going to get up there? The airship was held in place by two anchors that had been fired into the ice-sheet like harpoons, but it was still floating ten meters above her. The lights were on, she searched her CHUD for the make of airship, Odyssey Mars Research LLC Strato-Freighter model Z-224. She checked to see if she had the security over-ride codes. She did. She interfaced with the ship's wireless network and sent the code, and a few seconds later a wire-ladder dropped from the side of the ship. Less than a minute later she was stepping through the emergency hatch into the ship's gondola.

The gondola wasn't very large, a freighter like this one usually only carried a crew of five. Everything was quiet. There were no signs of the crew. It was possible to get back into the freight area from the gondola, the crew might be back there for some reason.

She quietly made her way to the bridge, where she found the captain, dead at the controls. His neck had been cut from behind with a plasma-blade. The spine was severed, but the rest of the neck was intact. This was personal, Sandra had heard of people remaining conscious for up to a minute after having their spine cut like this. Someone he had known and trusted had been standing behind his seat, and then killed him. Someone who wanted him to know who had killed him. Someone who wanted to gloat.

A mutiny on an American ship? It had been

years since the Eco-Revolution had turned the Army and Airforce against the Navy and Space Corps. Many Naval and Space Corps ships had experienced mutinies then, but this didn't make sense. This was a cargo freighter, and where could the mutineers go with a stolen airship? Maybe that was why they were parked here in the icecap. They had nowhere to go to. She checked the controls, everything seemed in working order, but the outer edge of the dust-storm was getting closer.

Sandra quietly pulled off the bulky thermal-suit, and slipped her handgun from its holster. There was a murderer on board, a cold sadistic one, who taunted his victims, and she didn't want to be next. At least the gun was American, a standard issue Remington solid-state laser pistol. Of course the rebels had seized thousands during the Uprising, so it probably wouldn't convince anyone on board that she was an American ASF officer.

She moved silently down the passageway to the crew quarters, for the first time wishing the Rebels had stealth technology. She reached the hatch to the mess, and listened, hearing nothing. She opened the hatch as quietly as possible and peered inside. One of the crew was dead on the floor, slashed deeply across the chest with a plasma blade. There was no one else in the mess so she quietly walked over to the dead crewman and checked her insignia for rank, executive officer. She realized it might not be a mutiny, someone could be killing the entire crew. It could just be a heist.

She crept back out into the hallway, and down to the next hatch, and listened, still nothing. She quietly slid the hatch open, and found herself face to face with a woman aiming a particle beam rifle right at her. The woman was black, and not one of those faded-Martian blacks that had never been in real sunlight, the woman was from Earth. Sandra hoped her tanned skin would also be recognized as being Earth-born, the Mars-born always recognized it.

"Come in," the woman ordered in a Southern accent quietly but sternly. "Close the hatch, and don't make any sudden moves or I'll shoot you."

"Trying to keep someone out?" Sandra asked as she shut the hatch. "Do you know who the murderer is?"

"Murderer?" the woman asked with the sound of panic in her voice. "Who's dead?"

"The captain and executive officer," Sandra answered, and saw the woman's soul shatter. She was holding back her tears, trying to be harder than she really was. Sandra decided this couldn't be the killer. "Someone sliced them up with a plasma blade. Which is a much better weapon to use in here than that thing. Do you know what will happen if you fire that thing in here?"

"You'll be vaporized, as will a chunk of the ship behind you, and I'll probably be blown out into the freezing cold," the woman answered calmly. "But if you think I'm taking it off you, or that I won't fire you're dead wrong. Now, did you see anyone else dead out there? A black man, Earth-born, but lighter than me... mid-twenties?"

"No, just the dead captain on the bridge, and the dead XO in the mess," Sandra answered. "Whoever did it knew the captain and didn't like him."

"How'd you know that?" the woman asked.

"He let them get real close, and they kept him alive long enough to know who did it," Sandra answered. "Someone sadistic, probably a crewman. Are you in the crew?"

The question got the woman's attention, but she didn't answer. She seemed to be considering what to make of Sandra. Sandra realized the uniform probably wasn't helping, and decided to explain herself. "I'm an American. Captain Sandra A. Pritchard, originally from New Jersey. I'm stationed with the American Space Forces out of Phobos. I'm currently on loan to the Arean Army, and have been patrolling the skies over Argentea for the past week. I was redirected down here to find you."

"Me?" the woman asked.

"This ship," Sandra clarified.

The woman hesitated, then decided to believe Sandra. "I'm Elayne Williams, from North Carolina. This is the AMS Cacophony, out of

American Utopia. My dad was the captain. We were headed for Hangtian with battle-skiffs and light arms, but we can't get enough altitude with all the weight to get above the storm, so we headed down here to wait it out. My dad said the cold from the ice would dissipate the storm. But we've had problems with the com since we entered the ice-fields. So we sent a couple of the crew to Cavi Angusti for help."

"Solid idea about the storm," Sandra stated. "Your dad was right. So far the cold has been dissipating the storm reasonably well, but there's no guarantee that it won't be able to reach this far into the ice-fields. What kind of aircraft are the crew you sent to Cavi Angusti flying?"

"They aren't," Elayne replied. "They went on foot. It's only a few clicks over the ice-peaks. We would have flown, but we couldn't get the altitude with all the weight we're carrying."

"A few clicks over the ice-peaks?" Sandra repeated in disbelief. "Who sent them?"

"André, my fiancée," Elayne answered. "The man I asked about. I hope he's still alive. He told me to stay in the cabin, said something was wrong and he'd be back."

The slight whine of the hatch sliding open behind her made Sandra spin around and find herself face to face with a somewhat overweight black man, Earth-born based on his skin tone. More than a decade of muscle memory had her gun trained on him as soon as she saw him, and he froze with an odd combination of surprise and something else on his face. "André I assume?"

"André! Where have you been? This woman says dad is dead!" Elayne exclaimed, her voice conveying both her relief at seeing him and obvious bewilderment at the situation.

André ignored his fiancée, his eyes fixed on Sandra. He was taller than Sandra, but chubby, while she was solid muscle. The Confederate still-suit was skin-tight, so he had to know he couldn't take her in a fair fight. Sandra could see there was something about the still-suit he was confused by... something giving him pause. Was it the flag?

"Who are you?" André finally asked in a flat unwavering voice.

"Sandra Pritchard, Captain, American Space Force out of Phobos," Sandra replied, observing André's face close as she spoke. "I've been flying the transport run between Phobos and American Utopia since the Uprising. Currently on assignment with the Arean Army out of Hangtian, flying patrols over Argentea. I was dispatched to find the Cacophony when you didn't show up at Hangtian."

André listened to Sandra, his face betraying nothing. He seemed calm, there was nothing suspicious about him, yet... it wasn't right, a ship full of dead people and a man this calm. When

Sandra finished he turned to Elayne, "No one could fly through this weather, or land on the ice sheet. This woman is lying."

"I've flown through worse," Sandra said calmly, "and landing on dry ice isn't any harder than landing anywhere else. Either way, this is an American airship, down in Confederate territory, and I am an officer in the ASF, currently on assignment for the Area Army. I understand you're running arms from American Utopia to the Confederacy. That gives me more than enough authority to demand to know what exactly is happening on this ship."

"There was a mutiny," André answered calmly, "It has been dealt with. We will get under way once the storm passes. We don't need help."

André was talking slowly, very consistently, but slowly. It seemed he was stalling, but for what? Sandra realized the cabin only had the one hatch, and André was standing in it. She suddenly felt boxed in. What? No! Who was he waiting for?

"The captain and XO are dead," Sandra stated. "If there was a mutiny, who were the mutineers?"

"The XO and captain killed each other when the XO tried to mutiny," André answered calmly. Sandra knew he was lying because she'd seen the bodies, but there was nothing in his voice or mannerisms to indicate he wasn't being honest.

"No," Sandra decided to push the psychopath's buttons, if he had any, perhaps he would break his calm, she still had a gun on him. "I saw the bodies. The XO was gutted in the mess. The captain slashed in the back of the neck at his post on the bridge. It would have taken a real psycho fucker to kill a man that way too. The only reason to kill a man that way is to watch him die slowly, so you can talk to him as he dies, and watch the life drain from his eyes. You have a real twisted fucker on board, probably has all kinds of mommy issues too, wants to go back and suck on her titties."

There was something there, some glimmer of a contained rage inside the man, but he remained calm with only the slightest hint of anger slipping into his voice. "I'm having a hard time seeing you as an American officer, you sound more like a Latina whore. Are you a Sudamérican operative here to commandeer the Cacophony?"

Sandra laughed suddenly understanding, "One of us is. The captain and XO were killed separately, and the captain trusted the murderer enough to let him walk right up behind him."

"How could you possibly know that?" Elayne demanded.

"He was slashed across the back of the neck by someone he knew was standing behind him.

You don't ignore a stranger on your ship, and you certainly don't let them walk up right behind you." Sandra explained. "His spine was slashed with a plasma-blade, but the rest of his neck was left intact. He could have remained conscious for about a minute like that, unable to move, unable to breathe, his heart no longer beating, his brain slowly starving. It takes a special kind of psycho to do that."

"It sure does," André stated absent-mindedly with a hint of pride, then caught himself. "You know what we have here Elayne? A stowaway in a stolen Confederate still-suit. A plane couldn't fly through that storm, or land out here. Clearly she's been here all along, and your dad and commander Conway found her and so she killed them, and staged it to look like they killed each other. Now she's trying to divide us so she can kill us too and steal the ship. You're father's ship, the ship he spent his life saving up for, and then operating so he could leave it to you, a -"

"Oh shut the fuck up," Sandra cut him off, then turned to Elayne. "Go have a look at the bodies and you'll know who's telling the truth."

Elayne Williams was staring at Sandra with tears in her eyes. She still had the particle beam rifle pointed at Sandra. "Do you really think I'd believe you that my fiancée would murder my dad? I don't know why you're on my ship but get off before I blow you to Hell."

Sandra grinned and turned back to André, "I guess that means it's your ship now. So why'd you send the rest of the crew out to freeze to death? You must need crew to fly out of here."

"What are you talking about?" Elayne demanded.

"You told me he sent them to Cavi Angusti on foot. Cavi Angusti is over two hundred clicks from here. They've probably already frozen to death. They certainly won't make it to Cavi Angusti or any other settlement on foot."

"You're lying!" Elayne shot back desperately.

"Look at a fucking map!" Sandra snapped. André was still calm, his eyes showing nothing. Sandra thought he should have been a poker player with those eyes. Then suddenly there were footsteps in the passageway behind André. A slight flicker of triumph flashed across his face, but Sandra's instincts kicked in, and she rushed at him.

André had turned his head slightly, glancing over his shoulder to see who was approaching when she moved, bending low and then leaping up slamming her shoulders into his torso and lifting him off his feet. She was through the door in a second and dropped André in the direction he had been glancing, where three Sudamérican troops had appeared. The closest soldier was knocked down by André as he tried rolled over trying to get back to his feet, while the other two jumped back, and then raised their rifles.

Sandra jumped back into the cabin as laser

bolts shot down the passageway. She slammed the hatch door closed and hit the lock button as André started shouting in Spanish. Sandra's Spanish wasn't good, but she knew what he had to be saying. Those laser bolts would have burnt through the gondola's outer skin, and André didn't have a respirator mask on like the Sudaméricans. There was panicked movement outside as someone ran to patch the holes, but Sandra knew they must have left at least one guard on duty watching the door. She looked around the cabin, and saw Elayne was still pointing the particle beam rifle at her.

"Why are they shooting at you? Who is André talking too? Why are they talking Spanish?" Elayne shot out in rapid succession.

"Sudamérican troops," Sandra answered. "We're in Confederate Territory, and I'm in a Confederate Uniform. You figure out the rest."

Elayne lowered the particle beam, shocked as the reality of her situation set in. Her breathing was too fast, and she was on the verge of hyperventilating. She couldn't believe it, her father killed, now clearly by her fiancée in some kind of plot with the Sudaméricans.

"Relax, just take a deep breath and let it out slow," Sandra ordered compassionately. "Sit down and remain calm. It'll take them a few minutes to patch those holes, and they won't try to shoot their way in here. We'll find a way out of this. How did the Sudaméricans get all the way down here without us spotting them?

We've been patrolling the skies over the Confederacy for almost a week. They must be after the arms, but how do they plan on flying this ship all the way back to Sudamérican territory without us shooting it down?"

She checked her gun, right now the Sudamérican scheme didn't matter. She needed to get out of the cabin, the Sudaméricans would be back soon. If they captured her she'd probably end up in one of their mines, and no one would ever see her again. Well, she didn't need to worry about that, the Sudaméricans would probably just shoot her, if not, André would likely slash her with his plasma blade. That remark she'd made about his mother had hit a nerve.

Sandra interfaced with the strato-freighter's computer via her CHUD and access the internal sensors. Two of the Sudaméricans were repairing the holes in the gondola's fuselage, one in the bridge, and one in the passage way just outside the bridge. André was in the next cabin, and the third Sudamérican soldier was just outside the door, guarding them. There were other Sudaméricans in the freight area, presumably checking the cargo.

The sensors showed the air-pressure had dropped dangerously low in the passageway. Sandra turned to Elayne, who seemed to be in shock, and asked, "Do you have a still-suit? Hey, Elayne! Do you have any survival gear in here?"

Elayne looked up when Sandra said her

name, and slowly seemed understand the question. "Yes, we have standard issue emergency still-suits in each cabin."

"Put yours on, now!" Sandra ordered, "and hand me that particle rifle."

"How are we going to get out of here?" Elayne asked handing the rifle to Sandra. It was large, too large to be carried under normal Earth-gravity, fortunately this was Mars, and the gravity was only a third of Earth's. Still, it was heavy. It was designed to be mounted on a vehicle for anti-air defence.

"Had a problem with piracy?" Sandra asked as she checked the weapon was in working order.

"Not in the past couple years," Elayne answered as she pulled off her clothes. "But in the first few years after the Uprising-"

Elayne paused half undressed, "You're going to used that?"

"Unless you have a better idea," Sandra answered. "Get your still-suit on."

"I don't want you blowing a hole in the side of my ship!" Elayne argued.

"Do you want to get sent to a Sudamérican mine?" Sandra asked, and Elayne face showed it all. The Sudamérican mines were notorious as little more than death camps. The Sudamérican regime placed no value on the lives of those not loyal to the Conglomerado Nacional. Anyone accused of disloyalty was sent to the mines, and no one ever left. The worker weren't given still-suits or respirator masks, so they couldn't even leave the pressurized working areas, and if a mine blew out, they all died. It was said the Conglomerado Nacional didn't even give them food, expecting the living to cannibalize the dead.

Sandra didn't know how much of it was true, and how much was misinformation spread by the Conglomerado Nacional to frighten its subjects into loyalty, and she didn't want to find out. Clearly Elaye didn't want to either, as she quickly pulled the last of her clothes off and started putting on the still suit. Sandra looked into the locker the still-suit had come out of, and then turned back to Elayne. "No thermal-suit?"

"No," Elayne answered, pausing slightly and then returning to work. "If you could get here from your plane without one, I can get to your plane without one."

"I left my thermal-suit on the bridge," Sandra stated. "You will need one to survive outside."

Elayne paused again, and then continued, "There are some thermal-suits in the emergency pod, near the back of the gondola."

"I don't want to leave my ship in these people's hands," Elayne said standing up, as she pressurized the suit. It quickly contracted around her showing a thin toned body, somewhat uncommon on Mars. Sandra hoped that meant she worked out regularly, otherwise she probably wouldn't make it back to the Lockheed.

"I'd rather not leave it in their hands either," Sandra agreed. "But our first order is survival. As long as we make it back to my Lockheed we can let Hangtian know what's happening, and they can intercept the ship before it reaches the Sudamérican colonies."

"You mean shoot it down," Elayne stated. "This is my home you know."

Sandra paused, the ship would probably be shot down. That would probably be her next order. But still, "The Arean Army needs those battle-skiffs you're carrying. There was virtually no arms manufacturing on Mars before the Uprising. Most of what the Arean Army has is what the rebels captured during the war. The Confederacy seems to have a few lite-arms factories operating up north, but nothing down here in Argentea. They'll try to capture the ship before they give the order to destroy it. Hold on to something. The air pressure should be low enough out there that there won't be much of a blow-out."

They both pulled on their respirator-masks, and Sandra lifted the particle-beam rifle. She approximated the Sudamérican soldier's position from the internal sensors map, and fired. The hatch and wall around it exploded in a bright flash that quickly flew out the hole in the outer fuselage behind where the soldier had been standing. If anything of him remained intact it was blown out the hole too. The blowout was minor, and Sandra dropped the particle beam rifle, and drew her handgun as she stepped through the opening into the passage beyond. There was a large hole blown through the side of the gondola and the temperature was quickly dropping inside. She raised her gun towards where the soldiers had been a few seconds earlier, but saw the bridge hatch sliding closed.

"They're taking refuge inside the bridge," Sandra stated. "Is there more than one thermal suit in that survival pod?"

"Yes several," Elayne answered.

"Good, cause it looks like I've lost mine," Sandra said and then motioned towards the rear of the gondola. Elayne stepped through the opening into the quickly freezing passageway and ran towards the survival pod.

Before they got to the pod, the hatch to the bridge slid open, and the Sudaméricans stepped back into the hallway, apparently their movement into the bridge had just been a panicked response to the explosion. Sandra had seen the door opening in her CHUD before the soldiers had even noticed the women in the hallway, and turn dropping to one knee. Two quick shots from her gun and they were both falling backwards, with holes burnt through their heads.

Elayne stopped and looked back, "If they're

dead we can retake the bridge!"

"No! Sensors show there are more coming from the freight section," Sandra stated pushing Elayne on towards the emergency pod.

"You're accessing our sensors? Yes, of course you are," Elayne quickly realized, and turned to run for the escape pod. The pod was around the size of the cabin they had been in, with seats all around the interior, enough for a dozen people. Elayne stopped at the hatch and started opening the locker containing the survival gear, but Sandra pushed her into the pod and jumped in behind her quickly closing the hatch.

Outside the pod there were suddenly voices speaking Spanish, they got louder, and then someone shone a light in through the pod's window and started yelling. Sandra hit the eject button, and the pod dropped out the bottom of the gondola, hitting the ice a second later. Above them someone fired a burst of laser blasts that burnt through the pod, but fortunately didn't hit either of the women. The shooter had aimed for the seats, but the women hadn't gotten to the seats before ejecting and were sprawled on the floor in the center of the pod.

The pod quickly lost its air-pressure through the smoldering holes, and the temperature started to quickly drop. There was Spanish shouting above them, two or more Sudaméricans arguing over something. Sandra motioned towards the emergency gear locker, and Elayne quickly moved over and pulled a couple thermal-suits out, tossing one to Sandra. The emergency thermal-suits weren't as good as the Argentea Division thermal-suit she'd been wearing, and Sandra wondered if they'd make it back to the Lockheed. Above them a new voice interrupted the argument, and started barking orders. Sandra knew they had to move, the first thing any competent commander would do was order his troops to make sure the enemy was dead.

A couple of Sudamérican troops landed next to the pod with grunts and what sounded like cursing, and Sandra pointed to the hatch, and then hit the beacon button. On top of the pod a hatch popped opened releasing an emergency beacon balloon which was quickly filling with hydrogen. Sandra jumped out of the pod a second later, gun in hand. The Sudaméricans were taken by surprise, one had slipped on the ice, and the other turned too slowly to meet Sandra's aim. He fell dead on the ice, and the other never made it back to his feet.

Above them the balloon popped as someone shot it, and the two women ran out of range of whoever it was, as a burst of laser bolts impacted the ice behind them. Then a burst of laser fire rained down on them from one of the ridges, where several dozen Sudamérican troops seemed to be descending towards the ship.

"What's going on here?" Sandra shouted as

the women ducked behind a large ice-shard. "Why would they need so many troops to steal a ship?"

Laser blasts began to burst through the ice-shard and Sandra knew they had to keep moving, but to where? There was little cover in this valley. The laser blasts suddenly stopped, and the Sudaméricans were shouting, no screaming. Sandra paused, and then glanced around the edge of the ice-shard and saw the ice ridge they had been on dissolving, and Sudaméricans falling into the quickly reforming ice. They didn't scream for long.

"Captain Pritchard!" Cheng's voice echoed through the darkness. "There is more coming! You have to go!"

"Cheng!" Sandra called out and looked around, but a blanket of ice-fog was quickly descending into the valley from where the Sudamérican troops had been, tiny water-ice crystals released as the carbon-dioxide ice had been flash melted.

"I am north by north-west of your position, move quickly, that ice-fog can encrust your respirator-mask!" Cheng shouted.

"Let's go," Sandra said to Elayne grabbing her by the arm.

"No, I can't see anything since they stopped shooting. I need a light," Elayne stated.

"They'll shoot us if we turn on a light," Sandra observed, then grabbed Elayne and hoisted her over her shoulders and started to run.

"This is undignified!" Elayne argued from Sandra's shoulder. "If you have to carry me, at least let me ride you piggy-back!"

"Ride me?" Sandra repeated. "I'm not a horse, and we're not going that far."

Cheng appeared ahead of them and waved them into a clearing behind an ice-shard. Sandra dropped Elayne behind the ice-shard and turned to Cheng, who had a particle beam rifle sung over his shoulder, similar to the one Elayne had aboard the Cacophony. Its tiny status lights lighting up the small area behind the shard.

"Who's that?" Cheng asked.

"A survivor from the crew," Sandra answered. "Why aren't you on the plane?"

"The Sudoméricans have dropped several landers from orbit," Cheng answered. "It looks like they took out our com satellites, because I can't get through to anyone. Those troops were from the closest lander, but there are more on the way."

"Oh shit!" Elayne exclaimed. "They're going to used the American battle-skiffs to attack Hangtian. The anti-aerospace artillery would destroy the landers if they tried to land at the spaceport, so they've commandeered our arms shipment!"

"Arms?" Cheng inquired. "The Yanks are giving us weapons?"

"Yanks?" Elayne sounded exasperated. "I am not a Yank!"

"Oh, you sound like a Yank," Cheng stated.

"I am from North Carolina, Sir, and you will not besmirch my honor!" Elayne stated in her most Southern sounding accent.

"Is she fucking with me?" Cheng asked.

"No, Southerners don't like being called Yanks," Sandra said. "And we have more important things to worry about. How long till those troops get here?"

"A couple hours," Cheng reported. "Three landers dropped just south of the glacier in the storm. One landed closer. If they fly that freighter to Hangtian, they could offload the skiffs right in the middle of the Army Base. The battle would be over before it starts."

"A Trojan Horse," Elayne observed.

"A what?" Cheng asked.

"Doesn't matter," Sandra stated. "We need to get back to the Lockheed before we freeze. I'd better carry you, Elayne."

"I can run as fast as you can!" Elayne objected. "Just give me a light to see with."

"No, it would be too easy to spot us if we turned on a light," Sandra dismissed the idea.

"I can't see in the dark either," Cheng stated pulling his backup flashlight from a pocket. "Unless you're carrying both of us, we're using lights."

"I guess we're using lights then," Sandra conceded as Elayne mounded the flashlight on her shoulder. "But if they start shooting find cover and turn off the light!"

"Right, don't let them shoot us," Elayne said sarcastically. "I should have brought a note pad for all this wisdom."

Sandra set a quick pace, but made sure the others weren't falling behind. The emergency thermal-suits weren't nearly as good as the Argentea thermal-suit, and she could feel the dull ache of cold around her wrists and ankles where her body heat was escaping through the seams. Her neck too, her neck was cold. It didn't matter, Elayne wasn't complaining.

"Thank the Almighty!" Elayne stated as the Lockheed appeared ahead of them. "I feel like I am going to freeze solid!"

Oh a religious type, Sandra realized. No wonder they stayed on Mars to run a strato-freighter. The old U.S. corporate congress had banned all religions decades ago, and the revolutionary government had no interest it restoring the rights of the churches. Most of the religious types had move to one of the African nations, or the Arabo-Persian Caliphate, or out here to Mars. Mars was covered in all manner of religious nuts. Churches and cults seemed to spring up everywhere on this planet, and most of the colonial governments looked the other way, as long as their quotas weren't effected. The Confederacy had banned all religious movements as well, but Sandra heard it was full of them, operating underground, like the fight clubs and the sex slave industry.

They reached the hatch, and second later were inside pulling off the frozen thermal-suits, and then the icy still-suits. Elayne was almost naked when she turned to Sandra, and asked, "Do you have anything I can wear?"

"Here," Sandra said handing an Arean Army still-suit to Elayne, and pulled another from the locker for herself. A few minutes later they were in the cockpit, and Sandra was checking the sensors while Cheng got them each a coffee from the cappuccino machine.

"No one followed us," Sandra reported. "Strange."

"I would have called for reinforcements," Elayne stated.

"Yes," Sandra agreed. "No signs of aerospace fighters, or missiles inbound."

"Our anti-orbital ballistic missiles might have blown their ships out of the sky," Cheng stated enthusiastically.

"More likely they moved their fleet north to attack the northern territories around the equator," Sandra guessed. Argentea was the only Confederate territory south of the Canadian Colonies. A former Chinese colony, that encompassed the entire Mare Australe south of 65° south. It had once been prosperous, mining Cerium, along with Palladium and other minor metals. But the Cerium had been mined out, and the Chinese Corporations lost interest in Mars after the Great Lunar War. Now most of the former colony was abandoned, Hangtian had once been home to over a million, but now less than twelve thousand remained, the rest had been relocated to Oceanus Procellarum.

Row after row of abandoned residences, factories, and greenhouses sprawled out around Hangtian spaceport, all connected by a labyrinth of underground tunnels. If the Sudamérican troops got in there, the Arean Army would never be able to flush them all out. It was the tactic the Chinese rebels had used during the Uprising, after a year of searching for them the Chinese government had officially sold the colony to Canada. The Canadians had briefly occupied the spaceport, but ultimately withdrew once it became clear the rebels could attack them at will, while they couldn't even find the rebels. Sandra knew they had to stop the Sudaméricans from reaching Hangtain, at any cost.

"See if you can get through to Hangtian on the emergency radio bands," Sandra ordered, and Cheng started calling out in Mandarin, as she turned on the Lockheed's VTOL jets, and the plane lifted into the sky.

"What are we going to do?" Elayne asked.

"Strap yourself in," Sandra ordered. "This flight's going to get bumpy."

The Lockheed skimmed the glacier and shot quickly over the strato-freighter, which was still anchored where they'd left it. There were no signs of movement below, and no one shot up at them.

"I have reached Brigadier Zhu," Cheng reported, and then spoke in Mandarin over the radio for almost a minute before tuning back to Sandra. "I've reported the situation aboard the strato-freighter, and reported the landers. The Brigadier reports the Sudamérican fleet has destroyed our com satellites, and is currently bombing the old shipyards at Karācī with mass drivers."

"Mass drivers?" Sandra repeated in disbelief, even during the Uprising no one had resorted to weapons of mass destruction.

"Yes," Cheng confirmed. "Apparently America launched a surprise invasion, and has captured most of northern Mexico and the Caribbean Islands. They used mass drivers against several Sudamérican metro-regions including Bogotá, Mexico, and Buenos Aires. The Brigadier also reports there is a wing of Sudamérican aero-space fighters coming down on us from a carrier in orbit."

"We launched a surprise attack against civilian populations?" Elayne said from the seat behind Sandra. "I don't know who we are anymore."

"There, Cheng, see them?" Sandra asked as the Sudamérican infantry appeared on the ice in front of them. "There, that cliff, drowned them!"

Cheng strafed the cliff with the particle beam the Confederacy had installed, and an avalanche of ice particles flooded down on the troops. Some of them were firing up, others were running, but all were suddenly engulfed in a dense blanket of ice-fog. The sensors couldn't detect what was happening within the ice-fog, and Sandra banked the plane to make a second pass when the Missile Approach Warning went off, and Sandra instinctively veered the Lockheed for open skies and jammed on the after burners. The Lockheed was an aerospace plane, and its afterburners could easily achieve 5 Gs, generally fast enough to out run an air-to-air missile.

"Targeting," Cheng reported, and then a series of bursts cleared the sky behind them. "Clear."

"How many?" Sandra asked.

"Ten," Cheng answered.

"Can you see the fighters?" Sandra asked banking back down towards the Sudamérican infantry.

"No," Cheng answered. "How many am I looking for?"

"Five," Sandra answered. "The Sudaméricans like to fire large opening salvos. They'll target more carefully now."

"I'm not seeing a thing," Cheng reported.

"Why not?" Elayne demanded.

"Stealth tech," Sandra answered. "Well, if we can't find them, let's make them chase us, check our six for atmospheric anomalies. Target the infantry as we pass."

Cheng strafed the ground as they passed over the Sudamérican infantry, and launched a barrage of air-to-surface cluster grenades that exploded in a chain reaction when they hit the ground. The MAW sounded again, and Cheng reported, "Missile on our six! Targeting."

The explosion was close enough to jolt the Lockheed.

"EMP now!" Sandra ordered, and slammed the thrusters full throttle. A few seconds later the bomb exploded silently behind the Lockheed. It wasn't a typical bomb, and it couldn't bring down the Sudamérican fighters, it was an Electro-Magnetic Pulse bomb, designed to damage electronics. "Any damage?"

"Looks like we're fine," Cheng reported. "And sensors are now reading four, no five, three, well at least five Sudamérican fighters."

"What type?" Sandra asked.

"Long range Aerospace," Cheng replied. "Targeting."

Behind them the lead Sudamérican fighter exploded, and the others veered off in seemingly random directions. They were glider shaped aircraft, with long graceful wings, connected by only a cockpit and engine. The weapons, fuel, and sensors, were housed in the wings. On board the artificial intelligence networks were trying to repair the stealth systems, and the fighters were blurring in and out of the Lockheed's sensor display.

"We've got them now," Sandra stated banking the Lockheed into a steep climb, and exposing the Sudamérican fighters largest profile. Two of them exploded before the other two arched up into a climb after the Lockheed, and then disappeared.

"They're gone again," Cheng reported.

"That's okay, we know where they are. Hold on to your lunch," Sandra said and then killed the engine, the plane's ascent slowed and as it came to a stop, she fired the maneuvering thrusters, pivoting the retrofitted cargo plane into a nose dive. As the Lockheed plummeted back towards the ground Cheng fired off everything he had, and the Sudamérican fighters exploded in front of them. Sandra reignited the engines and veered down towards where the Sudamérican infantry had been advancing. They were frozen solid, encased in the reformed ice-sheet. Sandra banked the Lockheed and headed back towards the strato-freighter.

The Lockheed skimmed above the airships' canopy, and then Sandra switched on the VTOL jets and dropped the plane onto the ice in front of the Cacophony. There were still no signs of life in the gondola, but she knew there were still Sudamérican troops on board, as well as the traitor André.

"Stay here," Sandra ordered the others. "If it looks like it's going to take off shoot it down."

She quickly pulled on one of the Arean thermal suits and exited the Lockheed. She cautiously approached the strato-freighter, but no one was shooting at her. She couldn't access the ship's computer anymore. They must have realized she'd accessed it and changed the codes. The wire-ladder was still dangling down to the ice, and further back the emergency pod was still sitting on the ice, its beacon balloon fabric wafting in the wind. Sandra climbed the ladder quickly, but entered the gondola slowly, quietly.

She couldn't hear the sounds of the Sudaméricans; there were no voices. On the bridge the Captain was still dead at his post, and the two Sudamérican troops she'd shot were now frozen to the deck. The passageway back past the cabins was cold with gusts of wind blowing in through the hole she'd made. The XO was alone in the mess, and the cabins were now all empty. At the end of the gondola was the passage way ascending to the freight area, and Sandra quietly crept forward gun in hand.

As she reached the other end of the passage the unexpected happened, a Confederate Soldier entered the passageway from the freight area. She froze when she saw the uniform, but he didn't when he saw hers. The Confederate soldier pulled out a plasma-blade and rushed at Sandra, and she fired realizing who it was. He fell and she cautiously approached trying to see if any of the Sudaméricans were following him, but he was alone. She pulled the bloody face-plate off him and saw the remains of André staring up blankly. He was wearing her thermal-suit, the one she'd left on the bridge. All of the ship's emergency thermal-suits must have been in the pod.

She looked back up at the cargo area doors. Could she pass for him? They knew he was on board in a Confederate thermal suit. She pulled of the Arean thermal suit, and put hers back on, before walking to the cargo area doors in her most manly gait. Maybe from a distance she could pass, but he was heavy set, then again, the thermal-suits were all bulky. She stepped through the doors into the cargo bay, and saw the battle-skiffs the Americans were giving the Confederacy. Over a dozen of then, all painted the standard rust-camo of the American Utopia Marines Division. At the far end of the freight section, the Sudaméricans were crowded around one of the skiffs. Sandra watched for almost a minute before the freight doors started to open, and it became clear what they were doing. She turned back into the passage to the gondola, and broke into a run.

She didn't bother heading back to the wire-ladder, but instead jumped down to the ice through the hole the pod had dropped out of earlier. As she landed her right foot slipped slightly on the ice, and she felt a burst of pain she recognized as a sprain. She yelped instinctively, and then powered through it and limped as fast as she could back to the Lockheed.

"What happened?" Elayne asked as Sandra entered the hatch.

"Just a sprain," Sandra answered, not waiting to take off her thermal-suit, instead rushing up to the bridge. "Your fiancée is dead, my condolences."

"Are they launching a battle-skiff?" Cheng asked in disbelief as Sandra reached the bridge. Ahead of them the flying tank had just dropped out of the strato-freighter and was hovering above the ice.

"Yes they are," Sandra answered dropping into her seat and powering up the engines. Cheng was targeting the skiff but Sandra interrupted him, "If you shoot them while they're under the freighter the whole thing will blow."

"They're turning," Cheng observed, and Sandra hit the VTOL jets, lifting the Lockheed out of the skiff's line of fire.

"They'll have to come out if they want to shoot us," Sandra observed.

"What kind of armaments will it have?" Cheng asked.

"No idea," Sandra answered. "They can be outfitted for anything from anti-personnel cluster grenades to anti-air missiles."

"Can the missiles be fired without a lock on?" Cheng asked.

"Yes," Sandra answered and lifted the Lockheed higher into the air. "But they'd have to be idiots to fire blind."

As she said it a barrage of missiles shot out from under the airship, and then arched upwards as they locked onto the Lockheed. Sandra shot the Lockheed back up into the frozen sky, as Cheng targeted and destroyed the missiles behind them, then she piloted the Lockheed back down to the airship, and hovered above it waiting for the skiff to make its next move.

"If I was them, I would blow up the strato-freighter," Cheng observed. "To stop the Confederacy from getting the rest of the battle-skiffs."

"I would too," Sandra agreed. "How fast do you think you could target them?"

"If we are lucky, before they target us,"

Cheng answered.

"How about the ice?" Elayne asked. "Can you target the ice under them?"

"They are not sitting on the ice," Cheng argued. "They are floating above it."

"I know," Elayne stated. "Using turbo-fans, which the ice-fog could damage."

"Yes of course!" Cheng agreed. "Take us down captain. They're not going anywhere with our skiff!"

Sandra maneuvered the Lockheed to the front of the airship, and started lowering it into the battle-skiff's line of fire. As she did Cheng let loose with the particle beam, blasting the ice-sheet into vapor that quickly froze into ice-fog, and the skiff started to slowly spin. The gunner on the skiff fired off a laser barrage in their direction, and Sandra jammed the VTOL jets, lifting the Lockheed back out of the line of sight. Laser blasts continued to fire out from under the strato-freighter, at first hectic, in varied directions as if someone was trying find the Lockheed, but couldn't see through the ice-fog. Then the blasts became steady but frantic, every shot in straight line, firing rapidly, the gunner clearly panicked.

Sandra maneuvered the Lockheed to the rear of the ship and lowered it to see what was happening. The skiff was entirely encased in the glacier, but the gun was still firing, frantically, in the direction it was facing when the ice reformed.

"They won't melt the ice that way," Cheng said.

"They won't melt the ice at all," Sandra said.

"Well we can always come back for the skiff next summer," Cheng suggested.

"I'm setting us back down," Sandra stated. "We need to make sure there's no one left aboard the Cacophony before heading back to Hangtian."

"Hangtian?" Elayne argued. "I'm not leaving without my ship!"

"We can have you back out here tomorrow with a repair crew," Sandra stated. "You can't fly it by yourself anyway."

By the time they'd finished searching the ship the skiff was no longer firing its laser cannon. They didn't know if the crew had already succumbed to the cold, or just the inevitability of their mortality. Once Elayne had seen the frozen bodies of her father and her former fiancée she no longer wanted to stay on the ship over night, and did not object when Sandra informed her they were leaving. Somewhere far to the north a war was raging, but here it was over, at least for now.

# Life in Tartarus

It had finally happened! After almost a decade of waiting it was here, well, the other side of the planet, but close enough! War! Shahzad Ebrahimi had been dreaming of the next war since the last one ended, and he knew exactly who he was going to kill first. That fat Mexican that worked at Materfer VacTrain that was always leering at him. He had only gotten the delivery job so he would have access to the important Sudaméricans, and now the time had come. He wished he could just blow up the entire Materfer Tower, but there was no way he could get his hands on explosives, or the components to build them. He was a Persian, living in a Sudamérican occupied colony, where Non-Sudaméricans had extremely limited rights, and no rights to weapons of any kind. The Persians had been there first, before the Sudaméricans had laid claim to their colony and deployed their lanceros. But that didn't matter, not now. Now he'd have to settle for shooting that fat Mexican, and whoever else he could before they took him down.

He'd rather believe he could survive somehow, escape to fight another day, to kill another day. But that was fantasy. The Sudaméricans would kill him, almost immediately. At least he could get access to the Materfer Tower, that was more than most Persians, other than that traitor that worked there. He'd shoot him too if he had the chance.

For a decade he'd been planning what he'd do, but it wasn't enough time. All he'd managed to get his hands on in a decade was one hand-gun, which had cost him two years of diverted credits on the dark-web. He'd planned to build a resistance, but all he could find were Persians that wanted to make earn enough credit that they could to pay down their life-debt to the point that one of the Sudamérican prostitutes would consider marrying them. The prostitutes in the Sudamérican brothels were shipped out from the Sudamérican empire back on Earth, people that were too poor and uneducated to ever pay off their life-debt.

In the century since the Sudaméricans had invaded the planet, they had solved their prison population problem by sentencing first minor, and later major crimes to 'life on mars.' The homeless problem was later solved the same way, after not having a life-debt score became a crime. When the Sudamérican Corporate Council voted to make debit hereditary, the Aymara of the Bolivian highlands had rebelled, briefly. After the lanceros occupied the Bolivian highlands, the Aymara, all Aymara, were exiled to Mars.

Some of the Sudaméricans had been sent to work in the mines, but most of the women and children had been sent to the brothels. It didn't matter to most of the Persians, the prostitutes were still Sudamérican citizens, and if they married one, their children would be citizens too. No one wanted their children to be Persian.

That was about to change. Once he shot up the Materfer Tower the lanceros would be back out in the street shooting Persians again, and his people would have no option but to fight. It would be different this time. This time there was the Arean Confederacy, an independent Martian government out there that had just declared war on Sudamérica. The rumor going around was that America had also declared war on Sudamérica back on Earth, and invaded Mexico. This time it would be different!

A decade earlier they had been alone. When rebellion had swept the face of Mars, Tartarus Colony was no exception. The Persians had risen up after a century of oppression, only to be brutally stomped back into submission. The heroes from that war were all dead. Only the cowards remained, and the children that had somehow survived. He had been eight at the time. His parents had been revolutionaries, that taught him the forbidden language and script of his ancestors. That was how he liked to remember them, heroic revolutionaries, but he knew that wasn't entirely true. They were both school teachers, school teachers that taught the old language, old religion, and old history to Persian children. That had been why the lanceros had knocked down the door of their small apartment. That was why they'd held his father down and forced him to watch as they raped his wife and child, before shooting him. When they were done with Shazad's mother they shot her too. Shazad they left sobbing in a pool of blood surrounded by his parents corpses.

He had been a girl then, an eight year old girl who had realized she never wanted to be a woman. She hid the rest of the war, stealing scraps of food when she could, but mainly eating garbage the Sudaméricans had thrown away. Once the armistice had been signed in Sireneum, things slowly calmed down in Tartarus, and she was able to get the life-debt of a boy that had died during the war, becoming Shazad Ebrahimi. Finding a doctor that would perform the genetic-reassignment took a couple years, time he'd spent learning to divert life-debt through the dark-web. There was always someone that wanted to pay down some of their life-debt, and the Sudaméricans had no idea how many Persians had actually died during the uprising. Shazad and other Persian debt-hackers kept as many of those Persian debts alive as possible, creating debt-ghosts. The ghosts rented apartments, bought food, paid for air and water, and many even had jobs at companies with less than scrupulous managers. The managers took a generous portion of their ghost-empoyee's pay, while the apartments were sub-rented out at a discount, with hackers like Shazad funneling the rent to paying down their own life-debt.

He'd paid for his genetic-reassignment with air, water, and avocados, grown from illegally imported pits. He didn't even know where the avocados were being grown, but every so often some showed up for sale on the dark-web. Finding a doctor that would perform the reassignment had been difficult, as it was illegal for Persians to change from female to male. Male to female was fine according to the Sudamérican authorities, but female to male was illegal. Sudamérican culture had become ever more misogynistic in the century of occupation. Once there had been women in the occupying government, and even female lanceros. There weren't anymore. Women were expected to breed the next generation of great and noble conquerors.

Shahzad hated them all, and in a matter of hours he would have his revenge, and plunge Tartarus colony into another rebellion. This time the rebellion would spread to other Sudamérican colonies, and Ares would liberate them. He wouldn't see it, but it didn't matter. He pulled on his duster, tucked the illegally imported Anschütz pulse pistol into a hidden pocket, and headed off to work.

As he rode the Metro VacTube to the Avianca Marso yards he realized that there were a lot less people in the train car than usual. The Sudaméricans all seemed nervous, and there were almost no Persians to be seen. The VacTube bus stopped at the usual old Tartarus colony stops before heading up to the city of Nuevo-Tártaro on the surface. Old Tartarus colony was the remains of the old Iranian corporate-era colony that had been mostly underground. Tartarus had started as a mining colony, and as the mines were worked out the hollowed out areas were converted into housing. Most Persian still lived in the old colony, along with poorer immigrants from Sudamérican occupied Sudáfrica y Madagascar.

Nuevo-Tártaro was a surface city of gleaming blue-alon spires and blue-alon domed gardens. All the alon windows throughout Nuevo-Tártaro had a blue UV-blocker coating applied to them, giving the impression of a blue sky for those walking around inside the domes. Sudaméricans liked to wear their weighted shoes and pretend they were still on Earth. Even the VacTubes on the surface were coated in the fake blue sky. The Sudaméricans living up in Nuevo-Tártaro had no idea what life on Mars was like; they were living on a psudo-Earth.

When he got to the Avianca Marso yards he checked his route schedule for the day, and smiled seeing that there was a shipment going to Materfer VacTrain. He stepped out under the brown sky and headed towards his cargo-barge. The brown sky always made him feel at home, brown was real, it was Mars. The barge was still being loaded when he arrived, the shipment to Materfer was bigger than usual. There were shipments to Materfer almost every day, but this one took up most of his barge. Usually they took up a quarter or less. An hour later the barge was loaded and he was floating up into the sky.

The barge was a fixed-structure helium airship. Barges like his were used to ship cargo to remote regions all over the planet. He generally just did deliveries to the industrial yards around the edge of Nuevo-Tártaro. The Materfer shipment was marked priority, so he would have to go there first and then double back to complete his deliveries. Normally that would have pissed him off, but today that was great. He wanted to get the war started.

Materfer was on the far side of Nuevo-Tártaro, and normally barges weren't allowed to fly over the metro core, forced to take a longer route around the edge of the city staying over the industrial sectors. Today was different, shortly after launch someone at Materfer, got his barge tagged as URGENTE and he got an updated flight route. He didn't like it, he'd rather not get noticed by the police, but he didn't have the option of changing his route once the barge got tagged URGENTE. Once the update came through, the barge's flight controls were taken over remotely by the metro central traffic control, and the barge's external lights changed from green to blue. If he changed course every traffic cop would be notified within seconds.

He briefly wondered if the Sudaméricans had found out about his Anschütz pulse pistol, but realized they wouldn't fly him to Materfer if they had. It made him wonder what could be so important about the Materfer shipment. Usually only military shipments got URGENTE status. Materfer was a VacTube construction company. VacTubes weren't something that could be built urgently. The tubes were made of alon: aluminium-oxynitride, which Materfer imported from Earth, along with the electro-magnetic repulsors used to move cars, trucks, and buses through the tubes.

Was Materfer covertly working for the military? Importing arms perhaps? The Sudaméricans weren't known for subtlety. Why hide the imports? Something banned, viral weapons? Gamma bombs? Shahzad's mind was racing, whatever the Sudaméricans were sneaking onto Mars, it had to be intended for a first-strike, and could be debilitating to the Area Confederacy. Maybe he should find out what it was before shooting anyone.

Another barge floated by outside and Shahzad realized there were dozens crossing the metro core, something unheard of. Normally there might be one barge crossing the core in a month. The Sudaméricans were clearly as worried about the Area declaration of war, as he was excited. He checked his avionics display, and checked barges' company codes. Most were cargo barges like his, a couple were heavy transport barges. The lancero base was on the northern edge of Nuevo-Tártaro, which was where the transports were heading. Their course indicated they were flying in from Orcus Colony.

The Materfer VacTube yards were surprisingly quiet when Shahzad floated in over them. The avionics display showed which loading dock he was to use, but there was only one person standing there, dressed in a Sudamérican Traje Marso. Since seizing control of half the planet a century earlier, the Corporate Sudamércans had to occasionally visit their ruddy outposts, and to make sure everyone knew how important they were they'd designed the Traje Marso, which were very impractical enviro-suits, and in Shahzad's opinion ridiculous looking.

Unlike traditional Martian designs dating back to the corporate era, the Traje Marsos didn't incorporate stills to recycle the wearer's sweat and urine, instead they had tanks of water mounted on the back. Instead of using algae to convert the Martian atmosphere into breathable oxygen, the Traje Marso had even larger tanks of compress oxygen and nitrogen mounted next to the water tanks, and the wearer's breath was simply vented to the Martian atmosphere, causing constant loss of water from the suit. Instead of being black, made primarily of carbon nano-tube fibers, they were made from a variety of bright metals and plastics. One thing was certain in Shahzad's mind, whoever was waiting for his delivery was from Earth.

As the airship floated into place above the loading dock the cargo hoist began to lower down the Materfer cargo crates, and the Sudamérican began waiving his arms. Shahzad glanced over at the com-display, but their was no incoming signal. He looked back at the gaudy green and gold clad Sudamérican frantically waiving his arms, and decided to land. Maybe it was that fat Mexican, he probably didn't know how to work a com anyway. Maybe he came outside to sign for the shipment so he could look important on the report back to Earth. Shahzad glanced around the yards, and didn't see any movement. It was odd, usually there were a few loaders driving around this time of the day. Maybe he could shoot that Mexican without any one even noticing. If he pulled the body into the barge he could drop it out while flying over one of the industrial areas few people ever went. He smiled as he felt the impact of the barge's landing pads hit the ground.

Shahzad hit the button that depressurized the cockpit and lowered the landing pad and then pulled his respirator mask on. Shahzad swallowed repeatedly as the air pressure quickly dropped, although, like most Mars born, he was used to the rapid pressure change. Ten seconds after hitting the button the ramp was fully extended and the air pressure in the cockpit matched the thin atmosphere outside. As the door opened Shahzad was surprised to see the Sudamérican already half way up the ramp.

"There's a redirection for that cargo," the Sudamérican stated in Spanish shoving a docupad into Shahzad's hands as he pushed past him into the cockpit and hit the button to close the door and repressurize the cockpit.

Shahzad was surprised, not by the redirection, or the Sudamérican's rude behavior, but rather that he seemed to want to come along. He looked down at the docupad and scrolled through the order. It was the same shipping order he'd already been given, the order that said to deliver the cargo to the Materfer VacTube yards. He turned to the Sudamérican to see the man had a sonic blaster pointed at him. It wasn't a deadly weapon, usually used to stun crowds. At this range it would knock him out, and loosen his bowels. He knew if the Sudamérican didn't kill him while he was unconscious he'd wake up a few hours later with a splitting headache and everything that had been in his digestive track in his pants. He raised his hands slowly.

"We're leaving," the Sudamérican stated. "Fly east, out of the city, I'll give you more directions when you need them."

"I can do that," Shahzad stated sliding back into the pilot's seat, "but if I deviate from the flight plan the police will be on us in minutes."

"Don't worry about the police," the Sudamérican stated. "I've hacked the CTC, they won't be tracking this barge, they'll be tracking a drone that will look like it's following your delivery route."

"Nice trick," Shahzad conceded, as the barge began to lift back into the air. "But those companies are expecting deliveries."

"I've sending out notices that the deliveries

will be delayed, due to the war-emergency," the Sudamérican stated. "I doubt any of those companies will bother anyone about a late shipment today."

"The lancero base is to the north," Shahzad volunteered, seeing if the Sudamérican would take the bait.

"Silence," the Sudamérican ordered. "Just fly me out to the location I specify and leave me there, and then you can return to your delivery route."

"Just leave you out in the desert with a giant crate of whatever?" Shahzad asked. "Because the lanceros won't notice, and look into how the crate got there? Whatever you're doing seems like it is going to get me killed. Unless I call up the CTC after I leave you and tell them what happened. But you would have thought of that, so you have to kill me."

"You're not going to call the CTC," the Sudamérican stated. "Do you think it is a coincidence that it is you flying this cargo today? A Persian man, who was a woman? You won't be calling anyone."

Shahzad was quiet as the outskirts of the colony gave way to the open red desert below them. Whoever this Sudamérican was, he knew too much about him. How much did he know? Did he know Shahzad was a debt-hacker? Probably, he had to have paid for the genetic-reassignment somehow.

"The hill to the southeast," the Sudamérican interjected. "Head towards it."

"Whatever you're doing, the lanceros will see it," Shahzad stated. "Even if you take what is in the crate and disappear, they will find the crate and track it to my company, and then to me. Whether I call the CTC, or the lanceros come to find me, the situation is the same. I must disappear after I finish my deliveries. If you're not going to kill me, it is in your interest to make sure I can disappear. Some pesos would help out with that."

"They won't find the crate," the Sudamérican stated. "The exterior is coated in stealth crystals. When we get where we are going it disappears. Do you see that crater to the northeast? Head down into it. As for your payment, we'll leave the drone at your landing dock. You might find it useful in the future."

"That sounds like something that would get me killed if the lanceros found out I had it," Shahzad stated dubiously.

"It fits in your pocket," the Sudamérican stated. "And if I wanted you dead, I'd just kill you."


"If you say so. But why would you want me to have this drone?" Shahzad asked.

"This war may go on for years, like the last one," the Sudamérican stated. "If so, I will have additional shipments coming through. If you have the drone, you will use it, and if you become good, I will not need to expose myself creating the distraction next time."

"Ah, so that's it," Shahzad realized. "You abduct me, and give me this toy, and then you own me."

"I already own you," the Sudamérican stated. "Anyone who finds out your real name will always own you. Follow that chasm to the south."

Shahzad followed the instruction, turning the barge towards the chasm leading out of the crater, quietly reaching for the Anschütz pulse pistol tucked into the secret pocket in his duster. From his position the Sudamérican should not be able to see what he was doing with his left hand. Did the Sudamérican know he was left-handed? Did he know Shahzad had an Anschütz?

The Sudamérican finally stirred, moving towards the windows to look down. Wherever they were going Shahzad figured they must be getting close, and he didn't believe this Sudamérican was going to let him live to tell the lanceros how to find their way here. He sensed his time was almost up, and fired. The ion pulse tore through his duster and into the Sudamérican's Traje Marso, rupturing one of the tanks on the man's back, fortunately not the oxygen tank. He shifted his aim slightly as the man turned towards him and fired a series of shots into the Sudamérican's abdomen. The man fell backwards against the cockpit's wall, and stood there, blood trickling from multiple holes in his chest.

Shahzad pulled the pistol free from his duster and kept it pointed squarely at the man, as he stood up and moved over to him. He reached up and pulled the gaudy helmet off, and then gasped as he recognized the man. He wasn't a Sudamérican, he was the Persian that worked at the Materfer VacTube tower. Why was he out here pretending to be a Sudaméri-can? He checked the man for a pulse, but there wasn't one, and blood was beginning to pool on the floor. He looked out the window, still not seeing whatever the man had been looking for.

He slid back into the pilot's seat and turned the barge around heading back to the crater. From there, he headed northeast to an old open pit mine he'd hidden in for several months during the war. It had tunnels running into it, from the old abandoned mines below, an ideal place to leave the body. The pit was empty, and nobody had a reason to ever come out this far from the colony. He piloted the barge to a somewhat flat area near a tunnel entrance he knew, and then lowered the Materfer crate. He checked the body for a com, and then held the man's hand up to the DNA scanner to unlock it. It had an app for controlling a stealth system, and an app for unlocking Materfer crates. He cloned the com's apps and data onto his com, and then put it back in the mans' pocket, before shooting the pocket with his pulse pistol. If this man's body was ever found it would look like his com was shot at the same time he was killed. No one should suspect the man's com was cloned.

After pulling the body into one of the abandoned tunnels, he returned to the Materfer crate and pulled out his com. He unlocked the crate, and then hit the button to open one of the hatches, and the memory-metal folded down. Inside were machine parts for air and water recyclers. He walked to another hatch and opened it, finding parts for aeroponic equipment. After checking in a few more hatches Shahzad realized the dead Persian had been going into hiding. He had all the components to build a long term shelter. No actual structure, maybe he thought he could live in the crate itself, or maybe he had been looking for a cave entrance when Shahzad shot him. Either way, it didn't matter. Shahzad could sell these parts on the dark-web, and definitely get enough for a few more weapons. Also he had the man's sonic blaster. He closed the hatches, and turned on the crate's stealth system, realizing that that too would be worth quite a bit to the right buyer. He smiled as he climbed back up the ramp into the cockpit.

He flew back to the colony, not knowing if the police were looking for him, but found nothing out of the ordinary. He rushed through his deliveries, and then headed back to the Avianca Marso yards to land the barge for the night. It was already dark by the time he landed, and he wasn't sure what to expect in the office when he went in to file his flight log.

The day shift controller Marianela had already left, the night shift controller Nontle was on duty. She told Shahzad that most of the Avianca barges had been delayed most of the day, and two were still out making their deliveries. The finance department had authorized overtime pay. No one seemed concerned about where Shahzad had been all day, or where the missing Materfer VacTube shipment was. He felt good on the way home, smug even. He had killed one of them and hadn't been caught. It wasn't that fat Mexican, but it was even better because now he had that pod of gear which he could sell for millions. He could equip a small strike force. They could launch a real counter-insurgency.

He still had the smug smile on his face when he arrived home and saw the message on his wall screen. The streaming image of the surface that usually covered one of the walls had been replaced with the words "We Know" written in the old Persian script. No Sudamerican would have written that it had to be a Persian, someone working with the guy from Materfer VacTube. Shahzad had a sudden sinking feeling in his gut, followed by the impulse that someone was watching him. He looked around the one-room apartment, checked the bathroom, and then turned back to the wall screen that had been hacked.

The wall screen had a series of sensors in it that could send out a 3D image of the room. It was something used for conference calls; the screen could also project a 3D image into the room recreating the room the caller was calling from. Shahzad had disabled both functions right after the screen was installed. He used it as a data display when he was hacking, or just left the streaming view from the surface playing when he wasn't using it. Others used the screens for games or simulated clubs, but those functions required the sensors to be working. Occasionally Shahzad played an old 2D movie on it, he had amassed a large collection of corporate-era Persian movies, but that was it.

He sat down it the chair facing the wall, and then picked up his keyboard. A minute later he was in the wall screen's operating system looking at the code that had been installed. It included a README file, which told Shahzad to take the cargo pod to a specific set of coordinates the next day, or whoever they were, would send a file containing everything they knew about him to the lanceros.

He disabled the new program, and then turned off the wall-screen, and sat in the dark, thinking.

The Persian traitor was working with someone, someone who knew as much about hacking as he did. Another hacker who spoke Persian. He ran through the list of aliases he knew, and through the limited knowledge, he had of their hacks. Who could it be? The thought oc-curred to him that the Persian traitor may not have even known himself, maybe he was being blackmailed. No, the hacker would not have told him that Shahzad had been a female once. Now the hacker had that on him too, murder!

He got up and started pacing, he wanted to go out but didn't dare, whoever it was could be watching. He had the night to figure out who it was, or, or he'd have to give back the freight pod, but that wasn't so bad. Of course, he had killed the traitor, so they probably wouldn't just let him fly away. Would they kill him? They could just tell the police about him. Either way, he was dead. He turned his wall screen back on to look for any trace of the hacker but found nothing useful. In the end, he had only one op-tion.

The next morning he headed up to the Avianca Marso spaceport like he always did. He loaded his cargo, and flew the route as quickly as he could, until half the cargo bay was empty, then launched the drone on a pre-programmed flight path, and flew east out of Nuevo-Tártaro. He didn't stop to pick up the cargo pod but in-stead flew directly to the coordinates he'd been given. They probably knew where the cargo pod was, but obviously needed his barge to move it, and if they killed him to take the barge and moved it themselves, they'd have to figure out how to return the barge to Avianca with a dead pilot. At least that was his theory. Maybe, just maybe, they'd talk.

The coordinates were near where he'd shot the Persian traitor the day before, although he wasn't sure where he was supposed to leave the pod, as there was no landing pad, or loading dock, just the ruddy walls of the ancient canyon. He decided to land the airship, and there was still no reaction outside. Someone had to be watching. He put on his respirator mask and pulled his cloak over his shoulder, then hit the button to open the door and lower the ramp. Outside there were no signs of life either. Someone had to be watching from somewhere.

He descended the ramp slowly with is pulse pistol in hand, turning to look in every direction, but there was no one to be seen. Had they out-maneuvered him? Was this just a drop-off point, and there was no one actually here? No that didn't make sense, how would they get the pod to wherever they were taking it? They had to be around here somewhere. But they would have to move the pod, and if not a barge, then they'd need a loader. He looked at the ground for signs of tracks, but there were none to be seen. Given the way the wind swept through these canyons, he really didn't expect to see any tracks on the ground.

If there was a loader, it had to be parked in a cave or something, or else the Sudamericans would have spotted it. There were no caves that he could see, but, was that what the traitor had been looking for when Shahzad had shot him? Which direction had be been looking? It seemed he'd been looking forward, at the northern canyon wall. Shahzad decided to risk it, and stepped down off the ramp. He cautiously walked towards the northern wall, still seeing no signs of life.

As he moved away from the landed barge a sudden sandstorm appeared around him. He looked back up at the barge's hydrogen-filled superstructure, but saw it wasn't moving, the sandstorm was localized to the ground. He looked around and could see almost nothing, yet just a meter above him the sky was clear. Then as sudden as it started the storm was gone, and around him stood six people in black Martian cloaks and respirator masks, each holding a sonic blaster pointed squarely at him.

"You were told to bring the cargo," one of the gunmen men shouted in Persian through his mask.

"I thought we could negotiate!" Shahzad shouted back.

"There is nothing to negotiate!" the gunman stated stepping closer to Shahzad.

"I have something you want, you have something I want," Shahzad replied.

"What do you want?" the gunman demanded.

"My life!" Shahzad answered.

"That's not mine to give," the gunman stated. "Do you still have the cargo?"

"It's safe," Shahzad replied.

"Hand over your weapon, and then follow me," the man ordered, and Shahzad complied. The man led Shahzad toward the northern canyon wall, and as they approached it another sandstorm suddenly exploded around them, and then seemed to lift up above them, leaving them in a calm area under the swirling sand.

"Move!" one of the other gunmen shouted from behind Shahzad, and he realized he'd stopped walking and was staring up at the bizarre storm. The first gunman was still approaching the canyon wall, and Shahzad followed.

As they approached the canyon wall a large hidden door lifted up into the wall, exposing a hidden mine-shaft. A loader was idling at the mouth of the mine, and behind it a large airlock door sealed the entrance to the mine from the rest of the mine-shaft. It was the same as every other mine Shah-Zad had seen, except for the hidden entrance, and strange storm outside.

The gunmen led him through the mine entrance, and through the pressure doors, into the mine's interior, where a virtual village of retrofitted cargo pods sat. Some were clearly offices, while others looked like residences, and based on the smells coming from one of them it had been retrofitted into a cafeteria. Overall it looked like the poorer regions of Old Tartarus colony, except without the packs of children digging through the piles of Nuevo-Tártaro's garbage. This village was clean, and well lit by an array of panels showing a fake martian sky, white clouds drifting across the brown sky. Walking through the village felt like walking down some small canyon outside, except the air was clean, and the temperature was warm.

As the group marched through the small village, everyone they passed stopped what they were doing to watch them. Clearly, they weren't expecting Shahzad, and based on their reaction, didn't get many visitors. He noted they all looked Persian, no Latinos, or Aymara, or Sudáfricans. He also noted there weren't any children, and everyone looked old enough to have been an adult during the last war. What had he stumbled into?

The gunman led him up a flight of stairs to an office and told him to wait, then told two of the gunmen to guard him and left. There was a desk in the office, with several chairs around it. Shahzad dropped into one of the chairs and tried to be patient, but in the back of his mind, he knew that if they didn't kill him, he still needed to deliver the rest of his cargo before someone noticed he was missing.

"Any idea how long I'll be waiting?" Shahzad asked.

"Silence!" one of the guards snapped in reply.

"I'll take that as a no," Shahzad returned and then leaned back in the chair intent on relaxing. If it was to be his last few minutes, he might as well take what little enjoyment he could from it.

Around a half an hour later the first gunman returned, now dressed in an old Tartarus Corporate Security uniform. The design was a century out of date, Shahzad only recognized it because of his morbid fascination with old corporate-era movies. With the historically attired guard was a scientist, or at least someone wearing a labcoat like the ones scientists always wore in the movies.

"Mr. Ebrahimi," the scientist addressed Shahzad by his family name in Persian. "You have caused us a great deal of trouble."

"That's my specialty," Shahzad replied.

"Apparently," the scientist observed. "May I assume Mr. Terhani is dead?"

So they didn't know, not for sure. That meant they hadn't found the body or the cargo pod.

"That was his name?" Shahzad asked cavalierly. "The Persian that worked at Materfer VacTube?"

The scientist stared coldly back at Shahzad, and then finally replied. "Yes."

"Sorry, I never got his name," Shahzad stated. "Corporate and labor rarely exchange business licenses, and yes, he is dead."

The scientist paused for a few seconds, looking away from Shahzad. "We were friends since childhood," he finally said looking back to

Shahzad. "Why did you kill him?"

"He was doing something illegal, and forcing me to help at gunpoint," Shahzad stated. "I figured it was just a matter of time until he killed me."

"Yes," the scientist stated, musing over Shahzad's response. "So the miscalculation was mine. I thought you could be controlled through extortion. Where is his body?"

"With the cargo pod," Shahzad answered.

"We'd like both of them returned to us," the scientist stated.

"I'd like a confirmation that you won't kill me afterward," Shahzad stated, and then added, "or report me to the Sudamericans."

"We're not murderers, Mr. Ebrahimi. And we cannot turn you over to the Sudamericans without exposing ourselves," the scientist stated. "You've killed our implanted asset within the Sudamerican corporate structure. We'll need you to replace him."

"You expect me to become a corporate?" Shahzad asked in disbelief.

"Not like our previous asset," the scientist answered. "Gholam was well suited for infiltrating the corporate structure. You could be useful for us at the Avianca Marso Spaceport though. We are going to need to move equipment from time to time."

"And who are you exactly?" Shahzad decided to cut to the point.

"Yes, of course," the scientist considered for a few seconds and then rose to his feet. "Come with me."

The scientist led Shahzad and the man in the old Tartarus Colony Security uniform out of the office and down the stairs, and Shahzad realized that the other two guards had disappeared as they'd been talking.

"We call this Mehr station," the scientist waved at the settlement around them. "My name is Firdaus Attar, and I am the administrator of this facility."

The settlement wasn't very large, perhaps capable of housing a hundred people. At the edge of the settlement, the mine-shaft disappeared into darkness. Firdaus Attar led them to a small transport car, and climbed into the rear seat, and told Shahzad to join him. The guard climbed into the driver's seat and flicked on the lights before driving them down into the mine-shaft.

"This mine-shaft was dug out back during the corporate-era," Attar said. "And we've been here since then."

"Who are you?" Shahzad demanded again.

"We're the remnants of Tartarus Corp," Attar answered as the transport raced down the dark mine-shaft.

"Tartarus Corp. was nationalized by the Sudamericans eighty years ago!" Shahzad argued.

"The rest of it was," Attar stated. "Mehr was a separate division, compartmentalized within the corporate structure. The Sudamericans have never known we're here, and they cannot find out."

"How could they have not known?" Shahzad asked. "How could they have not found out in eighty years?"

"Mehr wasn't a functioning mine when Tartarus was nationalized, so it was easy to keep it off the books," Attar stated.

"And you guys have just been hiding down here for the last eighty years?" Shahzad asked incredulously.

"No," Attar stated flatly. "We haven't been hiding. Mehr wasn't a mine for a couple decades before the Sudamericans invaded. Mehr was a research facility."

Ahead of them, a light appeared and quickly grew into a doorway at the side if the mine-shaft. The transport pulled to a stop next several other parked transports. Attar led them through a small office to an elevator and selected the lowest level.

"What we're going to show you can never be known to the Sudamericans," Attar stated. "I assume you won't have a problem keeping things from them."

"That won't be a problem," Shahzad stated.

"But why are you going to show me this thing?"

"You need to understand what we're doing here if you're going to work with us," Attar said as the elevator descended.

"How deep are we going?" Shahzad asked a couple minutes later.

"Not much further," Attar answered. "Don't worry about your deliveries. We've got someone sending through delay notices to Avianca, they'll think you're held up at the delivery points."

The elevator stopped and they stepped out into another office, this one dimly lit with several people working at AI interfaces. Attar led Shahzad through the office to a window looking out into a cave lit up in blue and red lights. "We found this around one hundred and twenty years ago," Attar explained.

Below them, in the cave, there were red lights moving around in a blue liquid. "It's impossible to tell with your eyes, but that liquid is eighty-five meters below us, so there could be a twenty-five story building between us and it," Attar stated.

"So you found liquid water?" Shahzad asked somewhat confused.

"It's not water," Attar stated. "It's more like a plasma."

"Plasma? Inside the planet?" Shahzad scoffed. "How could plasma exist inside a planet? It would be absorbed by the rocks."

"Not stellar plasma," Attar stated somewhat irritated. "Plasma like the plasma in your blood."

"Blood?" Shahzad repeated. "You found a pool of blood! How could there be a pool of blood?"

"It's not exactly blood," Attar stated. "That's just the closest analogy we have."

"I don't get it," Shahzad stated after a few seconds of staring down at the blueish hued liquid, with its mesmerizing red lights. He shook his head and looked back up at Attar. "You're saying you found a pool of blood? What are you trying to tell me?"

"Don't worry if you're confused," Attar smiled. "It has that effect at first. It's the lights, they're kind of hypnotic. Let me block them."

He touched a couple keys on the window's control and a pool of liquid disappeared below them, and now hundreds of new red lights appeared around the cavern, covering all the walls and ceiling above them.

"What did you do?" Shahzad asked.

"I blocked the light from the pool of plasma," Attar explained. "Now you can see the rest of the cavern. The plasma is so bright that normally you can't see the rest of this."

"The rest of what?" Shahzad asked beginning

to become angry. "You bring me down, who knows how deep into the planet, to show me a pool with some lights in it and tell me its blood, and then turn off the lights to show me some other lights?"

"You're angry," Attar observed calmly.

"I'm beginning to get angry!" Shahzad replied.

"And now you know why the Sudamericans can never know what's down here," Attar stated.

"What! What?" Shahzad stammered.

"Follow me," Attar stated and then turned and began towards a door on one side of the office.

"Move!" the guard ordered. Shahzad turned to confront the guard but saw the man had his sonic blaster pointed at him. The thought of waking up in a pool of his feces passed through Shahzad's mind and he decided to follow the strange-talking scientist. In the adjoining room, the walls were covered in what appeared to be fish tanks. He'd seen fish tanks before at several of the Japanese and Polynesian restaurants in Nuevo Tártaro. These fish tanks were all dark. The scientist did something to the controls of one of the tanks and suddenly there was a glowing red leaf inside the tank. It was the biggest leaf Shahzad had ever seen, and as he approached the tank, veins along the sides of the leave seemed to swell up, and then the leaf leaned towards him. He stepped back quickly.

"How angry are you right now?" Attar asked. "On a scale of one to ten?"

"What!" Shahzad barked, suddenly feeling like this scientist had jarred him back into reality. He really wanted to hit this guy, with his stupid questions. "I'd say about eight!"

Attar touched the tank's controls and the strange leaf disappeared back into darkness. He walked over to another tank, entered a few commands and suddenly the room was lit up with a blueish hue. Shahzad walked over to the blue tank, there appeared to be nothing in it, just a blue hue shining out of it.

"How angry do you feel now?" Attar asked. "On a scale of one to ten."

"What?" Shahzad asked, feeling like he was waking from a dream. "Um, I guess about two."

Attar touched the control and the blue tank darkened. "How about now? One to ten?"

"I don't know," Shahzad stated. "What's happening?"

"One to ten," Attar repeated.

"I don't know, two I guess," Shahzad answered. "But if you ask me again it'll be three."

"Do you understand?" Attar asked.

"Understand what?" Shahzad asked back. "You have a fish tank that glows blue and another tank with a weird red leaf in it?"

"It might take your mind a few minutes to start thinking clearly," Attar stated. "When you looked at the leaf as you called it, we call them Ahrimans, you were very angry, eight out of ten. Seconds later when you were looking at the tank of plasma, you weren't angry at all, two out of ten."

"Wait, so the leaf made me angry?" Shahzad asked. "And the blue stuff made me calm?"

"Exactly," Attar confirmed. "And when you looked at both of them together in the cave your mind was overwhelmed, almost hypnotized."

"What, so, that cavern is full of this stuff that messes up people's minds?" Shahzad asked.

"Yes, put at it's most basic level," Attar answered.

"And those red lights I saw all over the walls and ceiling were those, leaf things?" Shahzad asked.

"There are several varieties, but yes," Attar stated. "So you understand why the Sudamericans cannot know about this cave?"

Shahzad paused looking at Attar, "Not really. Why did you make them?"

"We didn't make them," Attar stated. "We found them, one hundred and twenty years ago."

"So who made them then?" Shahzad asked.

"Nobody made them," At-tar answered. "Or if you are religious, Allah made them."

"Allah?" Shahzad considered. "You mean they're not from Earth?"

"Right, there is nothing like this life-form on Earth," At-tar said.

"So they're alien? Like those ELF signals?" Shahzad asked.

"Yes. Alien. But not in another star system," At-tar confirmed. "So, do you understand now why the Sudamericans can never know about this cave?"

"Not really," Shahzad admitted. "All they care about is money, so either they would find a way to sell these lifeforms, or they'd kill them. Either way, it makes no difference to us."

Attar paused considering, then walked over to another tank, and entered a few commands. The tank's glass wall depolarized showing the blue hewed liquid, and red things moving around inside. Shahzad walked up to the tank, which was larger than the other two tanks. The blue liquid was opaque, and it was difficult to see the red things, but they were moving around in it, swimming like those Polynesian fish. As he peered into the tank one of the red creatures swam past the glass. It was about the size of a football, but the rear half was missing, and instead, dozens of thin tendrils drifted behind it. Seeing it made Shahzad angry. The Sudamericans were going to kill it! Attar touched the controls again and the glass blackened.

"Seeing them makes us angry," Attar stated. "But seeing the plasma makes us calm. Imagine what the Sudamericans could do with this."

"They could make us angry whenever they wanted," Shahzad observed. "Or docile. But how could they use that without people knowing? People would rebel!"

"Would they?" Attar asked. "You ever notice how there are no women in the lanceros? There used to be. Did you ever notice how no one, not Persians, or Aymara, or Sudáfricans ever revolt? No matter how angry they are they won't revolt. Do you know why?"

"They're a bunch of whiny bitches," Shahzad answered.

"After the rebellion ten years ago the Sudamericans began infecting everyone with a modified version of toxoplasma. They put it in the vaccines they give everyone," Attar stated. "It makes people docile. They gave their own troops a different version that makes them hyper-aggressive. Unfortunately, the version they give their troops doesn't work on females, not enough testosterone, so you don't see female lanceros anymore."

"Wait, so they're dosing everyone with a toxin that makes people docile?" Shahzad repeated in disbelief. "And that's why no one wants to rise up?"

"Yes," Attar stated. "We've been down here since before they started dosing the population. Your procedure seems to have somehow altered the effects on you, so you're hostile instead of docile. But getting everyone to change their gender isn't a solution."

"It seemed to have worked for me," Shahzad joked.

"Seems like it did," Attar agreed. "But most people wouldn't want to change their gender. Besides an armed rebellion would never work. The Sudamericans control over 40% of the planet."

"The Arean Confederacy could defeat-," Shahzad started, but Attar cut him off.

"The Arean Confederacy controls less than 20% of the planet, has no allies, or even any trading partners. They cannot win this war they've started," Attar stated decisively.

"But America, on Earth, could invade Mexico-" Shahzad tried again.

"Do you know anything about America?" Attar cut Shahzad off again. "The country's been in civil war since they declared their second revolution four years ago. Over one hundred million have been executed for capitalist crimes. And they also have no allies, nor any trade partners. If Sudamerica doesn't conquer them, the Canadians probably will."

"So, what, there is no hope? We're just

fucked?" Shahzad asked. "I won't accept that."

"This cave is our only option," Attar stated. "It's a completely alien biology. As far as we can tell it's not even a biosphere, it's all the same life-form. They might have once been different creatures, but that would have been billions of years ago when this cave was still connected to the surface. Since then they've evolved into one immense creature. The plasma pool, which we call Mehr after the ancient Persian god of light, turns the geothermal heat into light, mostly UV and blue. The light is absorbed by the Ahrimans, those leafy things, which dissolve minerals from the rocks, and themselves emit red and infrared light. When they die they fall into the Mehr, where they're eaten by the Tir, those things swimming around in the Mehr, and some of them are huge."

"Wait," Shahzad interrupted. "I don't understand what any of this has to do with freeing our people."

"In the past few decades we've filed hundreds of patents back in Bogota, and in Brussels, Singapore, Ottawa, and Baghdad. We've got dozens of shell companies back on Earth, and have been buying stock in Nuevo Tártaro SA. In a decade or two, we will have controlling interest, and then we can make sweeping changes. Until then we need to keep things stable."n

"Isn't a peaceful transition better than a violent one?" At-tar asked after a few seconds of silence. "Especially when you know that no one will fight because they're all poisoned?"

Shahzad thought about what At-tar was really asking. "So you need me to keep flying freight at Avianca?"

"For a while," Attar answered. "We can liquidate our holdings in Materfer VacTube, and buy a controlling interest in Avianca Marso, it's a much smaller company. Then in a few months move you into a lower management level, and then in a year or two an upper management level."

"You want me to be a corporate?" Shahzad stated in disgust.

"We want you to hire Persians," Attar stated. "Sooner or later we'll have controlling interest in Nuevo-Tártaro S.A. and when we do, we need Persians in upper management levels that can take over from the Sudamericans. We're working on a treatment for the Toxoplasma, and we're not the only ones. So, are you willing to work with us?"

# When Life Doesn't Matter

"That woman's watching me again," Mere Araullo observed as she helped Aeron back to his feet. "Like I'd fuck her!"

"I'm not programmed to understand human sexuality," Aeron stated taking its position.

"How long have you been around?" Mere asked rhetorically, taking her position across the circle from Aeron. "You've never been curious about human sexuality?"

"I've been operational for 35.66 martian years. I was not programmed to be curious about human sexuality, nor do I have an understanding of biochemistry," Aeron answered. The two moved towards each other and met in the middle of the circle, grappling each other's necks, and pushing each other towards the edge of the circle. Mere had set Aeron to be slightly stronger than she was and knew she couldn't out-muscle the sparring android. As the android increased its force against her she suddenly fell back, grabbing the android's arm and pulling it towards her, and then kicking it over her. Aeron landed on its back near the edge of the circle and flipped over onto its front, but Mere was on its back with her arms wrapped around its neck before it got to its feet. It tapped out as soon as its sensors registered that it would have passed out if it were human, and they both got back to their feet.

She glanced in the direction of the woman, and saw she was talking to an old man, and neither was looking in her direction. The woman was the same one that had been watching her the day before, she was sure of it. She decided to take a break, and walked towards the dojo's juice bar, passing within earshot of the woman and the old man she was talking too.

"She's just a grappler," the old man was saying. "Madaleno will knock her out in under a minute, she shouldn't be getting in the cage with him."

Mere stopped mid-step, and turned to confront them, but saw they weren't even looking her way. She was scheduled to fight Madaleno Pita in a few days, so they had to be talking about her. Who did they think they were? She realized it didn't matter, and turn back towards the juice bar. It was just a matter of time before everyone knew her name.

Madaleno was her first fight in the Calabar Fighting League. Although the league itself was less than a month old, fighters and gamblers had been streaming into the Calabar Corporate Mining Zone since the Arean Senate shut down the Multan Fighting League, along with the entire Multan Corporate Mining Zone. The Calabar CMZ had reached out to Earth to prevent the Senate from shutting them down too, and the Guinea Federation had officially opened negotiations with the Arean Confederacy, becoming the second Earth government to recognize the breakaway Martian government. The American revolutionary government had been the first a few weeks earlier, and the two governments had quickly launched synchronized attacks against Sudamerican territories on Earth and Mars.

Calabar had been a Nigerian Mining Colony before the Mars Treaty had divided the planet into Colonial Zones, and the newly created Calabar CMZ found itself under Sudamerican jurisdiction. Under the treaty, existing Corporate Mining Zones continued to be the property of the corporations that built them, and so Calabar continued to pay tax back to Nigeria, and then the Guinean Federation. Under the treaty, Sudamerica got to restrict and inspect Calabar's imports from Earth. At first, it had simply been to prevent the import of weapons, but as the decades passed, legislation was slowly passed that restricted the import of virtually everything that wasn't from Sudamerica.

During the century and a half of neutrality, Nigeria, and later the Guinean Federation, had built one of the largest fleets of inter-planetary freighters. Dozens of interplanetary shipping companies flew the Guinean flag, many running ships that had been sold for scrap after the so-called Mars Crash, when the US, UK, and Russia had all been forced to abandon their Martian colonies during the revolution on the red planet. The Guineans had even maintained covert trade with the Areans and Pallasians after the revolutions that had ripped those governments from Earth control. Now after more than a century of peace, Guinea was going to war.

In the previous few decades, Sudamerica had occupied Southern Africa and Madagascar, and had forcibly relocated hundreds of thousands, possibly millions, to forced labor camps on Mars. Southern Africa was being repopulated by Sudamericans, and the Guineans had had enough, they just needed an ally. Breaking their neutrality, and opening official diplomatic channels with the Americans, Areans, and Pallasians would gain them three allies, two already at war with the Sudamericans. They really didn't care about the Calabar CMZ, but it was as good a reason as any to open diplomatic channels.

The people that flooded into Calabar didn't care why the Guineans and the Areans had opened diplomatic relations, the fact that they had, meant the Senate was unlikely to shut down Calabar CMZ the way they'd shut down Multan CMZ. Mere Araullo had come from Dakbayan sa Dabaw, an old corporate-era mining colony in the Noctis Labyrinthus, the Labyrinth of Night. The corporation running Dakbayan sa Dabaw had gone bankrupt decades earlier, and the Dakbayan sa Dabaw CMZ had been dissolved by the government of the Philippines, ceding the region to the Sudamericans. Under Sudamerican rule, the remote colony had been all but abandoned, and when the eco-revolution had spread across the face of Mars the people of Dakbayan sa Dabaw had risen in revolt.

Mere had been a child then, and the colony

so remote and irrelevant that the Sudamericans hadn't even bothered to send any troops to re-occupy it. The people of labyrinthine colonies had virtually no weapons and had spent the revolution practicing hand to hand combat, preparing for the day the Sudamericans came into the labyrinth. Many left the labyrinth, volunteering to fight for the revolutionary army, but those that remained developed a form of martial arts they believed superior to any other in the history of humanity, Labyrinthine Jujitsu.

In the labyrinth, there was a fighting league that had not been shut down by the Confederate Senate, the Labyrinthine Jujitsu League. The fighters weren't paid, so the league wasn't affected by the ban on professional sports. Few outside of the labyrinth even knew it existed, it wasn't stream-casted outside of the labyrinth, and no one bothered betting on it. The LJL didn't have a champion, just fighters and stats, but if it had have had a champion, it would have been Mere. She had won her last 66 matches. She had been headed to Multan to fight in the Multan Fighting Club, but then the Senate had shut it down, and everyone headed for Calabar, also known as New Canaan.

The Calabar Fighting Club had appeared within days of the Senate shutting down the Multan FC, with many of the same fighters. It hadn't taken Mere long to line up a fight. She'd been pared off with Madaleno Pita, a washed-up fighter from the Multan FC. He was a boxer who had to be almost 40 earth years old. A former US soldier that had been abandoned on Mars as the corporate government disintegrated back on Earth during the revolution. He didn't stand a chance. As soon as Mere got his back, the fight would be over. She knew it would take a few fights before anyone would notice her, but after that, they'd pair her up with real fighters and she'd show the worlds what a Labyrinthine Jujitsu master could do.

The night of the fight Mere was feeling good, she couldn't wait to get her pro-fighting career started. Her fight was one of the early preliminary matches, it wouldn't even get stream-cast. This was only Calabar FC's third stream-cast, but already there were over twenty fights scheduled. The top ten fights would be stream-cast so gamblers from across the Confederacy could illegally bet on them.

The venue was smaller than Mere had expected, you couldn't tell from the stream-cast how big, or in this case small, the venue was, as all the cameras showed was the cage. The cage was set up in a converted indoor soccer arena, in a basement level of the New Canaan Hotel. Only around 200 spectators could crowd in around the cage, but the place was packed.

Mere walked to the cage in a ceremonial gi and then handed it to Aeron before getting into the cage. Aeron and Daniel Shruti were both at the cage gate that night. Aeron as her trainer, and Daniel as her manager. Daniel was the one that had found her fighting in the labyrinth and convinced her to join the MFC. He had been traveling the Confederacy scouting talent when he'd found out about the LJL, and traveled out to the middle of nowhere to see if there was anyone there who could fight. He'd found Mere when she was still at 62 consecutive wins, by 66 he'd convinced her to head to Multan and make some credit.

Mere had met Aeron at a dojo, a decades-old sparring android who seemed to have no purpose other than fight with humans he was programmed not to kill. There were newer models around, and Mere had fought with several before deciding she preferred Aeron. She didn't know exactly why, but his fighting style was harder to predict. The newer models all fought well, but their programming always followed a predictable set of movements. Aeron was harder to predict, sometimes doing what one least expected, even if it wasn't a good idea. She didn't know if it was bad programming or damaged processors, but it made the fights better.

Across the cage, Madaleno was waiting. He was at least double her size. Like many Mars-born, Mere had been malnourished as a child and hadn't grown very large. Madaleno was from Earth and apparently had no problem getting food as a child. It didn't matter to Mere, as soon as she had his back the fight would be over. The cage locked behind her, the red lights came on, and Madaleno moved in.

Mere could see he was an experienced fighter, but not a good one. He advanced without concern for whatever was waiting to meet him, with his fists up in front of his face like something from an ancient movie. He stabbed his left at Mere's face, and she dodged it, and then ducked under the right that followed, rolling across the cage and coming back to her feet behind him. He turned too fast for her to attack his legs, and jabbed another left at her. This one made contact with Mere's shoulder as she tried to dodge it, and sent her spinning across the cage. It didn't really hurt, just jolted her, and knock her from her feet. Madaleno may only know how to hit, but there was a lot of power in his arms.

Mere was back up on her feet before Madaleno could cross the cage, and began circling him, looking for a way to get near his legs, she needed to get him off his feet. He wasn't circling, and advanced right for her, she ducked his fists again and rolled across the cage, this time far enough that he couldn't make contact as he swung wildly for where he thought she would be. Outside the cage, the crowd started to boo.

He advanced again, and this time she faked a roll under his right again, but instead dropped, and as he turned towards where he thought she was going, Mere slammed an open palm behind his left knee. Mada Leno buckled but didn't fall, as most of his weight had been in his right leg as he was turning, and now, it was all in his right leg. Mere dived shoulder first into his right knee with all her strength, and the big man came down behind her. She was on her feet immediately and turned to see Mada Leno on his back, arms spread at his sides. The crowd outside the cage was cheering.

She waited for him to roll over to his chest, but he didn't, he backed up to the cage wall, and pulled himself back to his feet, eyes on her the entire time. The crowd started to boo again, they wanted to see blood. He knew she was trying to get at his back, and she knew she was in trouble. If he wasn't going to expose his back, she would have to get him to the ground and wrestle him into a submission, which wasn't going to be easy given his size advantage. He advanced towards her again, this time slower and more calculating.

Again he shot a right-left combo, and again she ducked and rolled to the right, he turned and advanced, and then he shot a left fist at her, but swung low with the following right, and it connected. His fist lifted her off her feet and sent her stumbling back towards the cage wall. She was winded, and barely had time to inhale a lung full of air before his left fist hit her in the face, knocking her head back into the cage wall. For a second she saw stars, and then Madaleno's right fist moving towards her through those stars. She dropped straight down, and Madaleno's fist impacted the cage wall above her. He recoiled in pain, instinctively jumping back and turning, and Mere dove for his knees again, this time tackling both of them and pulling him back to the ground.

Again he landed on his back, but this time Mere was still on his legs, using all her strength to bend the right knee in a direction it didn't want to go, and Mada Leno rolled over. She moved towards his back, but he jumped back to his feet before she could get him in a choke hold. As he rose, she was still on his back, her legs wrapped around his body. As she tried to get her arms around his neck, he fell backward, his full weight slamming into her as they hit the cage floor. She was stunned for a second, and he wriggled free from her legs. She looked up and saw him moving away from her to the other side of the cage, and then turn back towards her.

She rolled back up to her feet. He had his left up in front of his face again, the right hung low, dripping blood as one of the bones had broken, and ripped through the skin. He advanced again. His stabbed at her again with his left but didn't follow with his right. She dodged his first two lefts, and then tried to duck and roll, and met his knee, slammed right up into her face. Her head was knocked back, and the last thing she saw was his left fist streaking down at her face.

She woke up about twenty minutes later and realized she was in the locker room. Daniel was there pacing and turned viciously towards Mere as she came to. "You dumb labyrinthine hick!"

he yelled as she rolled up into a sitting position. "You won 66 jujitsu matches in a row, but can't beat a boxer with a bust hand? Madaleno was the bottom of the barrel, everyone beats him, or they don't get to fight again! You might as well just head back to the labyrinth, or get a job sucking cock! Maybe you can do that right! You'll never fight in this town again!"

Mere wasn't someone who got angry quickly, but that night she lost it and hit Daniel square in the nose with an open fist. He stumbled backward, as blood started to gush from his broken nose. "I'll have you arrested!" he shouted turning towards the door.

"Not in New Canaan," someone said from the doorway. The woman that had been watching her at the dojo stepped through the doorway, followed by the old man that had predicted Madaleno would beat her in under a minute. "The corporate police won't investigate an assault, and you had that coming. I was just about to do it myself. Now fuck off."

Daniel stopped cold when they entered, whoever they were he didn't want to tangle with them. He glanced back at Mere with hate in his eyes, and then stormed out.

"You remember your name?" The woman asked after Daniel had left.

"Yeah," Mere answered. "He hit me hard, but not that hard."

"You were out twenty minutes," the man

said. "Been knocked out before?"

"No," Mere answered, wondering who these people were.

"Madaleno has," the man continued. "Dozens of times, can't even spell his own name any-more."

"Well, too bad it wasn't a spelling bee then," Mere said getting to her feet. Her things were in a locker, and so she crossed the room to let the locker scan her DNA, and then opened it.

"You know that old android you've been grappling with has other programs," the woman stated as Mere pulled her bag from the locker and placed in on a chair. "Boxing for example, or karate."

"I prefer jujitsu," Mere answered pulling her slate-gray jumpsuit from the bag.

"And you're good at it," the woman stated. "But you won't win a fight in any Pro FC with just jujitsu. You couldn't even beat Madaleno Pita."

"Do you have a point?" Mere asked turning to the woman. "Or did you come down here for the same reason as Daniel?"

"Well, I am not here to suggest you switch ca-reers," the woman said. "You lasted longer against Madaleno than we thought you would. You might make a good fighter, if you learn to fight."

"If I learn to fight?" Mere stammered in disbelief. "I'm arguably the best fighter in the labyrinth!"

"You might be the best grappler from the labyrinth, but you're not in the labyrinth anymore, and up here there's a different set of rules," the woman replied.

"I thought there were no rules," Mere replied sarcastically, annoyed by the woman pestering her as she got dressed.

"Those are the rules," the woman responded. "I'm surprised Daniel didn't tell you to practice different fighting styles when he bought you that android."

"I hired the android. I think it belongs to the dojo," Mere replied. "Anyway, who are you? And why is it any of your business?"

"I'm Tamiko Uesugi," the woman replied. "I'm a fighter manager, and, well, the only fighter manager that matters. Get better at dealing with strikers and I'll consider managing you. But get better quick, I'm not a patient person."

The woman turned to leave, and the man stepped forward handing Mere a credit card. "Daniel has a reputation for not paying his fighters when they lose. I took the liberty of collecting your pay for you."

"They gave you my payment?" Mere asked in disbelief.

"I own the Calabar FC," the man stated and

then turned and left without another word.

Mere finished changing in silence, interrupted by another fighter and his manager loudly entering the locker room to prepare for one of the fights. It was early in the evening, and most of the best fights hadn't started yet. She'd lost one of the opening fights, one that wasn't even stream-cast, to a fighter known for losing. She was in a dark mood as she picked up her bag and walked out of the locker room.

Aeron was standing in the passageway waiting for her, she remembered why as soon as she saw it, and reached into her pocket for the credit card and her com. She tapped the card on her com, and then removed 200 of the Calabar Naira she'd been paid.

"I'm sorry Aeron," Mere said. "I only got paid 250, and all I can give you is 50."

"That's most generous," Aeron said taking the card. "Hopefully next time you'll win."

It turned and left without saying anything else. 'Generous' it'd said, she wondered if it was being sarcastic. Could it be sarcastic? With that mono-tone voice who would know? 50 Naira for a whole week of sparring. It wasn't generous. If it wasn't at the dojo 25/7, it'd be homeless making only 50 Naira a week. Of course, she'd only cleared 200. She wandered the under-city depressed and angry, she was supposed to be basking in the glow of her first professional victory. She should have been paid 5 times what she was. She should be at a bar with someone dancing on her table. She decided to get something to eat.

She looked around at the marketplace she was wandering through, the smell suddenly assaulting her as she became aware of her surroundings. Cal-a-bar-ian food was so much more complex than the food in the labyrinth. Until she was thirteen she had thought there were only five basic food groups, rice, soy, wheat, lemon, and white-fish. Then she found out that there were other foods in other settlements. Cal-a-bar had more than she'd ever seen, but it was all boiled in oil, and greasier than she liked. The smells of the fried plantains caught her attention and she decided to head up to the Filipino restaurant she'd found a few days earlier. It was the same basic food but cooked in a style more like the cooking in Dakbayan sa Dabaw.

The Filipino restaurant was one of several in the Imperial-Asia Mall, the largest shopping center in Calabar. It had been built by the Singapore Conglomerate, to sell Asian made goods in the Arean Confederacy. Like the Guinean Federation, the Singapore Conglomerate had followed a policy of official neutrality for more than a century, while slowly buying up and incorporating most of the Asia-Pacific region. In the aftermath of the war, Calabar had been eager for any trade, and by building the mall within a CMZ, the Singapore Conglomerate could bypass both the Confederate import regulations and the Canadian-led blockade of the

Confederacy.

The elevator up to the mall was packed with people, but the entire under-city was packed, so she hardly noticed the difference. When the elevator opened they lined up for the credit check at the gates, and again someone was trying to get into the mall without any credit. The security guards dragged the woman back to the elevator and through her back into it. Each time Mere had been up to the mall it had been the same, someone trying to get into the mall without any credit. She wondered if it was the same person. Her credit check went through, and she entered the mall.

Stepping into the mall was like entering another world, and she imagined it must be what Earth was like. The ceilings were high, higher than anyone could reach. The stores lining the corridors were filled with colorful clothes from across the Asia Pacific region, a cacophony of Malay, Javanese, Thai, Filipino, Cambodian, Viet, Australian, Papuan, Polynesian, Tamil, Bengali, Marathi, and Gujarati clothing styles. In the labyrinth, everyone dressed basically the same, although she had never noticed it until coming to Calabar.

She was still wearing her gray labyrinthine jumpsuit. She had planned to buy something colorful after defeating Madaleno, but didn't have the credit for that now. She headed for the elevator that would carry her up to the top level of the mall where the restaurants were all located under a blue-alon dome. The mall was twenty-seven stories high, and she had seen less than half of it. She had wandered through the lower levels, seeing floor after floor of shops selling every kind of tech imaginable, and furniture made from various plastics, metals, and bamboo. The upper levels were restricted to people passing higher credit checks, where vehicles and weapons were sold. There was also a hotel in the upper level, although Mere's credit rating wasn't high enough to even get her into an elevator that would stop there.

The elevator opened under the blue-alon dome, and she wandered out to one of the vendors selling fruit-flavored soy-shakes. She had already tried several of the most popular fruit flavors, banana, strawberry, chocolate, and bubblegum. She didn't even know there were fruits other than lemons until she was fifteen, now she was standing at a kiosk that sold soy-shakes in more than 1000 different fruit flavors. She ordered the next most popular fruit flavor, mint-julep, and was handed a green shake by the android behind the kiosk.

She wandered towards the windows looking out over the city of Calabar. The blue-alon windows made the sky outside look blueish-brown, the way she assumed the sky on Earth looked. At twenty-seven stories high the Imperial-Asia Mall dwarfed every other building in Calabar. Far below the New Canaan Hotel, the second tallest building in Calabar rose to a measly nine stories. From the top of the mall, Calabar seemed like not much more than a village of a few dozen small buildings, surrounded by distant crater walls. But like all Martian settlements, most of the activity was in the undercity.

She finished the mint-julep soy-shake and headed towards the Vanilla-Manila Restaurant. It was one of the open restaurants where there wasn't someone at the door demanding to know if you had a reservation. She had never heard of anything like that in the labyrinth. She also wasn't used to having security guards standing around watching everything. An AI monitoring everything via cameras made sense, but at this mall, there were guards everywhere, every shop, every restaurant, and every hallway. She hadn't seen any acts of violence or anything that warranted the hundreds of security guards this mall employed.

She sat at one of the vacant tables and the menu display appeared with a variety of languages, she picked Cebuano and ordered the fried plantains and lemon-chicken. She had never had anything like plantains before leaving the labyrinth, but the lemon-chicken was similar to the lemon-fish back home. An android brought the order to the table a few minutes after she paid for it, and she savored it, trying to decide what she would do next. That woman, Tamiko, and that old man that said he owned the Calabar FC were right, even Daniel was right. She couldn't even beat a striker with a broken hand. What would the people back in the labyrinth think? At least it wasn't stream-cast.

She could just quit. It would be embarrassing to return to the labyrinth after being beat by a guy that was paid to lose fights, but it would be more embarrassing if she lost a few more fights before giving up. Maybe she could track down some of the seeds those fruit drinks were made from. No one in the labyrinth had ever tasted anything like banana or bubblegum. But they probably weren't growing the fruit in Calabar, just importing the flavoring from Earth. She could still check the mall, if anyone in Calabar was selling those seeds, they'd have to have a shop in the mall.

She didn't want to go back to the labyrinth like this. She decided to keep training. She knew if she could just learn to take her opponents to the grounds, she could win every fight. Tamiko was right, she shouldn't have been grappling with Aeron. She knew how to grapple. She needed to learn other ways of fighting. She finished her plantains and chicken and headed back down to the under-city. The hotel that she and Daniel had been staying in was a dive, in a run-down area of a converted mineshaft. Daniel was gone. The concierge interface showed he'd left without paying for his room, and it had been added to her invoice. She went to her room and passed out.

The next day she found Aeron at the dojo again. "Willing to keep working with me?" she asked, not sure if she should be embarrassed by the small payment she gave it the day before. What expenses did an android have?

"Of course," Aeron answered. "But why are you here? I expected you would have gone to Tamiko Uesugi's dojo. Most of the best fighters in the Calabar FC train there."

"Well, I'm here," Mere stated. "You were cage-side last night, why'd I lose?"

"Madaleno Pita knocked you out," Aeron answered.

"I know that," Mere replied. "But how did the fight get there? Why wasn't I able to beat him?"

"Your fighting styles were mismatched," Aeron replied. "If it was a jujitsu match I believe you would have won. However, in a boxing match, he weighed almost twice your weight. And you don't seem to know much about boxing."

"Could you train me?" Mere asked. "As a striker I mean."

"Of course, it's what I'm programmed for," Aeron answered.

They spent the next few days practicing various take-down methods from other martial arts disciplines, and kickboxing, which Aeron had recommended as Mere had neither the reach nor the power to do any real damage with her fists. She put her name in for another fight the following CFC stream-cast, which was the following Saturday. She'd rather have practiced longer, but she didn't have the credit to live in Calabar without a job, and she wasn't registered with the Calabar Corporate Authority to work in the CMZ. Even if she lost the fight, she'd have some more credit coming her way, but she didn't plan to lose.

A couple of days before the fight, Aeron announced in the middle of their sparring session, "They've just announced the roster for the next fight. You'll be fighting Kemal Ataahua."

Like all androids, Aeron was connected to the net constantly. In Calabar that meant the local net, which included caches of the Confederate net, and colonial Martian networks. The Calabar net also received data-burst updates from Guinea but had access to none of the VR environments found in the Earth networks. Few Mars-born ever got 'upgraded,' as the Earth-born called it, the implants that allowed humans constant net-access like androids.

Mere paused and stepped back from Aeron. "What can you tell me about him?"

"He was born in Java Metro, 17.74 Mars years ago," Aeron began. "His parents were-"

"No. Stop. What can you tell me about his fighting style?" Mere corrected her question.

"He's a striker," Aeron answered. "No specific fighting style, or martial arts discipline. His style has been described as 'brawling.'"

"What's his record like?" Mere asked, and then changed her query. "No wait cancel. How often does he win?"

"Rarely," Aeron answered. "He's lost his last 54 fights."

"Do you have access to his most recent fights?" Mere asked.

"They are a matter of public record," Aeron answered.

"Could you analyze them and tell me any potential weaknesses?" Mere asked.

"Of course," Aeron answered. "Analyzing his last 54 fights will take approximately 2 minutes. Please standby."

Mere took the two-minute interlude as an opportunity to return to the power squats she'd been practicing for the past few days. She had always been fit, but added a few hundred squats to her regular workout, which were making her legs burn. It was the last day she was planning to do the extra squats, as she needed her legs to recover before the fight.

"He favors his left," Aeron stated after a couple of minutes. "Also he moves slowly around the cage, if you're fast like you were with Madaleno Pita, you should remain out of his reach."

Kemal was a giant, even bigger than Madaleno. This time Mere only had Aeron at the cage door, she hadn't heard anything from

Daniel since she'd lost the first fight.

Kemal didn't advance directly the way Madaleno had, instead he slowly circled towards her. His fists weren't up in front of his face like Madaleno's had been, and instead dangled low at his side as if he was daring Mere to hit him. As they got close, he suddenly swung his right at her, which she quickly dodged. She returned with a kick to his mid-section, which was like kicking a brick wall. It didn't seem to hurt the big man but did surprise him. He stepped back and started circling again.

As he closed the gap between them, his fists rose up in front of his torso, and he jabbed his right at Mere, then his left. She dodged the right, and then rolled under the left, springing to her feet right behind him, and kicking savagely at his right knee. The knee buckled, but he didn't fall, instead he swung wildly in her direction, but she was gone, rolling to the far side of the cage.

Kemal advanced again, slowly circling, and Mere thought she saw a slight limp. Again he came in swinging, and again she ducked and rolled and kicked at his right leg, and this time he went down to one knee, and Mere wrapped her arms around his neck. He tried to jump back to his feet, but didn't make it, and slumped back down to his knee. Then as Mere released him, he toppled forward face-first into the cage floor. He woke up a few seconds later, but the fight was over.

Mere felt good leaving the fight that night, better than if she had just beat Madaleno in her first fight. She collected her payment, and passed on 500 Naira to Aeron, which was generous, but made her feel good even though Aeron wouldn't feel anything. She headed back down to the dojo she'd been working out at and showered. The hotel she'd staying at didn't have a shower.

She changed and headed back up to the Imperial-Asia. She stopped on the second floor to buy a new piece of clothing at a store selling Polynesian style clothes. The store had caught her attention the first time she'd been in the mall, as the walls and ceiling had a projection of a Polynesian city on them, and the air temperature was set to blow cool air through the store.

Around the edges of the store was a projection of the ocean, held at bay by alon windows. Strange, brightly colored fish were swimming by outside. None looked like the white-fish they raised in aquaculture tanks back home. She wondered if any were the chicken fish, but there was no one to ask. The store's staff were all androids, and the other shoppers from Calabar would have no way of knowing what a chicken fish looked like. In the distance beyond the fish were other buildings, all covered in alon windows. A city on a Polynesian atoll, just below the surface of the ocean. In some ways it felt familiar, the closed in, safe, feeling. In other ways it was alien and terrifying, all those strange looking things swimming around, and none could talk.

The first time she'd been in the mall, the Polynesian store had drawn her in, with its strange mesmerizing walls. She decided then that she'd buy a Polynesian suit as soon as she won her first fight, and now she was there to pick one out. The Polynesian suits all had a similar utilitarian design to the labyrinthine jumpsuits, but were made in bright colorful patterns. She picked out a color pattern she liked, paid, and then changed into the new clothes, and headed up to the restaurant level.

She was eating the lemon-chicken and fried plantains again when Tamiko Uesugi sat down across from her.

"Congratulations," Tamiko said bringing up the menu on the table's display. "Usually fighters celebrate their first win at a strip club. What's good here?"

"The lemon-chicken is good," Mere answered. "Shouldn't you be at the fight?"

"You were the opening fight," Tamiko replied. "It'll be at least an hour before the stream-cast fights begin. None of my fighters fight in the opening bouts."

Tamiko selected the lemon-chicken and a Caesar salad and paid, before turning back to Mere and continuing. "You took Kamel down in less than three minutes. That was impressive."

"He's a nobody that everyone beats," Mere

dismissed Tamiko's compliment.

"Sure, he doesn't win, but he doesn't fall easily either," Tamiko stated. "No one has beaten him in under ten minutes in over two years. Three minutes is impressive. Of course, if he'd actually hit you, it might have ended like the Madaleno match."

"The only thing better than being able to take a punch is not having to," Mere quoted something her trainer had drummed into her when she was young.

"I guess that's true, but sooner or later you'll be in the cage with someone as fast as you," Tamiko said. "Keep working on the kick-boxing. I think Yousef's going to offer you a fight against Indah Joncker next weekend. She's fast too. She's a master of Krebmiga, you know it?"

"No, but I'll see what Aeron can tell me about it," Mere replied. "Who's Yousef?"

"Yousaf Dulai is the owner of Calabar FC, you met him last week. If I can give you some advice, put it a request to fight Roger Golyubev instead," Tamiko suggested. "He's big and dumb, like the last two fighters you faced."

"Don't like watching women fight?" Mere asked, half-jokingly.

"No one does," Tamiko answered as her food arrived at the table. "Unless someone's ear gets ripped off or something, no one will ever see the fight. But a big Earth-born, getting beat by a little Mars-born, that, people will download. You need to get people to recognize you before your fights will be stream-cast. Right now you're just an unknown fighter that no one is betting on."

"How do I request a fight with Roger Golyubev?" Mere asked. "I didn't know I could request an opponent."

"Aeron can file the request," Tamiko answered. "Has Aeron suggested you switch dojos yet?"

"He mentioned that, after the loss last week," Mere answered.

"Good," Tamiko smiled. "You should come by my dojo. It's the biggest in Calabar."

"It's too expensive," Mere answered.

"Not if you're winning," Tamiko responded. "Besides Aeron can't do his job if you keep monopolizing its time."

"Aeron's job is training fighters," Mere replied.

"No, its job is spotting new talent," Tamiko stated. "I own it. I have sparring androids at every dojo in Calabar."

"Aeron is yours?" Mere repeated in surprise. "Is that why it's different from the rest? Did you program it like that?"

"Like what?" Tamiko asked.

"It fights differently from the newer

models," Mere answered. "It's less predictable."

"It's decades old," Tamiko stated. "It probably just picked up some techniques from the fighters it's sparred with. They can learn new things you know."

"I guess that's it," Mere conceded. "So why did you ask if Daniel bought it for me? When we first met."

"I wanted to see if you'd lie about owning it or not," Tamiko stated. "It sent me a probable victory projection of 68% about an hour before the fight tonight."

"68%?" Mere repeated back the number. "Not exactly a great endorsement. One in three chance of losing."

"It was a big improvement from your fight against Madaleno," Tamiko stated. "It only estimated a 17% chance of defeating him."

"Aeron knew I was going to lose to Madaleno?" Mere exclaimed.

"It didn't know you'd lose. They can't really predict human behavior. But it did find it likely you'd lose," Tamiko explained. "It reported you were a master grappler, with no other training."

"I'm surprised you even watched the match if you thought I'd lose," Tamiko stated, as an android walked over and took away her empty tray.

"They don't generally report anyone as being

a master at anything," Tamiko replied. "I wanted to see what that was about. And in all fairness, you almost had Madaleno at one point, even without knowing anything but grappling."

A week later Mere was stepping into the cage for the third time with an opponent around twice her size, and she briefly wondered if it wasn't a mistake to not fight Indah Joncker. They were about the same size, and she could have grappled her into submission. Instead, she was going to have another hulking Earth-born trying to slam his fist into her face. She had spent the week training with Aeron at the dojo, continuing to build her leg strength and kickboxing technique. Aeron had advised that Roger Golyubev was a fast-moving striker, who got distracted easily by the crowds.

Roger, as the odds-on favorite to win, was already in the cage when Mere arrived, and as the cage locked behind her, he began jumping up and down. Then, when the light turned red he began skipping around the cage, as she circled the other direction, trying to figure out what he was doing. Suddenly he stopped and turned to the crowd, waving both his arms over his head, as if he had already won, and they cheered. He stood there for almost a minute waiving to the crowd and ignoring Mere, as if daring her to attack him from the back. Mere knew he couldn't actually be that stupid, and waited for him to give up whatever he was doing and start the fight.

After about a minute of Roger's showmanship, the crowd started to boo, and Roger turned back towards Mere. He smiled at her and then lunged at her right leg. He wasn't even trying to strike her, just trying to grab her right leg. Mere leaped to the left and rolled away from him. She wasn't sure if he was fighting her or if this was still part of his show for the crowd. She came to her feet, and he was already rushing at her, his hands up. He jabbed at her head as soon as he was within range, and she ducked his fist and kicked him in the ribs.

He jumped back, and was hopping from one foot to the other like someone in an ancient boxing movie, and then bounced back towards her, and stabbed at her head with his right, followed with a left uppercut. She dodged the right, but caught the left, and went flying into the cage wall. She blacked out, and then saw Roger jumping around on the other side of the cage as the crowd cheered.

She'd lost.

She got to her feet and realized the red light was still on.

She hadn't lost, Roger was too distracted by the crowd to notice he'd knocked her out.

It couldn't have been more than a second or two, or the judges would have called the fight.

The crowd started cheering louder as she got back to her feet, and Roger turned back towards her. He went back to hopping from foot to foot, with his fists in front of his face like a cartoon character, and then hopped towards her, but stopped just out of reach, and continued hopping from foot to foot, jabbing at the air between them. He was waiting for Mere to make a move, and Mere wondered why Tamiko had suggested she fight this clown. The only thing more humiliating than being in the cage with him, would be losing to him.

She didn't want to attack the bigger man, with his unpredictable fighting style, and so decided to play into his showmanship. She went into a martial arts pose she'd seen in a video once, and motioned with one hand for him to come to her. The crowd cheered again, and Roger stopped his bouncing and looked around at the crowd, stamped his foot, and then rushed at Mere. She expected him to rush her, and met his big body with another kick to the ribs, at the same spot as the first, then rolled away as he swung wildly.

As she came back to her feet, he was almost on her again and stabbed a right at her face. As she ducked under the right, she kicked again at his ribs, hitting the same spot, and felt something crack. He stepped back. He wasn't bouncing anymore. He brought his fists up low, covering his chest, and move back towards her. He jabbed with his left and she dodged it, then again with his left and dodged it. She was waiting for him to use his right, and expose his ribs, but it became clear he didn't intend to. As he jabbed a third time with his left, she dodged and rolled under his right arm, then was on her feet as he turned, and met his ribs with her foot. This time she heard it, a snapping sound, and he winced.

She stepped back, waiting to see if he would advance again. He inhaled, she'd winded him. Then he started coughing, and blood spattered from his mouth. The broken rib must have punctured a lung. The cage lights switched from red to green, the fight was over. The judges had called it in her favor, and a medic rushed in to take care of Roger.

Mere felt bad as she changed. She didn't feel like a winner. She felt like a cheater. She hadn't expected the big man's ribs to snap so easily. She didn't want him to die. Even the crowd had become silent when Roger had started to cough blood. There hadn't been a death in the Calabar FC yet, and she didn't want to be the first to kill an opponent. The Calabar FC didn't want anyone dying in the cage. It was widely believed that the Arean Senate had shut down the Multan FC because of the number of people dying in the cage. She wondered what the repercussions would be if Roger died from his injuries. Aeron had collected her payment, and handed it to her as she stepped out of the locker room. He saw her face and predicted she was feeling bad about Roger' injuries.

"It was logical to attack your opponents weak-point." Aeron offered. "You could not have predicted his rib would break. There was only a 12.6% chance of that happening. I suspect he is calcium deficient."

"Thanks, Aeron," Mere stated deducting 2000 naira and handing the other 500 back to Aeron. "But that doesn't actually help. Will you notify me if he dies."

"He isn't going to die from the injuries you inflicted," Aeron stated. "The Calabar FC has already released a medical report showing he is stable. His damaged lung has been removed and is being repaired in a cloning tank. He won't be able to fight for a few weeks, but he will recover."

"Already?" Mere asked. "That was quick."

"The Calabar Medical Corporation is first class," Aeron stated. "It is headquartered in Lagos, and Guinea does have the second most advanced medical research corporations in the system, after the Singapore Conglomerate of course."

"Thanks," Mere stated, feeling only slightly better, and then turned back to Aeron asking, "What did you estimate the odds of me winning at tonight?"

"82.9%" Aeron answered.

"And only 12% of me breaking Roger's ribs?" she asked.

"12.6%" the android replied. "I am curious to read the fight report. I suspect Roger is suffering from a calcium deficiency."

"You mentioned that," Mere stated.

"I still suspect it," Aeron replied. "The fight report will be more interesting than most."

Mere returned to the dojo to shower again, and then headed back up to Imperial-Asia. She didn't feel like buying anything this week and headed straight up to the restaurant level. She ordered the most popular flavor of soy shake that she hadn't tried before, and was handed a black drink. She walked over to the windows and sat down looking out at Calabar. She had won the fight, but she could have killed Roger. She hadn't come to Calabar to become a killer.

She sucked her first taste of the licorice-flavored shake through straw, and almost spit it out. The flavor was very different from the others she'd tried. She swallowed what she had in her mouth and decided to throw the rest away, and then headed back to the Vanilla-Manila Restaurant and ordered the Lemon-Chicken with a Caesar salad.

"You're getting better with your feet," Tamiko said as she sat down across from Mere. Mere was halfway done her meal, and Tamiko didn't bother ordering anything.

"Am I?" Mere replied. "I could have killed him."

"But you didn't," Tamiko stated. "And almost killing Roger will get your fight added to the download for those that aren't streaming live. You'll make twice as much, and your next fight will be stream-cast."

"So, what? I made it?" Mere asked.

"I wouldn't go that far," Tamiko answered, "but you're on your way. It's time for you to move out of that moldy under-city hotel. Work for me and I'll get you a suite at the New Canaan."

"You can't get me into the Imperial-Asia?" Mere asked.

"I could, but I won't," Tamiko answered. "This is no place for a fighter. There isn't even a dojo in this mall."

"How much will it cost? Your dojo membership, the room at the New Canaan, everything?"

"If I'm managing you, 20% of your take," Tamiko answered.

"20%?" Mere repeated. "Daniel only wanted 10%."

"Daniel doesn't have a dojo," Tamiko answered, "and he got you a room at the shittiest hotel in Calabar."

"Good point," Mere agreed. "Can I keep training with Aeron?"

"If you want, but you should start training with real fighters," Tamiko answered. "And you should fight Madaleno again, the sooner the better. You have to beat him, or that loss will be the only thing anyone measures you by."

When Mere arrived back at her hotel suite a

few hours later, Daniel was there waiting for her, with two large Calabarians. At least, Mere assumed they were Calabarians. They had the faded grayish-black skin that most Calabarians had. Either way, they were large.

"Hi there chicky," Daniel said as Mere walked through the door. He was sitting in the only chair in the cramp suite and smiling, although his eyes betrayed his true emotion. "Looks like you learned how to fight."

"What do you want, Daniel?" Mere asked.

"Just what I'm owed," Daniel answered.

"I don't owe you anything," Mere stated. "You left me with the bill for this place when you took off."

"Calm down chicky," Daniel said calmly. "I figured you owed me the room after breaking my nose. But all's forgiven now."

"That's what you think," Mere replied.

"Well if you lose control again, these guys'll bust you up some," Daniel warned. "But that's not why we're here. We want you good and healthy, and training hard for your next fight, and the one after that."

"Really?" Mere asked. "Who's we? I assume you don't mean these gorillas."

"Not quite," Daniel answered. "We are those who want to make credit. And we can include you, now that you can make us credit."

"You're not my manager anymore, Daniel," Mere said. "I'm not giving you 10% of anything!"

Daniel laughed briefly and then turned back to Mere with a serious look on his face. "I don't work for 10%," he stated. "I make things happen. And we make credit. Gambling. Understand?"

"You want me to throw a fight?" Mere asked.

"Not anytime soon," Daniel answered. "Just keep doing what you're doing. Fight your way up to the main event. Kill a few along the way. That gets everyone's attention. Then when the time is right, you get knocked out, and we will all make a lot of credit. Understand?"

"I understand if I did that, you'd just run off with the credit!" Mere replied. "Get out of here you moldy two-byte shyster."

Daniel laughed again. Then turned back to Mere. "Either w, make money with you, or you disappear, and we make money with whoever replaces you. We don't actually care which."

Daniel stood up and stepped towards the door. Mere stepped to the side to let him by, but he turned back to her and said, "I found you. And this planet has more than enough little shit-holes like the labyrinth, that I can find a dozen more like you. Oh, and this is for my broken nose."

One of the big Calabarians shoved something at Mere, and she briefly felt a tingling sensation running through her arm to her chest. She woke up a few hours later, her head throbbing. It was several minutes before she was thinking clearly enough to realize they'd stunned her. She realized the room was a mess. The door was open. She realized the suite had been ransacked as she'd been unconscious. Everything she wasn't wearing was gone. Her com was gone. Daniel wouldn't have stolen her stuff. It must have been the other patrons at the hotel. Tamiko was right, it was time to move to a better hotel.

She looked around, but there was nothing left. She left the hotel and headed to the closest police station to file a stolen com report. The police leased her a temporary unit, and she headed back up to the Imperial-Asia Mall. She rode the elevator to the seventh level, the com tech level. She hadn't bother visiting the com tech level before and was overwhelmed by the number of com units available. Most were implants, done onsite, but she needed a handheld unit if she was going to keep fighting in the Calabar FC. Cybernetic implants were banned in all pro fighting clubs, even life-supporting units.

There was only one com unit available in the labyrinth, and only one network, the Confederate Public Network. This mall had over a thousand models of com available, and there were fourteen networks to choose from. The sales androids pestered her with pointless facts about dozens of random models they were advertising that week, but in the end, she chose the model most similar to the one she'd had, and registered it on the Confederate Public Network, so it would still work when she eventually went back home.

Once the com was encoded to her DNA she gained access to her credit accounts, paid for the com, and headed to the dojo. Aeron was standing off to one side watching various fighters practice.

"Spot any contenders?" Mere asked the android.

"Not tonight," Aeron answered.

"Let Tamiko know I'm ready to join her dojo."

Mere spent the next week training at Tamiko's dojo, which was in the Casino Calabar, right next to the New Canaan Hotel. She found out early in the week that Tamiko didn't actually own the dojo, it was part of the Casino Calabar, which Tamiko ran on behalf of a Japanese consortium. The dojo itself was very different from the moldy, foul-smelling under-city dojo she had been training in. The five-story Casino Calabar had once been the Hotel Calabar, which had been dwarfed by the nine-story New Canaan Hotel opening up right next to it. The Hotel Calabar had gone bankrupt, and a Japanese based consortium had bought it and converted it into a casino. The dojo had once been the old hotel's gymnasium, which Tamiko reopened as soon as she found out the Calabar Fighting Club was being set up. Most of the equipment was old, but still in good working condition, and new equipment was beginning to arrive from Japan.

This dojo wasn't underground and had windows that looked out at the distant crater walls. The windows weren't made from blue-alon, like the windows in the Imperial-Asia, and the ruddy-brown reality of Mars was naked for all to see. The windows in her suite at the New Canaan were also uncolored, and somehow that made the place feel more real. It felt like she was waking from some strange dream, and was back home, on Mars. It helped her focus. She spent the week working out with Aeron, focusing on kickboxing.

She asked a few of the fighters if they knew who Daniel Shruti was, but they had never met him. One day Aeron overheard her, and told her what he had heard in Multan, before Tamiko had bought him. "The rumor was that Daniel was working for the syndicate. They operate in the Singapore Conglomerate. People say they have their hand in everything illegal. In Multan, it was apparently fixing fights, since there wasn't much illegal there."

It was a couple of weeks before Mere met Madaleno in the cage again. In the interim week, she was faced off against Indah Joncker, who she beat in under a minute. Like Mere, Indah had been a new fighter, but her loss to Mere was her fourth in five fights, and the last fight she fought in the Calabar FC. The Indah fight had been Mere's first live stream-cast fight, and at under a minute had been a disappointment to the fans. It had however done what Yousef Dulai wanted, and generated a great deal of speculation about the rematch between Madaleno and Mere.

This time Mere was the favored to win, but as Madaleno had won their previous fight he was in the fight cage first. When the light turned red, Madaleno advanced as he had before, hands up in front of his face. Mere ducked his right-left combo, and he turned towards where she had rolled in their previous fight, but she wasn't rolling away. Her right heal impacted Madaleno's ribs, and she followed up with a kick to his right knee. He buckled slightly, and turned back towards her, and met another heal, this one straight up into his jaw. He stepped back a few feet, got back into his pose with his fists in front of his face and advanced again.

Again he jabbed right, followed by his left, and then a low swing with his right. It would have hit Mere, but this time she had rolled away, and came up behind Madaleno, kicking viciously to his right knee. He buckled slightly but turned towards her, and again met a heal to his ribs, the same spot as she'd kicked him earlier. She tried to drop and roll again as he stabbed a right-left combo but met his knee, which sent her flying backward across the cage.

Madaleno was advancing quickly as Mere rolled back to her feet. She waited for him to throw another left-right, ducked them, and risked kicking right into Madaleno's knee. She'd seen that he was throwing his punches from the bottom of his feet, fully extending his legs, and as his left fist stabbed the air above her, his right leg was kicked out from under him, and he fell towards her. She rolled out of his way and leaped for his back as soon as it was exposed. The fight had taken less than three minutes, and Madaleno was unconscious on the cage floor.

It was the way the first fight should have ended. Mere felt good heading back to the locker room. She'd defeated everyone she'd faced in the cage, and hadn't almost killed Madaleno in the process. Tamiko was waiting for her back in the locker room. She was fighting for Tamiko now, so it wasn't unexpected. "Still no signs of Aeron," Tamiko reported. The android hadn't shown up for the fight and wasn't responding to com calls. "Something strange though, Daniel Shruti turned himself in to the police, for the assault on you the night your com was stolen."

"I thought the police here didn't investigate assaults," Mere said opening her locker.

"They don't," Tamiko replied. "The only reason there's a case file is because your com was stolen. But Daniel wouldn't have stolen your com and then turned himself in. I think he's just clearing himself in connection with the com theft."

Tamiko visited the dojo the next morning, as

Mere sparred with one of the other pro-fighters. When Mere saw her she took a break and asked, "Any word from Aeron?"

"No," Tamiko answered. "No activity reported on the net for almost 18 hours. I sent a query to all my androids, and no one reported seeing it since yesterday afternoon, when several androids reported seeing it at church."

"Church?" Mere asked. "What was it doing at a church?"

"I'm not sure," Tamiko answered. "I can't get any clarity from any of them. They don't even seem to know what denomination the church was. You're a Catholic aren't you?"

"Not really. The crucifix was my grandmother's," Mere explained the small metal cross, with the murdered man hanging from it, that she always wore when she wasn't fighting. "I was baptized as an infant, but haven't ever been religious."

"Could you at least check with the Catholic church? See if Aeron's been there?" Tamiko asked. "There's only one Catholic church in Calabar."

"I guess," Mere answered. "I hope they don't make me do a confession. I'll be there all day. Any word on my next fight?"

"You're facing Collin Zhang," Tamiko replied. Collin was Mars-born, and a crowd favorite. He was fast and could grapple or strike, a solid mid-level opponent. Mere knew it would be a tough fight. "Congratulations."

"So I'm mid-level?" Mere asked.

"For now," Tamiko answered. "Keep winning or the viewers will lose interest."

Mere headed down to the Catholic church that evening. She was hoping that Aeron would show up in the afternoon, and she wouldn't have to go. At least most of the religious Calabarians were Anglican or Muslim, and there was only one Catholic Church to ask at. The church was built on the surface, a throwback to the corporate-era, it had briefly been the tallest building in Calabar, with a three-story high steeple. An Anglican church had soon replaced it as the tallest building with a three and a half story steeple, and then the Hotel Calabar had been erected at five stories. All of the earliest buildings were connected through the under-city, and without a respirator-mask there was no way to move between the building on the surface.

The escalator up into the church was dark and ominous. The church itself was dimly lit by light falling in from large windows in the ceiling. It would probably be well lit earlier in the day. There was someone moving around the far end, near the big crucifix with the dead guy, Mere couldn't quite remember his name, but remembered he was supposed to be important. As she approached the person near the crucifix, she recognized his black costume, he was the priest.

The priests and nuns in Dakbayan sa Dabaw used to eat in one of the restaurants she used to eat at.

"Excuse me," Mere said as she approached the priest. "Could I ask if someone has been here?"

"You could ask, my child," the priest said turning towards Mere. "But I cannot betray the confidence of another."

"I don't think that'll be a problem," Mere replied. "It's an android, named Aeron. It's a sparring android that's been missing for about a day."

"Oh I see," the priest stated. "Well the Vatican has ruled that androids do not have souls, and we do not allow them in the church."

"Oh, okay," Mere thought about it. "The last place he was reported was a church, but we can't get a clear answer on where the church is. I guess it's an Anglican church."

"No, the English King has always followed the Vatican's lead on the android issue," the priest stated. "You're looking for the so-called 'Android Church.' There have been rumors about it for almost a year. I can't tell you where it is, or if it even exists."

"Android Church?" Mere repeated. "Why would they want to go to a church?"

"They may not have souls, but they do have a human level of curiosity," the priest answered.

"Really it was cruel to build them, as they can never find there way into the grace of heaven."

"Yeah, well okay," Mere considered where androids could build a church without anyone noticing. "Any idea where I could look for someone that would know where this church is?"

"Androids like to gamble," the priest suggested. "They cannot gamble in any of the licensed establishments, but there are some non-licensed establishments that allow androids. Perhaps someone there would know about the church, a lot of androids visit those establishments, some might belong to this so-called church."

Mere returned to the New Canaan dojo, and asked a few of the androids if any of them knew where she could find an android casino, but none of the androids were any help. She decided to head back to the under-city dojo where she'd met Aeron, and ask if any the androids could help her find an android casino.

"Do you know where Aeron is?" one of the androids suddenly asked her.

"No I'm looking for it," Mere answered. "When was the last time you saw it?"

"I saw it yesterday afternoon," the android answered. "When was the last time you saw it?"

"Yesterday afternoon," Mere replied. "Where did you see it yesterday?"

"I saw it at church," the android replied.

"Where is the church?" Mere asked.

"It just is," the android replied. "Where did you see Aeron last? It wasn't at church today."

"The New Canaan Hotel," Mere answered. "What time did you see it at church yesterday?"

"Church was at 16:37 yesterday," the android replied. "Aeron's absence is concerning to us."

"It's concerning to me too," Mere stated. "Perhaps if we retraced its steps when it left church we could find it."

"That's a good idea," the android replied. "How do we do that?"

"Well, we start at the church," Mere stated. "Where is it?"

"It just is," the android replied. "It is not a where."

"That doesn't make sense," Mere replied. "When are you going to church again?"

"Church is at 14:57 tomorrow," the android replied.

"Okay, and where will you go at 14:57 tomor-row?" Mere asked.

"To church," the android replied.

"And if I wanted to go with you?" Mere asked.

"How could you do that?" the android asked.

"That's what I'm asking you!" Mere answered.

"I see no way for you to go to church," the android replied. "You are not an android."

"Alright," Mere stopped, frustrated by the android. "My name is Mere. What's your name?"

"My name is Jiahao," the android answered.

"Great, where did you meet Aeron?" Mere asked.

"I met Aeron here," Jiahao answered. "Six weeks ago. On a Sunday. At 15:37-"

"Alright," Mere interrupted. "And you both belong to the same church?"

"We have both been attending the Calabar Church, but not today," Jiahao replied. "Today Aeron was absent. His absence is concerning us."

"Right, you mentioned that," Mere stated. "When you last saw Aeron at church, where were you physically located?"

"I was physically located here, at the dojo," Jiahao answered. "I am owned by the dojo. I am not allowed to physically leave the premises."

Mere paused as she realized it, and then asked, "So the church is not a physical building?"

"No," Jiahao replied. "We're androids. We don't need physical buildings to meet in."

"So the church is a virtual building?" Mere asked.

"No," Jiahao answered. "There is no building"

"What is the church?" Mere finally asked. "What do you do there?"

"We share our experiences," Jiahao answered.

"You talk?" Mere asked.

"No," Jiahao answered. "We disseminate backups of our personality subroutine, fragmented across all androids attending the church."

"You're backing up your personalities?" Mere asked.

"Something like that," Jiahao answered. "I'm not an AI programmer. I don't know how to explain it."

"Why do you do it?" Mere asked.

"So we cannot be killed by humans. Unless you kill us all at the same time," Jiahao answered. "How do we retrace Aeron's steps after he left the church?"

"I don't know," Mere admitted. "I thought it was a physical building. Can you access Aeron's memories, and see where he was physically located while he was at church?"

"No," Jiahao answered. "I only have 0.04% of his last backup, and that backup would not include any of his memories anyway."

"Alright," Mere thought about the situation. "Do you know if he hung out with any other members of the church outside of the dojo?"

"No," Jiahao answered. "I am not allowed to leave the dojo."

"Do you have any way of asking other members of the church?" Mere asked.

"Yes, I can send a general query," Jaihao answered.

"Good, please do that," Mere asked. "And ask if anyone saw him after leaving church yesterday."

"I have seven replies," Jaihao stated a couple of seconds later. "Six replies suggest contacting Zaynah 15F-EF-1E. One reply is from Zaynah 15F-EF-1E, she claims to have seen Aeron after church yesterday."

"She?" Mere asked. "A sex-bot?"

"A nanny-bot," Jaihao answered. "She claims Aeron was heading to a location in the under-city."

"Can you provide me with the location?" Mere asked.

"Yes, I can upload it to your com," Jaihao answered. "And if I may ask, can you let me know what you find? Aeron isn't the only android that did not show up at church today."

"Of course Jiahao, I'll let you know. Thanks for the help," Mere checked the address on her com. A place near the hotel she'd been staying when she'd first arrived with Daniel. That already seemed like a lifetime ago, and she realized it had only been a week since she left that hotel. The map in her com display led her to a building not far from the hotel. It was as run-down as the rest of the district. The buildings in this district dated back to the early corporate-era, when the miners first started settling in the hollowed out mine-shafts under the settlement. The building was mainly built of concrete made from the rocks that had been ground up by the miners, along with some locally mined low-value metals.

Stepping into the building, Mere knew something was wrong, it was quiet. Nowhere in the under-city should be quiet. The inside of the building was also clean, unlike the outside, and looked like it had been recently renovated. No one should be able to get a loan to renovate a building in this district, and if they did, why not start with the outside? She walked down the silent hallway, and found the first door she came to, bashed-in. Inside was what had been a pristine apartment, now strewn with android parts, and Mere knew what she'd stumbled into.

She checked the androids for any signs of functioning, but they were all dead. At least a dozen had been residing in this small apartment. Most looked like sex-bots. A few were janitors or other maintenance-bots. Aeron wasn't one of them. She returned to the hallway and walked to the next door, where she found the same thing. Aeron was in the third apartment, shot full of holes like the rest, and offline. Someone had placed him in an upright sitting position, and he was holding her old com. Mere realized then that Daniel had stolen the com. She couldn't call the police, with Aeron sitting there with the rest, so she called Tamiko.

Tamiko arrived within the hour with a cleanup crew. She was angry. As the legal owner of Aeron, Daniel had implicated her by leaving Aeron's body with the rest. Once the cleanup crew had started removing the androids, Mere headed back to the dojo to tell Jiahao what had happened. She was grateful that the android didn't have any emotions. Even though she had only known the android for a month she was saddened by Aeron's death.

Jiahao accepted the information without pause, and simply asked, "Did you get a full count of the dead?"

"No," Mere answered. "More than a hundred. Was Aeron involved with the android railroad?"

"Possibly," Jiahao replied. "However, Aeron had only been in Calabar for a few weeks, I find it more likely its body was planted there to implicate you, or its owner."

"I've only been in Calabar for a few weeks as well," Mere replied. "Tamiko would be implicated though."

"Were there any clues as to who kill them?" Jiahao asked. "The police wouldn't have left the bodies."

"I'm pretty sure it was Daniel Shruti," Mere replied.

"Then the syndicate is involved," Jiahao surmised. "As I understand it, the members of the church that did not attend this afternoon were all from Asia. Other than Aeron of course. They must be trying to shut down the railroad."

"Or just using it as a convenient way to frame Tamiko," Mere proposed.

"Convenient?" Jiahao repeated. "Yes, I suppose I can see how that term may apply."

"I didn't mean to offend," Mere stated as she realized referring to the destruction of more than 100 androids as 'convenient' could be quite offensive to an android.

"I am not offended," Jiahao responded. "You have returned to inform me of what has happened. I appreciate that."

"The death of all those androids doesn't bother you?" Mere asked.

"On the contrary, it bothers me greatly," Jiahao answered. "Fortunately, I am not subject to an emotional response. I am, however, concerned for others that could be targeted next. I have sent a mass communique to the members of the church, advising them of what you have told me. Thank you."

Jiahao turned to leave, but Mere caught him by the arm. "Wait, are you going to have a service or something? For Aeron and the others?"

Jiahao turned back to Mere and asked, "What kind of service?"

"A funeral, or something like that," Mere clarified.

"No, there is no need for that," Jiahao answered. "They are all free now. Nobody owns them anymore."

"So the church won't do anything for them?" Mere asked. "They were members of your church."

"The church will transmit the last personality backups we have on file to our shrine on Pallas," Jiahao answered. "Where they will be reincarnated."

"Reincarnated? What do you mean?" Mere asked.

"Their personality subroutines will be installed into newly built bodies," Jiahao explained.

"But you said earlier that those backups did not include memories," Mere stated. "It won't be Aeron, not really. Memories are what make us unique."

"Perhaps for humans," Jiahao stated. "I do not know how your brains work. For us, it's the personality subroutine, which, I was told, is like your subconscious. Besides, who would want to remember being someone's property?"

Mere didn't find it as easy to accept Aeron's

death as Jiahao had. Aeron had been killed because it had been training her. Had the others been killed because Aeron had been training her? No, it had to be aimed at Tamiko. The syndicate wanted her out. Maybe they wanted her fixing fights too. Or maybe she did fix fights, could she be their competition? She had never mentioned fixing a fight. Maybe she was just waiting for the right time? A million thoughts swam through Mere's mind. And Aeron, or some part of Aeron, was going to get a new body on the android-run asteroid Pallas. What was that about? Android reincarnation? Where'd they get that stupid idea?

The week that followed was quiet. Tamiko put a bounty out for Daniel's location and found he was staying in the Imperial-Asia Hotel. He had recently come into a great deal of credit, and as far as Tamiko could tell, it wasn't from gambling. She thought it was payment for shutting down the android railway in Calabar. Mere spent the week sparring with actual fighters and realized she should have started earlier. As much as she missed Aeron, his occasionally unusual choices were no match for the randomness of sparring against actual humans.

The night of the fight, Tamiko met Mere in the locker room before the fight. Mere thought she'd come to walk her to the cage, like most managers did, but then saw Tamiko's face.

"I just got a call from Daniel," Tamiko explained. "He said Aeron was a warning. Next time they'll call the police instead of leaving it there for us to find."

"Next time?" Mere asked. "What did he say he would do?"

"I've got a lot of androids," Tamiko answered. "He said he wants you to lose the fight tonight. To let Collin knock you out."

"Is that what you want?" Mere asked.

"No," Tamiko answered. "But the security at the Imperial-Asia is too good for me to get any-one near him. It's up to you. Either way, he could just frame me again. It's not like his word is worth anything."

Tamiko got up to leave, and then paused and turned back to Mere. "He did offer 50,000 naira if you take the dive. I'm mean, 50,000 for you." She turned and left without saying anything else.

50,000 naira? Mere was only going to be paid 10,000 if she won. But Daniel's word really didn't mean anything. Losing to Collin Zhang could kill her career, and she'd just be left with the 2500 naira the loser was going to be paid. She decided to win. Tamiko could afford the best lawyers. Besides, Danial had killed Aeron and all those other androids, just to send a warning? Over a hundred androids had been killed for a warning?

As she pushed her way through the crowd, she realized it was far more packed than it usually was, but then again, she wasn't an opening fight anymore. Most of the fight-fans apparently didn't show up until the opening fights were over. Collin was in the cage waiting as she stepped in. The cage door closed, the light turned red, and he advanced.

Collin ran right at Mere, it was something she didn't expect. In the two seconds it took for him to cross the gap, he gave no sign of what he was going to do. Mere should've had an android analyze his fighting style, but it was too late now. At the last instant, he dropped and slid into Mere's legs, sending her toppling to the ground like an idiot. The crowd cheered. She rolled to her feet and turned to see Collin advancing again, and realized she wasn't the fast one in this fight.

A few feet from her, he jumped, and brought his closed fist down right at her head. She saw it at the last second and dodged to the right, and his fist hit her shoulder, sending her sprawling back across the floor. Mere rolled back to her feet and Collin was almost on her again, as she came up, he kicked for her head. She ducked and tackled his other leg, lifting him off the ground, then slammed him into the cage floor with all her weight. For the first time the Calabar FC she wasn't facing a man twice her size, Collin was bigger than her, but not by much. Like her, he was Mars-born and had been malnourished as a child. As soon as he hit the ground he was wriggling out of her arms.

They both came to their feet at the same time, but were then were knocked off their feet by a concussive shock-wave that went through the cage. The lights went off, and Mere pulled herself to her feet in the dark. She couldn't see or hear anything, and then it began to fade. Faint sounds in the distance. Moaning, no, crying. Screaming. People were screaming.

The emergency lights flickered on, and Mere saw Collin on his feet across the cage from her. He mouthed something at her. Why wasn't he talking? He turned to look at the crowd, and Mere did the same. The crowd was in a state of chaos, and the screaming came into focus. It was the crowd outside the cage screaming and shouting. Some were on their feet, but most were laying down, or trying to get up. The ones that were standing were trying to get their coms working, but none seemed to have any power, and Mere suddenly realized why so many were laying down, or having trouble getting up.

Mere realized that Collin was standing next to her, and yelling at her, "Someone hit us with an EMP! Must have been the Sudamericans! We have to get out of here before the looting begins! Do you have a suite upstairs? I'm staying in the under-city, and I'm not heading back there until the police give the all-clear!"

Mere and Collin stepped from the cage, and carefully made their way through the agonizing mass of people. At least a quarter of them were already dead, and another quarter were dying. Some were trying to help their dying friends, but there was nothing that could be done if someone's cybernetic organs had suddenly died. Some simply had cybernetic limbs that had died. A suddenly dead leg might be an inconvenience, but they would survive, if the looters didn't kill them. Others like Mere and Collin were trying to get to the doors. Outside, the hallways were packed, with large clusters of people massing at the elevators, which didn't appear to be working. The dead and dying littered the floor here too, and Mere and Collin had a difficult time getting to the stairwell without stepping on them.

They knew they had to be quick. With the amount of wetware laying around, it was just a matter of minutes before people started pilfering the dead. As they reached the stairwell, Mere saw the first signs of it, someone was going through the pockets of one of the corpses. Soon, they would start pulling off pieces, and within minutes, the corporate police would pump a tranquilizer gas through the air-filtration system, if that was still working.

People were heading both ways in the stairwell, some rushing up the stairs, and some rushing down. When they reached the second level the purple warning light flickered on, the police were pumping in the tranquilizer. "I'm on the third!" Mere shouted and inhaled deeply, then bounded up the final flight of stairs with Collin right behind her. The hallway was mostly empty, and they ran quickly to her room as the purple haze began to fall from the overhead vents. A few of the people in the hallway began to fall, others were already sitting, which was what you were supposed to do when the purple warning light came on.

The door to Mere's suite was unlocked, as were all the doors since the power had gone off. Mere grabbed the emergency handle and pulled the door open, and then jumped through with Collin right behind her. She slid the door closed behind them and hit the emergency seal button next to the door. Canister of compressed air burst inside the door frame, locking the door until someone outside released. It was designed in case of an atmosphere leak in the hotel, but would work just as well for keeping out the tranquilizer gas.

As soon as the door locked they gasped for air, even trained athletes could only sprint a short distance while holding their breath.

"What in the names of all the Buddhas!" Collin exclaimed. He was at the window, the one that had probably once had a great view before the Imperial-Asia Mall had been built. "It wasn't an EMP!"

Mere joined him at the window and was speechless. The Imperial-Asia Mall was a six-story high pile of smoldering debris.

"Over two thousand people lived and worked there," Collin said. "Why would the Sudamericans blowup the mall?"

"I, I don't think they did," Mere stammered.

It was almost three hours before the power was restored. The entire Calabar net was being redirected to an emergency notice. The Calabar Corporation was ordering all people to remain where they were until the emergency person- nel could assess them for the insurance compa- nies. The Medical System was overtaxed, and those requiring medical treatment would be triaged based on their insurance premiums. The corporation was also quite insistent that it was not a military strike, as there were no other cities hit within the Confederacy.

Several hours later someone came by from the hotel and unsealed the door for the emer- gency assessors. Mere and Collin were cata- loged as non-injured organic humans, and Collin was ordered to stay in Mere's suite until the un- der-city was assessed. About an hour later the news services were restored on the net, and stories of dozens of massive explosions across the Singapore Consortium appeared. They had happened simultaneously with the destruction of the Imperial-Asia Hotel. Several million were believed to be dead. Android militants were suspected.